Sine Timore proudly presents

HANNAH SINGER,

CELESTIAL ADVOCATE

by Peter G

For God, my teacher, and my angels, who never gave up on me, even when they had every right to.

And for the Ramones, for showing what is important.

From the case files of

Hannah Singer

Celestial Advocate

Alan Levy woke up with a start.

His eyes flew open and he sat up straight. He had been lying prone on his back in an open field. The grass was greener than he ever thought possible. Flowers dotted the landscape, bursts of color exciting the eyes while the scents soothed the mind. The sky was blue, the clouds were white, and the birds sang the sweetest song.

It was terrifying.

All he knew was this was unreal. He quickly patted himself down. No broken or missing parts. He sprang to his feet and started running. He didn't know where he was running to, he had no real direction. He just hoped that he would eventually reach the edge of this place. He didn't care if he was heading somewhere dangerous, just as long as it felt real to him.

He ran out of the open field into a lightly wooded area. It wasn't any better. He didn't stop.

He came to a rough, rocky area. It still didn't feel right. He didn't stop.

He came to another wooded area. It was a thick forest. He was panicking now. He wasn't any closer to something that felt familiar. He stopped, bending at the waist and hanging his head down. He need to clear his thoughts, find some sense to it all.

As his mind sorted through all that his senses were feeding him, he noticed something.

A smell.

Brownies.

He pulled himself up, looking around. Brownies? In the middle of a thick forest? No sign of civilization anywhere? But it was there. Unmistakable. It wasn't an overpowering smell, either. It was natural. Real.

He carefully moved through the forest, peeking out from behind trees as he followed the scent. He noticed a small clearing up ahead of him. He moved slower and more deliberately, unsure of what he would find there.

In the center of the clearing was a small campfire, carefully ringed with stones. Two fallen tree trunks, just the right size to be benches, were on opposite sides. Sitting on the far trunk, holding a small tin pan covered with aluminum foil over the fire, was a woman. She looked to be in her early thirties. Average height for a woman. Golden hair that started out straight at the top of her head, but got wavy as it reached down to the small of her back. It billowed out a bit, just like the robes did, white with pale blue highlights and a blue overrobe. Her face was pleasant, a peaches and cream complexion complimenting her small mouth, small nose, and green eyes. She whistled quietly, harmonizing with the birds in the trees.

Alan gasped. Lots of guys do when they first see me.

I angled my eyes up to him. He was only peeking out from around the tree. I smiled at him. "Want some brownies? Kind of a shame to eat them alone."

Bingo. I had him right where I wanted him. He came out from behind the tree and crossed to the other trunk. He moved as if it was against his will but he was powerless to fight. He sat down, the look on his face a mixture of relief and fear. He really had no idea what to make of any of this. They never do.

I carefully took off the aluminum foil. The brownies were done. The scent was wonderful. I put a small butter knife in the center and held the pan out to Alan. He carefully cut one and picked it up. The brownie was a little gooey. Just the way they should be. He carefully took a nibble as I brought the pan back and cut one for myself. I set the pan down on one of the stones, closer to him so he could have another when he was ready. I knew he would.

I waited for him to speak. His voice was medium in pitch and soft. "Uh...I don't want to sound stupid, but...."

"You want to know where you are."

He didn't say anything. He just nodded at me as he reached for the pan.

He was partway through cutting another when I spoke. "You know what happened. You're hoping you're wrong."

He stopped and looked at me. His eyes were wide. I gestured to the pan. "Don't stop, have another. Enjoy them."

His attention was riveted to me as I spoke. He was actually rubbing the knife against the edge of the pan for a second before he moved it. "How far did you run? How long? And you aren't even winded. And you aren't in that great of shape."

He had a mouthful of brownie. He was chewing it slowly, like he wasn't even aware it was in there. "You aren't hungry, are you? You eat, and you don't feel any different inside. When's the last time you slept? Saw the sun set? Did you stop even once when you were running?"

He swallowed noisily. I offered him a napkin from the small pack at my side. "You're dead."

He took the napkin with trembling fingers. "I...I can't be."

"You are in the Valley Of Death."

His head jerked around, searching for threats. "Th-this is the Valley Of Death?"

"Not as imposing as you thought, huh? Probably expected a desert or something. Closest thing we have is a beach. It goes on and on, but you have water right there."

He looked ready to pass out. Strictly speaking, he shouldn't. Unconsciousness is a product of a living body, not the soul. But life conditions certain behaviors, and passing out was a possibility. "Relax," I told him. "You're perfectly safe here. No one is going to hurt you."

"How long have you been here?"

"Almost seven hundred years."

He seemed relieved, then confused. "Is this Heaven?"

"Nah," I said, pulling back the tin and cutting a brownie for myself. He hadn't been paying attention, and the last shape he cut curved in strange ways. I made as square a piece as I could with what was left. "This is just where the souls go after they die. Heaven is a different place. You'll see this big, beautiful white building with columns and stuff, like an old palace. That's the Celestial Court. You go in, introduce yourself, and say you want to get into Heaven."

He was scared now. "What happens then?"

"It's not like angels drop from the ceiling, grab you, and throw you to Hell. They won't do anything to you unless that is the judgment at trial."

"Trial?"

"Yes. When you petition, you are granted a trial. An angel decides if you are to be allowed into Heaven or not."

He bowed his head. "What if I don't petition?"

"Then you just wander around the Valley Of Death forever. You aren't forced to do anything. You may think it beats the alternative, but trust me, Eternity gets boring really quick."

He looked up. Tears were forming in his eyes. "I...I did some things wrong...."

I got up and walked up to him. I sat next to him and took his hands in mine. I felt his fingers constricting and shaking. "Of course, you did. Everyone does."

"I...I don't want to go to Hell."

I squeezed his hands. "Well, then. What you need is a Celestial Advocate."

He looked at me, completely confused. I felt his hands ease up a little bit. "A what?"

"A Celestial Advocate," I told him. "The Celestial Court hears two arguments. One is from a Church Advocate saying what you did wrong and why you should not be allowed in Heaven or Cast Down or whatever. The other argument is the Celestial Advocate. Their whole job is to appeal to the mercy of the Court."

He looked hopeful. "And they get me into Heaven?"

"Well, for the most part. I mean, if you aren't good enough to get into Heaven, something else might happen. You might be made a guardian angel to atone for your sins. You might be sent back to live another lifetime to try and get it right. But no one who has ever deserved to get into Heaven has ever been denied. And it's the Celestial's duty to make sure that, whatever happens to you, getting Cast Down is not one of the options."

His head drooped again. "How long do I have?"

"As long as you want. You petition when you are ready, and it goes from there."

"How do I find a Celestial Advocate?"

"They tell you where they are when you petition. Assuming you don't have one at that point. Sometimes, you don't have to find one. One will find you."

9

His hands turned to stone, cold and unmoving. He turned his head slowly until he looked me straight in the eyes.

I squeezed his hands before carefully putting them in his lap. As I stood, I smiled and said, "It's a pleasure to meet you. My name is Hannah Singer. I'm your Celestial Advocate. See you around, Alan Levy." I walked away, leaving him to think things over.

Dying is, obviously, a big shock to people. Most seek out the Courts or eventually stumble across them and decide to take their chances. But some people are stragglers, and can spend decades, if not centuries, wandering around the Valley Of Death. Advocates from both sides will come around, making sure they know what is going on and what their options are. The newly departed souls then get a crash course in the Celestial Courts. Well, more or less. It really depends on which side finds them first. Omniscience only applies to the living on Earth, not what comes next.

In the early days, God made a covenant with His people. Not everyone can talk directly with God, so knowing His will could be a bit hit and miss. So, God told them that, whatever they held true on Earth, He would hold true in Heaven. Simple and direct, right?

Well, the wording was kind of vague. It didn't take long for churches to realize that it gave them a fantastic amount of power. They could determine who got into Heaven and who didn't. It became quite a bargaining chip. It could control the people the churches wanted controlled, and excused the ones they wanted to protect. Things like buying indulgences or forgiveness by high-ranking officials became commonplace. All the while, thinking that the covenant meant that they could guarantee their own eternal salvation.

However, the vagueness of the wording was actually part of God's plan. God knew full well that people would be tempted to abuse the covenant. I mean, He's God. He's no dummy. One of the things He did was set up the Celestial Court. God does not sit in judgment due to the covenant - He'd have no choice but to rule as the Church doctrines say. Instead, an angel presides, and there is a jury of twelve angels, the Tribunal. Advocates for either side, Churches and Celestials, argue what fate they feel the Petitioner deserves. The Tribunal makes its decision, and the Petitioner gets whatever. The presiding angel doesn't really make any decisions, but can influence how things go based on questions or what he will allow.

The churches, obviously, aren't thrilled with this set-up. They have tried contesting it, saying that it violates the covenant. But no one has ever been able to explain how, and the one time it went to trial, they lost badly. So they have no choice but to go along with it.

Churches are frustrated, but it's nothing compared to what Celestials go through. Churches have their rules set, it's pretty straightforward for them. Celestials have to consider the Petitioner and the arguments. In other words, the ruling, by default, will go to the Church and they will get the fate they seek unless we can give the Tribunal a good reason to disregard it. And it has to be a good reason. Much as we might like it, we can't just say, "Rule in our favor because the Churches are on a power trip again."

What I told Alan was a little bit of an oversimplification. Strictly speaking, the soul files a petition. The petition is then reviewed by both the Celestials and the Churches. If both sides say, "No contest," the petition is granted and the Petitioner heads straight to Heaven or whatever God has planned for them next. But if either side opposes, it goes to trial. Whichever side opted not to contest the petition becomes the Petitioner's Advocate. If both sides oppose, it's still a trial. The only difference is a Heavenly reward is off the table.

Petitioners sort of get their choice of Celestials. It really depends. Most Petitioners have very simple cases. For the most part, they're good people. The Church may contest the petition, but there's not much effort involved. The Churches know it's pretty daft to ask that people be Cast Down because they, say, stole some gum when they were kids. Cases like that, the Church's case is token and one Celestial is pretty much as good as another. But then, there are the more complex cases, where you can't really say they followed the letter of the law, if you will, or maybe they did follow the letter of the law but not the spirit, or maybe it's someone the Church feels should be in Heaven but they haven't done enough right. Those "grey area" cases go to special Celestials. They are known for thinking on their feet and being very sharp.

My crowd.

There aren't many of us greys. We still do regular Advocacies, but we also get these really unusual cases where things can't be decided simply and to everyone's satisfaction. Our boss is St. Michael. Yes, the archangel. He treats everyone well, although the two of us have become best friends. It took me a while to warm up to him. Basically, I was scared. I thought he would resent me for being an Atheist before I died, but nothing of the sort. He's sort of like my big brother.

It's very hard to surprise Michael. There are certain individuals he keeps a close eye on. He knows, when they finally die and if they ever petition, it's going to be fireworks in the Celestial Courts. Alan Levy was one such individual. Michael had stopped by my quarters about seven years ago, carrying the scroll with Levy's case file. He presented it to me and said, "Like it or not, I'm giving you this one."

Scrolls chronicle what people do in life. Levy's didn't have a tie holding it closed. That meant he was still alive. The tie doesn't appear until there is nothing more about the person's life to add. I took the scroll, unrolled it, and started reading it. I got to the most recent entries, and my eyebrows arched.

I angled my eyes over the top of the scroll without moving my head. I smiled. "Ha ha. You're such a kidder. Be serious, will you?"

Michael, standing there in a black camp shirt covered with pink flamingos and blue Bermudas with palm trees, arched his eyebrows back at me. "Do I look like I'm not being serious?"

I thought better of giving the obvious answer. "Come on, Michael. You're the most notorious prankster in history."

He rolled his eyes. Every once in a long while, he regrets his reputation. "This is not a prank. This is serious. Alan Levy is a real person and you are reading his current situation. I'm not sure when he's going to die, but when he does, he's going to need the best Celestial. He's a good guy. He shouldn't be Cast Down just because of that."

"Good health, decent lifestyle?"

"Yes. He's not part of the party crowd and he's only twenty-four, so he could have lots of decades left. But you know how the Churches are going to react, and I figure you could start working on your arguments now."

"Do I have to return this to Russell?" Russell runs the Office Of Records, where all the scrolls are kept.

"No. He knows it's in your possession, and I doubt any of the other Celestials will want to touch this one."

"Good guess."

"Naturally, Churches might want to see it, but I doubt they'll even be aware of him until he dies."

"I promise not to keep it from them."

Michael let out a sigh and looked to the side. "I'm not trying to make you uncomfortable here."

"I know that. You can't help how people live their lives. And that is the whole point of this job - to extend God's mercy, right?"

Michael looked at me, smiling a bit now. "Thanks. I know this is going to be tricky, and you're the best with these kinds of cases." He saluted me and walked out of my quarters, shoulders hunched like he was trying not to be noticed.

I took the scroll and put it on top of my modest bookcase, where I keep the books I absolutely cannot do without. Unless something unusual happened, in around fifty years, I was going to be advocating to get a porn star into Heaven.

Alan Levy started out like most of the world - a very unremarkable life. His dad was an administrator for a computer company, his mom was a paralegal. Both parents had to work. Where they lived required a certain amount of income to meet the cost of living, and neither of them were at the top of their pay scales. Alan and his younger sister were latchkey kids, and he watched out for her.

They did pretty good in school, although the sister didn't need much education. She was pretty and bubbly, and that got the attention of lots of boys, many of whom had been climbing the social ladder since they first went to preschool. She was chosen by one who was fast tracked to work at a Fortune 500 company. Didn't have to work a day in her life. However, she never forgot her parents. And she never forgot the big brother who kept an eye on her.

However, what she could do for him was limited. The family was too proud to take handouts from her and her husband. Well, what handouts were offered - he was still moving up and had to maintain his own life (complete with twins on the way about two years after they married), meaning the big bucks were still a ways off. The parents were doing okay, but Alan was struggling. He had taken bookkeeping and economic courses. Not a lot of places hiring, and those that were wanted a lot more than someone fresh out of college. He temped, doing the accounting equivalent of odd jobs, and frequently didn't know if he'd even have work the next day.

Most people don't realize how hard everyday life is. How, when you are just surviving, you no longer feel alive, like maybe death isn't a bad alternative. The feelings of powerlessness and despair push thousands of people over the edge. Alan had to cope with them constantly because of what he actually wanted to do. Like most teenage boys, he had dreams of being in a rock band. He and his buddies started a group called Smuggler's Cove. Alan was the lead singer. They were pretty good. Or, at least, I thought so - I mostly listen to classical music, so I'm hardly an authority on good rock. Unfortunately, they were from a more affluent neighborhood. Not a lot of the right kinds of rock clubs, where you build a following and get discovered. They were simply too clean cut to really get in that way.

The line-up of the band changed a few times as the other members gave up on their dream and became part of the ordinary world. Alan clung to his dream like a drowning man to a stick. It was the only thing that really made his life tolerable. He didn't have to tour the world or be a household name, just to continue making music for appreciative crowds.

It was after a couple of years, when Alan had sold his guitar for the third time, that his uncle Mick came for a visit. Alan didn't really know Mick aside from some family gatherings, nothing in depth. In fact, it was a family reunion a few months earlier when Alan last saw him. Mick had an unusual proposition - he had connections in the porn industry. He worked for one of the major producers' distribution channels. Mick's wife had mentioned that Alan had the sort of build and smoky vibe that porn actors have. Mick showed a few pics around, and the production company thought he might be a good fit.

Alan, naturally, had doubts. But Mick laid out a convincing case. No one was coming around to sign Smuggler's Cove, so it was unlikely he'd ever get to do it for his livelihood. If he did well with the porn company, he'd be making a good living, with a lot more cash than he was getting temping. And best of all, with that providing a good means of support, he wouldn't have to abandon his band. Alan had to decide quick, while he was still young. With no other real direction, he gave it a try. The producers were impressed with his professionalism. He was no ego case, so he was in demand.

This formed the crux of Michael's position. Advocating for sex workers of all types was nothing new. Admittedly, there were more such Advocacies happening since the start of the 21st Century, when far more people were casually taking part, either through their own web sites or just private pics for lovers. But Alan's case had a unique angle - it was just a job. He was good at it, but he tolerated it for the sake of his music. If the band took off, he'd quit the industry in a heartbeat. He avoided hanging with others in the industry, they weren't his scene. He just worked, saved his pennies, and dreamed of a different future. Strictly speaking, no different than most other people working their lives away.

Alan was doing fine, and even found his bookkeeping skills were a plus in this new world. Many in the industry were hesitant to trust people with their business funds. The fact that one of their own could help with their accounting and such was a huge perk. Alan soon found himself doing more of that and getting paid well. He eventually quit making the movies. And the band played on. The happiest day of his life was when he was doing a gig and, without prompting with the lyrics, the audience sang along to one of his songs. He thought, I could die happy now.

He came pretty close.

Alan, obviously, never lived those decades Michael and I had him pegged for. He was out driving in his new sporty little car, a convertible. It was night, and he had just finished rehearsing with a new rhythm guitarist for Smuggler's Cove. Pulling through an intersection, another car came around the blind curve. The driver was drunk and going way too fast. He approached from the left, hitting Alan's car square in the driver's side door. Alan might have had a chance to survive, but physics took over, and Alan's car went to the curb, flipping over and crushing his upper body. The driver, who hadn't bothered with a seat belt, smashed his head into his windshield. Brain trauma, instant death. Even if he'd lived, he'd have been too drunk to process the grizzly scene. Paramedics and accident investigators could only be on the scene after they emptied their stomachs. Involuntarily.

And so, at the ripe young age of thirty, Alan Levy was en route to meet his Maker.

I was in the middle of a fairly routine Advocacy. The Petitioner had, during his college years, turned the basement of the dorm into a hothouse, an undercover botany lab to grow marijuana plants. He knew he was safe. The police weren't about to bust one of the greatest college football teams during a drug raid - the Dean made sure of that. Once he got out of college, he abandoned his little sideline. It was the only real bump on the road of his life. The Churches put in their contest before the Celestials finished reading the petition. Their position was, the guy had broken laws, even if he was never caught, and drugs in general are bad because they alter the body and the consciousness, even temporarily. I could advocate this in my sleep (if I ever slept). I just kept the facts simple and few in number. The Church was a new guy who was so determined to show what an affront this was, he exaggerated everything. It didn't take long for his stance to seem absurdly overblown. The presiding angel was just about to send the whole thing over to the Tribunal (and from how they reacted every time the Church spoke, it was obvious it would be a fast ruling and what it would be) when a pair of putti flew into the courtroom. Generally, when the doors are closed during trial, no one comes in or out except those charming little childlike angels. They run messages. One went to the presiding angel, and the other, named Lily, came to me.

"Michael requests your presence now!"

Michael doesn't interrupt my Advocacies unless it is something crucial. "Where is he now?"

"His chambers. Lots of angels and Celestials in there."

Before I could move for a recess, the presiding angel had gotten his message and stated, "Miss Singer, would you object to being substituted?"

"No objection at all, sir." I was already gathering up the scrolls on the table.

"We are in recess for a short break so council can confer." He banged the gavel, the doors began to open, and I bolted through them as soon as they were wide enough to squeeze through.

Galileo Galilei was waiting in the hall for me. Michael clearly didn't know the trial was almost over. "What do I need to know?" he asked.

"Nothing. It's about to be sent to the Tribunal. You'll just be waiting, and I'll bet not for long. What's up?"

"Michael didn't tell me much, just told me to move and to tell you an Alan Levy has died."

I shoved the scrolls into Galileo's arms and raced down the hall. The speed of the angels is amazing. I'm not an actual angel, though, so all I could do was minimize my time.

I got to Michael's chambers. The door was closed, no doubt to keep any conversation from being overheard. I put my hand on the door, and it pulled me through to the other side without opening. Michael was taking no chances of anything getting out.

Inside, it was bedlam. Five angels and three Celestials were standing around Michael's giant desk, jawing amongst themselves while pointing to the desktop. Everyone was close enough, I couldn't see Michael in there. Then, I saw Michael's hand rise over the top of the crowd and wave me over. Thank God no one had their wings out, or I wouldn't have even seen that.

I came around, and Michael didn't bother with greetings. "Alan Levy just died. Car accident. He's in the Valley Of Death and will be coming around any moment now. We don't know where or how to find him, and I want to get to him before a Church does."

There is no fixed point of entry for the Valley Of Death. "Any idea where he might have gone?"

The crowd got quiet so Michael could bring me up to speed without fighting the din. "He was simple and pretty open, and the car wreck was in a residential area. We're figuring a meadow or plain, he wouldn't gravitate to the beaches or mountains."

"Who all is looking for him?"

"Just Advocates. He thinks he's got a one-way ticket to Hell, so he'll run from angels."

"So much for speed."

"Right. Any ideas how we can find him?"

Eventually, the idea was hit on to get Alan to come to us instead of us coming to him. The brownie idea was mine. Everyone started making them in

15

strategic locations. When Alan was noticed and started heading to one of the campsites, an angel rushed me to where he was going and took the other Advocate out. So it was just me when a confused, frightened, and alone Alan came along.

He didn't come to the Courts right away. A few different Churches found him but didn't know exactly who he was. They gave him a general spiel with lots of fire and brimstone for the unworthy, "but you are clearly Righteous, and have nothing to fear!" He eventually wandered over and submitted his petition. He did ask if he had a Celestial assigned to him already. The clerk said he looked a bit relieved to hear I was still on his case. But he still had that frightened look. He was scared. And he had every reason to be.

Souls that petition stay at the Interim. It's a very nice residential area, intended to be as calming and relaxing as possible. Alan was told I'd be along before he knew it. When I showed up, he was sitting in one of the shade gardens, propped up against a tree and surrounded by blooming plants. Even the branches of the tree were covered in blossoms.

He was lost in sensation. He didn't even notice my approach. I cleared my throat (purely a symbolic gesture), and his eyes popped open in my direction. "Hello, Miss Singer!" Then, his brow wrinkled. "Do I call you 'Miss Singer', or 'Advocate Singer,' or what?"

"We aren't in court. Call me 'Hannah.' Ready to go over your case?"

"I guess." He tilted his head up to the tree. "You know, I love the smell. I could never get near flowers on Earth. Allergies. My eyes would water so much, and I'd sneeze like crazy."

"I promise to bring you back. We haven't requested a trial yet, so you still have time."

He folded his legs and sat forward, resting his elbows on his knees. "So, what do you want to know about me?"

"Actually, it's not just us. Michael wants to be part of this discussion. To help brainstorm your defense."

His face lit up. "Michael Duffson?!? I haven't seen him in years!" He sobered up. "I mean, it's sad that he's dead, but…."

I held up my hand to stop him. "No, not that Michael. St. Michael the archangel. He's in charge of the Celestials."

"Oh," he said, squinting his eyes a little. "Isn't he the guy that fights the devil?"

"Yes."

"Why is he helping with my defense?"

"Michael takes a special interest in the harder cases. He likes it when people have the best shot possible."

"He wants me to get into Heaven? Even after the porn?"

"He likes everyone who deserves to get into Heaven to get there. He was with me every step of the way for my trial. I had a big problem myself. I was an Atheist."

16

He pulled his head back a little. "If that doesn't keep you out, why aren't you in Heaven?"

"Voluntary. I'd rather do Advocacies for now."

"Did you have a difficult trial?"

"You have no idea."

I pulled him up and we started walking. But we didn't get more than a few steps when I heard that voice.

"Hello, Singer."

As always, it wasn't the voice itself that got me. It was pretty generic. It was that smile. It oozed from each word. It was coming from by my left shoulder. The metaphor was just sickening.

Jeff Fairchild, the most senior Church, was walking up to me, a couple of other Churches in tow. Fairchild was tall and muscular. You'd think he and Michael were cousins or something. Fairchild's hair was short, reddish-brown, and curled. He looked like a poker player, willing to take all your money and smile the entire time. Because you would never be as good as him. Ever.

Each Advocate has areas of expertise. For example, there were Celestials who only handled cases dealing with Calvinistic church beliefs. They knew the stuff backwards and forwards and could argue all day. There were others who worked the Free Will angle. I got the grey area cases, where there was no clear cut right and wrong and the Churches couldn't wait to put their boot to the poor soul's face. That my specialty. Arguing those points was Fairchild's. We constantly faced off against each other in court. So much so, the presiding angels wondered when they saw one of us advocating and not the other.

I had been dreading this. I knew Fairchild was going to advocate for the Church. If someone else had the case, he'd pull rank just to get it and lead. I was just hoping the first confrontation would not be in front of the Petitioner. I decided to walk past him. I could have easily walked in the opposite direction and gotten away, but I didn't want Alan thinking Fairchild was someone who scared me. Annoyed me, sure, but not scared me.

I grabbed Alan's hand and started pulling him after me. I was walking quickly and was hoping to be too fast of Fairchild to intercept. "Great to see you, leading a tour of new guys, huh? We'll talk later, we have a conference with Michael."

Fairchild was still moving in until I said Michael's name. That brought him up short. "Oh, so you don't have time to introduce me to the Petitioner?"

I released Alan's hand and moved in, staring Fairchild right in the eyes. Alan and the other Churches were hanging back, staying out of the way of the two angry people ready to duke it out. "His scroll is already back at the Office Of Records."

Fairchild pulled it out of his robe. "I know. I already got it."

"Then you can exchange pleasantries with him later. We're late."

"This is Eternity. There's no such thing as 'late' in Eternity."

"You can discuss that with Michael." I wasn't in the mood for a philosophical debate.

Fairchild stepped deftly past me and walked right up to Alan, extending his hand and smiling. Jerk. "You must be Alan Levy!" he said happily.

Alan seemed to notice the vibe. He weakly shook Fairchild's hand, as if contact would turn him to dust. "Yes."

"Jeff Fairchild," he said, ignoring a look from me hot enough to make angel fire look like liquid nitrogen. "I'm an Advocate, too."

"I already have an Advocate," he said, nodding towards me. "But thanks for the offer."

"Aw, aren't you optimistic?" Fairchild still hadn't released Alan's hand. "I'm not asking to represent you. I represent the church."

Alan paled. The full ramifications hit him.

Fairchild released Alan's hand then came up to the side, draping his arm over his shoulder. "You really think you'll get into Heaven, don't you? Life of sin and debauchery you've lived...."

I leapt in front of Fairchild's face as if I'd been shot out of a cannon. "No tampering with the Petitioner!"

"I never got a chance to talk to him before he petitioned. Aren't I entitled to a little meet and greet?"

"No, and you know it." Fairchild had been Advocating for over two hundred years and knew everything back and forth. He was the toughest challenge any Celestial could ever face. Part of the reason I faced him so much was my skill. The other part was that no one else thought they stood a chance against him.

"I trust you aren't going to delay a trial any longer than necessary. Steve Gossling's trial has been stayed pending the outcome of Alan's here."

I didn't like this. "Who's Steve Gossling?"

Fairchild pointed to Alan with a smile. "The guy who hit him. The Celestials opposed his petition because he was drunk and killed Alan here. Because of my defense, we need a ruling on Alan first."

"Why?"

"The Church's official stance is that Gossling did a valuable service and performed God's work by removing a pornographer from the world."

My jaw dropped. "That's low. Even for you."

Fairchild returned his gaze to Alan. Alan had scrunched down a little bit, and Fairchild was now leaning on him. "She's good, but she's not perfect. Modern times require a better approach to keep undesirables from sullying up Heaven."

Alan gulped.

Fairchild put the cherry on his chocolate sundae of intimidation. "Had I been around to contest her Petition, that Atheist would be in a lake of fire right now. Where all your kind belongs."

"*Burn!!!*" I roared. I grabbed Alan by the front of his shirt and dragged him after me. It was a little while before I calmed enough to hear him begging me to slow down, he was barely keeping his balance. I eased up and released him, but still kept walking quickly, Alan sometimes walking and sometimes jogging to keep up with me.

We got to the Court building and I led Alan to Michael's chambers. I only knocked once, a short rap. The door opened immediately. I just pointed to it, arm straight out, and Alan slinked past me, watching to make sure I wasn't going to punch him as he went by.

Inside, Alan got his first view of the infamous St. Michael. People on Earth have ideas of angels being these beautiful, graceful beings of light. But Michael wasn't just an archangel, he was in charge of facing the Devil himself. Michael was specifically chosen because of his disposition. He's a prankster and a fighter. He's a frat boy with a heart of gold. You'd almost think he could take on the forces of darkness all by himself. But that's only in a crisis situation. When it's downtime, Michael likes to have fun. When the 20th Century hit and Americans created a line of businesses called "the joke shop," Michael had his own little piece of Heaven. He loved the giant foam cowboy hats in neon colors. He loved neckties that lit up and played music, and would pair them with an electric blue zoot suit. His office was full of charts, maps, records, and other reference material, but peppered with things like rubber chickens, dribble glasses, the bug-in-an-ice cube, a wind-up nun that shot sparks, and that pack of gum where the only piece actually has a springbar like a mousetrap on it. A word to the wise: if you ever get called into Michael's office, under no circumstances should you ever take from the candy dish. Any one of a variety of things will happen, none of them pleasant.

Michael stood by his desk and smiled warmly at Alan. He wore a T-shirt campaigning for "hoagies, not stogies," cut-off jean shorts, and reef sandals. He was wearing glasses with color wheels that turned. Gold foil stars on springs attached to a headband wiggled around at any movement he made. He extended his hand warmly and came walking up. "Alan Levy! Good to meet you!"

Michael's hand was actually angled a bit odd. I caught the hand and flipped it over. Yes, there was a joy buzzer there. I glared at Michael. I didn't think this was the time for these things.

Michael arched his eyebrows innocently. "Alan, why don't you have a seat over there?"

Michael had gestured to the two highback wing chairs in front of his desk. Alan crept over, watching Michael the entire time and wondering what exactly he had gotten himself into. Before he sat, I rushed up and shot my hand onto the seat of the chair. I pulled up a whoopee cushion.

I glared at Michael again. Michael shrugged. "What? I'm just trying to loosen the poor guy up."

I stomped over to the other chair. "Fairchild said hi. I think we should be serious for a moment." I plopped myself down.

PHRRRRRRRRRRRRRT!

I leaned forward, my elbows on my knees and my forehead on my hands. This was going to be a long meeting.

I snapped out of it when I heard Alan laughing. I looked at him. He looked away as if he was afraid I'd snap at him. Of course, suppressed laughter is even worse, it keeps reinforcing itself. Michael was already laughing. Alan broke down and laughed openly. I started laughing, too. What else could I do? Laughter is infectious.

Once we had pulled ourselves together, Michael sat behind his desk. "Okay, let's get down to brass tacks, shall we? We are going to brainstorm and come up with a whale of a defense against Fairchild and his buddies."

Levy dropped his eyes. "Didn't repenting do it?"

When anyone petitions, the first thing that happens is they are taken to Penance Hall to repent. It eliminates a lot of headaches with the Churches, since the only real qualification is people have to repent their sins, it doesn't really say when they have to. And the ones determining penance up here are a lot more lenient and understanding than on Earth. Not everything is granted penance. You rob somebody, you don't get forgiveness for that. But things like seeing a woman in a swimsuit and having a lustful thought gets tidied up really quick.

"Repenting is for the garden-variety sins," Michael explained. "It doesn't cover those grey area ones. Like making porn."

Alan seemed to be willing himself to become smaller. "I didn't think it would hurt anything."

"And that's why your case is being advocated," Michael said. "See, most things described as sins, everyone knows and understands why they are considered sins. Don't steal, don't sleep with your neighbor's wife, don't murder – not kill, don't murder – things like that. The whole reason for the Celestial Courts was people doing things that might or might not be sins or things that might be sins but they had a reason to do them anyway. For example, you kill someone trying to kill you. Whether or not it can be excused can be complicated."

Michael leaned back in his chair. "The official position of the Celestials is you needed a job to survive. Yeah, you may have gotten enjoyment out of it. I mean, how could you not? But you would have given it up if you could. In fact, you did when you switched to bookkeeping. Hannah? How do you think Fairchild will approach this?"

I shrugged. "I'm not sure yet."

Alan looked worried. "You mean you don't know?"

I smiled at him. "I mean, I don't know yet. I need to figure out all the possible angles and which ones he'll take. Fairchild isn't stupid. No matter what you anticipate, he'll come up with something you aren't expecting."

"Why are you fighting for me?" Alan asked. "I mean, maybe I deserve to go to Hell."

Michael looked at him like he was nuts. "You wouldn't say that if you knew what Hell was really like. No one deserves that. God doesn't think anyone deserves an eternity of pain and torture. That's the whole reason for the Celestial Courts."

"Other people have to be simpler cases. They didn't do porn."

"True, other cases are simpler. That's why I gave Hannah your case.

She's the best Celestial ever. Allow me to employ some visual aids to better illustrate how this is going to go."

Michael pulled out one desk drawer on his left and one on his right. His left hand went in its corresponding drawer and came up with a sock monkey. "See this? This represents the Church who is arguing you should be Cast Down."

Michael's right hand zipped into its drawer. "And this represents Hannah." His right hand reappeared with a boxing nun puppet on it.

"And this is how the trial is going to go." The boxing nun puppet then began punching the sock monkey as Michael did a really lame Rocky Balboa impersonation.

This didn't seem to be reassuring Alan, so I started talking. "The regular defenses for people in the sex industry are pretty well covered. But they don't apply to you. Fairchild is going to have to come up with another angle and hope that he catches me flatfooted. My main goal is to nullify his arguments and present you in a way that will make the Tribunal side with letting you in."

From there, the three of us went back and forth about Alan's life and what possible traps Fairchild would lay out. It wouldn't be long before Alan's trial, and we had to be ready.

The time of trial had arrived. By this point, there was nothing new to be learned. Fairchild had talked with Alan (in my presence, to make sure he didn't throw another scare into him), scenarios were tried, and there was no point in delaying any further. It was time to spin the wheel.

I walked down the hall to the courtroom with purpose. Behind me was Alan, flanked by two Guardians. Guardians always had their wings out and had swords in scabbards at their hips. You could tell a lot about how dangerous they considered the Petitioner by where they kept the swords and where their hands were relative to them. The scabbards were swung around enough for a quick draw, but their hands were at their sides. Clearly, they felt all they needed to keep Alan in line was a little muscle. And Alan seemed to be fine with that.

We rounded the corner to the main entrance of our courtroom when I saw him. Approaching from the opposite side was Fairchild, two other Churches behind him. They were carrying a variety of scrolls with them. Each scroll had a clasp. That meant they were history files. Fairchild might be looking at using precedent to win. Then again, he knows I watch out for those things, so it could have been to throw me off, too.

We got to the entrance at about the same time. Fairchild already had his haughtiness in place. "I hope Alan is ready for a real change of scenery."

"Pretty weak, you usually come up with something more intimidating than that."

Fairchild smirked at me. He then leaned over to the door and held it open for me. "Age before beauty," he smiled.

I pinched his cheek like an aunt would. "Aw, thanks, kiddo."

"Burn!" And he stalked through the door first. To his credit, Alan lunged for the door and held it open for me.

Alan entered the courtroom, and started taking it in. It was large, but it wasn't ornate. Everything was in varying shades of soft white. It was illuminated, but no one could tell how – there wasn't a light source anywhere, and no shadows appeared. The only other colors came from Alan's clothes, the green polo shirt and khakis he was wearing when he died. We walked down the aisle that split the Gallery at the back half of the courtroom neatly in two. There was a low wall, barely higher than the backs of the Gallery benches, separating the area from the rest of the court, a single opening without a gate in the center to pass through. It was wide enough for five people, or one person with a Guardian with wings out on each side of him.

The other side of the wall had a different feel. The Gallery felt like a church with rows and rows of benches to sit at. The Advocates' Area, however, was open. A table in front of each half of the Gallery with four square stools each. The Churches took the table to the left, we Celestials got the one on the right, situated nearly in the center of the courtroom. Then a yawning gulf to the presiding angel's bench, raised up and paneled with a giant cross on the wall above it. To the right was the dock, a small square area surrounded with waist-high banisters where the Petitioner stood during trial. Against the right wall was the Tribunal's box. Two benches, six each, nice and wide to accommodate the wings, and a huge door in the wall, the Tribunal's entrance.

Two other Celestials were already at our table, sitting in the far seats. As we approached, Alan asked, "Where do I sit?"

"Right here for now," I said, motioning to the second one in. "You sit with your defenders. Since we aren't contesting your petition, that's us. Just follow my lead. I stand, you stand. I sit, you sit. Keep quiet and keep still, even in the dock. I'll let you know when you can talk freely. Don't give Fairchild anything to feed off of."

The Guardians went to stand in front of the bench. Alan carefully sat down, and I took the far seat. "By the way, these two fine Advocates are Claire and Del," I said. He waved weakly at the man and woman to his side, and they responded by reaching over, shaking his hand, and engaging him in light conversation, keeping him calm. With Alan distracted, I examined the table in front of me. Several scrolls were out in front of us, some already open to relevant cases and events. There wasn't much open space left.

I turned my head to my left. Fairchild's table was its usual flurry of activity. He had three other Churches there, huddled around the table like they were trying to keep prying eyes from seeing their secret plans. I noticed Fairchild was examining my table's activity as well. The left corner of his mouth twitched and he returned his attention to his group.

A few more came in to sit in the Gallery and watch the proceedings. Among them was Michael, who took a front seat directly behind me. Since this was a formal proceeding, he was dressed in proper robes. Alan actually did a double take. "Michael?" he asked.

"Yup," he confirmed.

"I almost didn't recognize you," Alan smiled.

"Must show proper respect. I'll make up for it later."

Alan seemed to settle a little more. So did I. Michael always has my back.

I was so lost in going over everything that I didn't notice the time. The chimes sounded and my head jerked up. Everybody immediately got to their feet. Out came the wings. None of the Advocates there were actual angels, so we had ceremonial wings. They aren't attached to our backs, but still move with us like they are. My wings were the plainest in the courtroom, a very rudimentary shape. The others had more detail or better definition. Ceremonial wings reflect the personality of their owner. Fairchild's were the boldest of them all. Alan looked even smaller now, surrounded by winged beings and no wings for himself.

The door behind the box opened and the Tribunal filed in. Twelve angels, wings already out. The sight never got old. The pride, honor, dedication, and wisdom came through in everything. I always said a little prayer that, someday, maybe, I can be one of them.

The presiding angel entered, carrying a record scroll. It was Sachiel. I immediately charted a new course for my approach. Sachiel was usually pretty hands off from trials unless someone really lost the point. This also meant that Advocates sparred with each other more openly. It wasn't unusual for most of their arguments to be made to each other instead of the bench or Tribunal. And that was just for regular Advocates. When it was down to Fairchild and I, it became a show. This was going to be rough.

Sachiel sat down at the bench and banged the gavel. The Tribunal and the Gallery sat down. Sachiel quickly opened and scanned the scroll, then set it down. He put his hands down on top of the desk and called out brightly, "Who is the Petitioner?"

I sensed Alan was about to say it was him. Force of habit is a powerful thing. Under the table, I put my foot on top of his. I heard him gasp a little. He had snapped out of it. I announced, "The Petitioner is Alan Thomas Levy."

"And who are his Advocates?"

"Claire Johnson, Del Sierra, and Hannah Singer, acting as lead."

"And who advocates for the Church?"

Fairchild's voice burst across the court. "David Tucker, Harold Lenska, Neil Amacker, and Jeff Fairchild, acting as lead."

Sachiel nodded to Fairchild. "Will the Petitioner please take the stand?"

Alan moved carefully across the court and climbed the few steps to the dock. He held onto the rail like he was on a ship rocking in a storm. After he entered the dock, the junior Advocates sat down. Other than the Guardians, it was just Fairchild and I standing.

"Advocate for the Petitioner goes first. You're up, Singer."

"Petition for entry to Heaven should be granted due to life situation. Levy was earning a living. It was what was available. What other option did he have?"

"What, he couldn't flip a burger?" Fairchild snipped.

Sachiel rapped the gavel once. He then leaned towards Fairchild like he was a child caught trying to steal a cookie. "It's still opening statements, Fairchild."

Fairchild had jumped the gun, so he nodded and buttoned his lip. I continued. "The Earth is not Heaven. Not by any stretch. Man has always organized into groups, whether for protection, companionship, or to achieve a common goal. Man has created various societies, some to pursue a better way of life, others to keep up with or compete with other societies. It is through this human cooperative that man can pursue things like art and knowledge and quality of life instead of just searching for something they can kill with a rock and eat. Ancient man didn't concern itself with anything other than survival. They just didn't have the luxury.

"The downside is, in order to live in one of these societies, there is a cost associated with it. The costs vary, but they aren't usually bad. You just need a certain level of income or a certain set of achievements. Given the choice between working and living in a shack with no plumbing and having to stalk their next meal everyday, reasonable people choose to get a nice little house. And who can blame them? Life is hard enough as it is.

"Alan Levy faced a choice. Like everyone, he wanted a good quality of life, to pursue enjoyments instead of wallowing in misery. However, to reach a level where he could live enjoyably, there was only one option available to him. And that was performing in adult films. Had he been presented with another option, he would have taken it. In fact, he did so when he switched to a bookkeeping job that paid well enough. Levy didn't do porn because he was an exhibitionist. He didn't get a thrill from thumbing his nose at social acceptability. He wasn't looking for an outlet for his prurient desires. It was a job. It was just something he did until something better came along. He was no different than anyone tolerating a job just to provide for their family or because they want to stay where they are instead of moving. His porn career was not a willful sin. As such, it should be excused and his petition into Heaven should be granted. Thank you."

Opening statements are simply a basic overview of the case. Specific strategies don't get revealed there. Not only would it bog things down, but it would give the opposition time to formulate counter arguments. A good Advocate knows how to shape openings without handing the other side anything they can use. They also know how to dig up hints of what's to come. I listened to Fairchild's opening statements with the same level of attention he gave mine.

"'A willful sin.' Interesting concept. You should not be punished for something beyond your control. This is the lynchpin of accidents. You didn't mean for something to happen. Everything happened around you and you were not in a position to stop it. We can all agree there are circumstances where that happens, when it truly isn't someone's fault.

"The question is, when is something a willful sin and when isn't it? At

24

what point have you done all you can and things happen regardless of your involvement? Singer's defense hinges on a sort of sliding scale, between 'I did all I could,' and 'I just didn't do enough.' Different events have different levels of involvement. People are less likely to be upset about certain things and will let some things happen instead of standing on principle. Things that they think are harmless. They didn't hurt anybody, so it's not like the sin was that great. Does it really matter?

"The simple answer is yes, it does matter. Not only did Levy willfully sin, having plenty of sex outside the sacrament of marriage, but to say he had no choice removes responsibility from him. He would have had to give up his band. What a shame, lots of people work horrible jobs with no dreams coming true, and they stick with it, out of principle, dedication to themselves, and to God. A man who is behind on his bills, his kids are sick, has far more justification for amoral acts like robbery than Levy has, but he will not do something he knows is evil. Levy is not to be excused. He is to be pitied, because he took the easy way out. His life was convenience, not sacrifice. His petition should be denied, and he should be Cast Down."

Sachiel leaned back. He looked at Fairchild and I and said, "Opening arguments are over. Go to it."

Fairchild looked at me. He wanted me to make the first move. It's the first tactic any Advocate learns. The opposition makes arguments, and the Advocate just has to nullify them. They bring the fight to you. However, it's also very easy for the smart ones to reverse. Just make a statement that will make them want to engage you. And I had a beaut. Fairchild should know better than to try that maneuver with me. "Extramarital sex is excused by God."

Well, so much for Fairchild's original strategy. "Singer, you really need to review your Bible."

"Sure. Let's start by reviewing the story of King David. Great family values with that guy. King Solomon built his house to hold his wives, plural, and mistresses, a thousand total. Not one complaint about that. And don't forget concubines. They're all over the Bible." First blood for Hannah Singer.

"David and Solomon were admired as great men!"

"Levy had sex with lots of beautiful women and got paid for it. I can think of lots of guys who would admire him as a great man for that."

"That lifestyle is counter to a good Christian life!"

"Not according to the Bible."

"Prove it!"

I smirked. Fairchild looked like his stomach just dropped to his feet. "Oh, no. No no no no no...."

I started reciting from Song Of Songs, chapter 7. "How fair and pleasant you are, O loved one, delectable maiden! You are stately as a palm tree, and your breasts are like its clusters. I say I will climb the palm tree and lay hold of its branches. Oh, may your breasts be like the clusters of the vine, and the scent of your breath like apples, and your kisses like the best wine that goes down smoothly, gliding over the lips and teeth."

I looked at Alan in the dock. He looked stunned. I started fanning myself with my hand and told him, "I'll bet your dialogue was never that poetic."

Fairchild commanded my attention. "You're taking Song Of Songs out of context!"

Fairchild had told me that before. And I responded the same way I had before. "Okay. What's the correct context? Enlighten me." Fairchild was still searching for words. I decided to take advantage of his mental distraction. "After all, if living a good Christian life is based on living with what the Bible says is okay, and the Bible clearly doesn't have a problem with...."

"The Bible has nothing to do with this!"

"I accept your statement."

Fairchild's eyes shot wide at that moment. He had just thrown out any Biblical basis for his arguments. It's such a rookie mistake, I'm amazed when any lead Advocate falls for it, especially one with the two hundred years under his belt that Fairchild likes to brag about. I found out later that Michael had caught Alan's eye in the dock. Michael licked his finger and "marked" a point for me.

Fairchild, to his credit, doesn't give up easily. He looked at Sachiel and said, "The Church requests the Bible be reintroduced into arguments."

Think fast, Hannah. I faced the bench and said, "The Bible is not necessary to support his arguments."

Fairchild wasn't about to let me get my way this time. "If arguments are based on Biblical teachings, how can I argue without a Bible?"

"The Bible is a repository of ethics and morals. They are universal truths, that people should love one another and be good to each other. Are your moral definitions so weak they don't stand on their own?"

"In order to argue from a Biblical point of view, I need the Bible. QED."

Can't stop his approach. Better speed him up, make him overshoot the landing. "The Bible is of no use to your arguments. Where in the Bible does it say, 'Thou shalt not make porn?'"

"There are plenty of things that add up to 'Thou shalt not make porn.' Several pronouncements, taken individually, that can be combined under that."

"So, individual Biblical punishments, which are extreme enough in their own right, combine to make something not so extreme. Which ones do you have to choose from where the punishment fits the crime?"

Fairchild was clearly trying to search his memory. He wanted to find some Biblical punishment that wasn't too bad. I wasn't going to help him. I continued, "Slaughtering Nabal and his family for not giving David and his men food? Elisha summoning a bear to kill kids making fun of him for being bald? Kill anyone who works on the Sabbath day? It's okay to beat a servant or maid as long as they don't die?"

Fairchild winced. We Advocates call that a Mousetrap. It's an argument you can't wiggle out of. If Fairchild tossed Biblical defense, most of his ammo went with it. But if it stayed, it would be a cinch for me to frame his recommended fate as being excessive and mercy as the only appropriate response.

Fairchild decided that, if I was going to win, I'd have to earn it. "The church withdraws request for reintroduction."

"Glad we got that settled," Sachiel said. "Please continue."

"Even without the Bible, you won't win," Fairchild snarled at me. "There is no excuse for his behavior."

"Plenty of sex workers with far more questionable motives and who are far less repentant for their lives get into Heaven."

"Not thanks to us! We oppose such things! Even you have to admit not everyone can handle sex!"

I couldn't respond right away. There's a reason so many religions become uptight when it comes to sex. Sex changes everything. It's a form of relation with no real analog in any other aspect of human interaction. Sex can deepen bonds, which is why it's so crucial in marriage. But if people are not mindful of its import, if they are being irresponsible, it can be hazardous to their well-being. It is the most intimate and direct way of expressing how you feel about someone. And if both people are not on the same page, it causes real problems in all realms -- physical, mental, spiritual, and emotional. However, if I didn't choose my words carefully, Fairchild would pounce and twist it to bolster his point. I wasn't going to let Alan get hung out to dry over this.

I chose my words carefully. "Well, he could handle it. He's clearly not maladjusted, is he?"

"That is our policy! People jump into sex without knowing the risks!"

"So, even though he's responsible, just because other people are not, he should be forbidden? What about earning privileges and rights?"

Fairchild knew I was chipping away at the fundamental reasoning for sex being a sin. I was well on my way to getting an exception for Alan, so he went for a change-up. "That concerns personal liberty. We are talking about a job here. People can't help who they are attracted to, but they can help what they do for a living."

"He had bookkeeping degrees, but no one hired him."

"No one in his area. He could have moved where the work was."

"And break up his family? Not everyone is fine with that."

"He didn't look hard enough. When presented with the offer to do porn, he stopped looking. He did bookkeeping later, after the work was coming to him."

I smiled. I had this in the bag. "It's that important to the church for people to remain sexually pure?"

"Yes," he said, but with uncertainty.

"So the church failed Alan Levy."

"What do you mean, 'We failed him?'"

"If keeping people safe from temptation is the church's goal, why didn't they step up with an offer for Alan? Churches need bookkeeping, don't they? They could have provided him with work at a decent wage, right?"

27

"The churches already have bookkeepers."

"Then how would they have provided Alan with an alternative to working in the adult film industry?"

"The church isn't required to provide jobs to their flock, just spiritual enlightenment!"

"'Spiritual enlightenment.' That's interesting. So, they are to guide people to the best lives they can have. They are to provide wisdom, not condemnation."

"We do provide wisdom. Condemnation is part of it to keep those who don't deserve Heaven out!"

"The church still failed."

"How so?"

"Who reached out to him? Who told him where other jobs were? Did they help his band so he could do that instead? Did they give leads? How about dealing with companies that just hired temps for indefinite assignments instead of actually hiring, which meant paying more and providing benefits? The church failed him. The whole world failed him, from business owners to neighbors to the church. If porn is a bad idea, and the only cure for bad ideas is better ideas, why did no one provide a better idea?"

"Each person is responsible for their spiritual lives."

"And he made his peace with his spiritual life. You are contesting it, not him."

"I have to contest it! It's my duty!"

"So, it's nothing personal, you're a good guy, you didn't have a lot of options, not a lot of awareness, so we're condemning you to Hell."

"Yes! It's exactly what he deserves!"

"And you don't think that's excessive?"

Fairchild froze at that point. He had backed into an argument that proved the Church recommendation was too harsh. He really had no other options to hit me with, because he told the bench, "I move for closing arguments."

Fairchild usually just starts closing arguments, he doesn't move for them. When he does that, he knows he's lost. The only question was, what would the Tribunal decide? They don't have to take our recommendations, they can come up with their own fate. The closing arguments are your last appeal to justice and mercy, even when those conflict.

The Petitioner's Advocate is entitled to the last word, so Fairchild started. His recommended fate would never happen. All he could do now was keep mine from being accepted. "The whole purpose of the Celestial Court is exceptions. People do things wrong all the time. No one is perfect. Even those who live in strict accordance with the Bible will do things wrong. Maybe their understanding enabled someone to do something horrible, like keeping a fighting family together. Or maybe they weren't understanding enough, and broke up a family that could have made it if they just stuck it out a little longer. Mistakes happen. Mistakes are unavoidable. This is the reason for penance, forgiveness, and mercy, the three pillars upon which the Celestial Courts are built.

"However, there are limits. People who commit crimes must atone for their misdeeds. There are some sins that only we know, the living either haven't figured out that they are sins or haven't accepted the truth yet. There are sins against the church. There are sins against society. No one will deny that robbery, incest, rape, murder, bestiality...these are not just sins, they are evil acts. These are not even granted penance here, they have to stand trial and account for what they have done. Everyone committing these acts doesn't see a problem with committing them, either in general or at the moment of temptation. There is no penance. There is no mercy. There is no forgiveness. There cannot and will never be.

"Alan Levy willfully committed immoral acts. Not for any noble reason, like a poor man who steals food to feed his family. He simply didn't want a life of hard work. Most of the world has to sacrifice. They do not lead the lives they choose, they have to do the best they can with what they have. Levy refused such a life. It is weakness in his character. There is no strength, there is no nobility. The point of being alive is to live in accordance with God's will. God's will is for us to be upstanding and noble, to resist the superficial and easy. He has not only not done anything to earn a Heavenly reward, but his character is fundamentally flawed. Reincarnation? If he winds up in a similar or more permissive family, we'll just be here again arguing these same points when he petitions again. There is nothing that warrants the compassion of the court. A Heavenly reward is earned, and he will never have what it takes. He deserves the simplest, most direct fate possible. He should be Cast Down. Thank you."

Fairchild nodded to the Tribunal. The Tribunal didn't respond beyond looking at me. I had to sell them, give them a good reason to disregard Fairchild's points and rule favorably for Alan. Alan looked at me in fear. I was his last hope of staying out of Hell. Fairchild had put a lot of effort into his speech. He wanted to Cast someone. And Casting someone I was representing would be the greatest achievement any Church had ever done. I couldn't blow this. Everything depended on me and my closing arguments.

It's star time.

I started with framing to keep Fairchild from objecting. "Biblical scripture is not allowed in this trial. However, there is no such restriction on Biblical history. As such, I would like to remind everyone of the story of Adam and Eve and the forbidden fruit. God forbade Adam and Eve to eat the fruit from two trees in the Garden Of Eden. The serpent talks to Adam about taking the fruit. Adam talks Eve into going first. Only after seeing his guinea pig is unharmed does he bite the fruit.

"The fruit was from the Tree Of Wisdom. They gained awareness. God kicks them out of the Garden Of Eden. Why? He might have been scared that they would eat from the Tree Of Life, making them immortal. But why have the Tree there in the first place, then? Why not put it somewhere safe?

Why put either tree there, especially given how simple it was to take the fruit. All they needed was the will, and they would do so.

"God did not kick them out of the Garden Of Eden as a punishment. He kicked them out because they couldn't stay there anymore. The Garden Of Eden was to protect them from a world they could not handle and survive in. By eating the fruit, they became intelligent, aware, and responsible for their own actions, and they were ready for the world. Otherwise, God could have undone the effects of the fruit. He's God, after all.

"God hands down orders and commandments and laws. And people have minimized or disregarded them at strategic times. Even the church has done so, unrepentantly killing during the Crusades and the Inquisition. When this happens, people are saying that, even though it is wrong, they have a good reason to do it and are taking responsibility for their actions. And that is where judgment lies. Was the reason good enough? How far did they go? What were their motivations? And so on.

"Alan Levy has never blamed anyone else for his making porn. He knew what he was doing and took responsibility for it. He never abused the situation. There are many things that can happen in that field. Levy treated it as a job, nothing more. He treated others with respect. He never took advantage of them. He acted with maturity and dedication when he had every excuse to cast it aside. And he emerged from the industry unscathed. Given how many people and businesses on Earth take advantage of people in ways other than sexual, crushing their spirits and owning their lives, Alan really made the best choice available to him, and the industry truly did treat him well.

"People have had sex outside of church approval since the earliest churches. They do it for a variety of reasons. Some have sex because they love someone and feel that commitment is important, not a stamp of approval from a church. Some do it out of desperation. Some do it for money. All of them defy the doctrine of no extramarital sex. Why? Some have simple reasons based on a misunderstanding of what marriage is supposed to be. Some do it for the thrill. In all these cases, the participants are taking forbidden fruit, and have to live with and own up to the consequences.

"Alan owned up to the responsibility. He was no rebel, he was no bad boy. He was making a choice and doing the best he could with it. Did he know God didn't want him to do that? Sure. So does everyone else living on Earth. But they do it anyway. And they come here to face judgment about what they did. For a decision made in a moment of emotion.

"Unlike the evil sins mentioned, sex is not evil. Sex is beautiful. People on Earth have a saying that they would rather watch a film of two people making love than two people trying to kill one another. But there is still harsh judgment associated with sex. People are taught that it is naughty instead of it being another adult responsibility like drinking. And when they see their lives are not being harmed by sex, and the only opposing reasoning is an overreaction, can we not all understand why people disregard the messages about extramarital sex?

"The key to remember is this: God and Jesus warned against extramarital sex. But at no point did they eliminate the sex drive itself. They could have made it easier to control. If its only purpose is reproduction, why make it feel good? Why bother making humans so that can't reproduce asexually? Sex is another area where if people are willing to take responsibility and do right by each other, sex becomes their right. And if they are not worthy of that right, if they are careless, that becomes the crime. Alan did right by others, he didn't descend into a life of debauchery. If he hadn't been filmed, we would not be having this trial right now. It would have been he had sex with however many women, some of us would be shocked, some of us would be impressed, he'd repent, and it would be over. He's on his way to Heaven. Literally, the only difference in his sin from every other case involving casual sex that we argue here is that he did it for a living. A living that wasn't coming any other way. He doesn't deserve mercy. He did nothing wrong to warrant a debate about mercy. He deserves what everyone else gets who is in a situation with analogous points but different details. He deserves Heaven. Thank you."

Sachiel tilted his head towards the Tribunal. "You have heard the Advocates for Alan Thomas Levy state their recommended fates. You may now make your decision. You wish to confer?"

The Tribunal whispered to each other for about a minute. Alan was starting to sweat. Finally, the lead Tribunal said, "We are ready to rule."

"And what is your decision?"

"Petition for entry to Heaven is granted."

Sachiel picked up the gavel. "So be it, court is adjourned." He banged the gavel and sauntered out of court, the Tribunal taking off at the same time.

Alan just stood in the dock, complete shock on his face. He wasn't even moving. Michael walked up to him and said, "When I snap my fingers, you will think you are a chicken," and snapped his fingers in front of Alan's eyes.

Alan shook his head. "Wait...what?"

"Glad you could rejoin us, Alan. Did you at least hear what the ruling was?"

"Yeah," he said, a bit distant. "I get to go to Heaven."

"I told you she was the best."

Alan raced out of the dock and started shaking my hand. Fairchild and his juniors just glared at me and stalked out of court. When the gushing gratitude eased up, Alan asked, "Now what do I do?"

I pointed to the door on the left side of the court. "That's the Petitioner's exit. Go through it, and the rest will happen."

He was snapping his head from me to the door. Michael came up and said, "Oh, go on through."

He walked backwards, gesticulating to us the entire time. "Thank you again! For everything! You don't know what this means to me!"

I smiled at him. "Oh, trust me. I know."

Alan smiled, turned, and dashed through the door. Michael, the juniors, and I gathered up the scrolls and headed out of court. After we returned them,

31

Claire and Del went their own ways and Michael and I went ours. As we walked outside onto the main grounds, I spoke. "Sex really makes people do weird things."

"You mean as far as sex goes, or how people react to it?"

"Yes," I responded. "You know, we wouldn't have half these trials if the churches on Earth tried to be more mature and understanding about sex."

"It's not just the churches that are immature about sex," Michael told me. "Everyone is. Once again, they don't know the effects it has so they figure it's harmless. Or they just don't care. People already seek out loopholes instead of understanding. Attempting a progressive position isn't going to fix anything."

"I know," I told him. "It just seems like there should be a better way. You know, some clarity."

"Sex is individual, Hannah. The official position may have its flaws, but ultimately, it still comes down what each person is ready for and when they are ready for it. Some are fine with waiting, others aren't. It's always their choice. That's why we have to create exceptions instead of the church changing its doctrines. It's imperfect, but the alternatives are worse."

All I could do was shrug. "So we'll be dealing with these cases for a long, long time."

"You know we always have, just not in these numbers."

"It'd just be nice to streamline things."

"Remember, the Celestial Courts weren't set up for us. They were set up for them." And Michael gestured in front of him.

We had come around and were in front of the clerks' office, where people start the petition process. The line was actually a little longer today, there were people waiting outside the door. They were shuffling their feet, shifting their weight, and looked scared.

I smiled. These people needed someone who wouldn't let them down. It was what I was good at. It was my duty.

I went to the Office Of Records and requested scrolls. It was going to be busier than usual for a while.

I have to admit, the Heavenly hosts are very nice and respectful. It was a surprise to me. First of all, I remembered being taught that angels were fierce and powerful warriors. They administered terrible, swift justice against all enemies of the Lord and his devotees. Conquering armies. Demons. Non-believers.

Especially non-believers.

My early days as an Advocate were nerve-racking for me. After all, I had been an Atheist. I didn't think there was any way I'd be more than tolerated. But not only was I welcomed to the ranks with open arms (and a standing offer to enter Heaven whenever I was ready), but they treated me like family. They didn't nurse any grudges against me.

So, how exactly does a person become one of the most unusual Advocates the Celestial Courts have ever seen? Simple. They are part of one of the most unusual trials ever argued before the Celestial Courts. The fact that things worked out is enough to convince any Atheist that God has a master plan.

The story of how I became Hannah Singer, Celestial Advocate, is reminiscent of a superhero origin story, with an ordinary person getting important responsibility thrust upon them that they have to rise to their best potential to handle (I will not discuss how I know about that stuff). I don't remember much about my childhood. I mean, who does? I was born in England in what is now referred to as the Medieval Age, sometime in the early 14th Century. I was a peasant, working and toiling in the fields for the most part. I was run out of my home village and pretty much just wandered until I found a new place to stay.

Why was I run out? I was an Atheist. That's really it. See, every Christian has doubts at least once in a while. Jesus did Himself. But I didn't have doubts. I never believed, full stop. Everyone I knew worked from sun up to sun down, some so poor they didn't even have clothes to wear and worked naked in the fields. There wasn't even time to mourn the deaths of family and friends - taking the time could cost you your own well-being. Travelers forced themselves into the woods and sometimes to kill marauders looking to rob them. Survival was the only thing that mattered. All the while, kings and lords lived in luxury off of our labors. To me, Heaven was just another tale parents told their children to teach little life lessons. That is, when it wasn't being used to control people. Violence? Revolt? Defying the established order? You don't want to risk losing the Paradise you can go to, do you? I saw the church as a tool, sometimes unwitting, sometimes in collusion with the king.

Everyone was supposed to be polite and subservient. Especially the women. Women weren't allowed to learn how to read, so I would listen to others read aloud from the Bible. The story of King David? The Book Of Job?

They would read those and smile about God's generosity and love. And I'd be sitting there in shock at how harsh, unfair, and unfeeling He was. So when I finally snapped and lashed out at phony promises and willful blindness...it didn't go over very well. First, everyone tried to save my soul, praying for me, performing exorcisms, everything except letting me reach what I felt was a reasonable conclusion. It was sometime around when they went for more extreme measures that weren't working (a hot poker against the skin that branded a cross on my stomach) that they realized my "true nature" -- I was actually a witch, there to destroy them. I wasn't with God, so I had to be against him. My life was truly in danger. I quickly repented my ways, lying through my teeth the entire time, and after being welcomed back into the fold, given lots of food and clothes, I snuck out in the middle of the night and never looked back.

I eventually wound up in another village. Becoming a part of it wasn't that tough. I just feigned Christianity. The branded cross, you should pardon the expression, made quite an impression. Everyone wanted to help me. I kept my mouth shut about my beliefs. There was nothing on the other side of life. Frankly, I didn't want to die. It's also why I never married. I was already living a lie, I didn't want to compound it. A couple of men tried courting me, but eventually got tired of chasing me.

Those of you familiar with history know what's coming. I was living as the Black Death was reaching its peak. The people in my village, naturally, were scared. So was I. When the plague first came, everyone banded together to help those in need. It was truly beautiful. But eventually, as the population dwindled, those with the sickness were shunned and run out of town in an effort to protect the others. I was the only one who still tried to help them. I would tend to them in the early stages of the disease, and would still try to bring food or whatever I could after they had been forced into the forest just beyond the village. Seeing the bodies was horrible, and I still remember the scent as if it was around me now.

And then, it happened.

I got the sickness.

I knew the early symptoms. I'd seen them often enough. I was going to die, slowly, painfully, and soon. I felt like I had a pack on my back. Each day, another stone was added to it, making it heavier. I had trouble shouldering it. I started to stumble. I was feeling faint. I strained with effort to do anything. When people in the village started asking if something was wrong, I knew I wouldn't be able to hide it much longer. I resolved I would jump before I was pushed. I would leave the village that night. Just like I had the last one.

It was really strange that night. I looked over what I would take with me, and weighed that against how long I expected to live. The cold calculations didn't seem the least bit morbid to me, I just wanted out of there. I had always felt alone because of my beliefs. I even felt alone when everyone was around me, because, if they knew the truth, I'd be ostracized again. I was alone in life, I wanted to be alone in death.

I don't know how long I was out there. I remember the sickness seemed to explode once I left, like trying to keep it from being noticed was the only thing holding it at bay. I thought about killing myself. It's not like staying alive would have made any difference. But the explosion from the sickness made travel to any place like a cliffside impossible. That pack suddenly became heavier than ever. I felt my heart strain, like it was forcing itself to beat. Breathing became harder. A chest full of air was too much effort, so I just did the best I could. The world became darker, a shadow settling over my eyes that became harder to see through with every passing moment.

I remember waking up, straining to lift my eyelids. I was leaning against the trunk of a tree. I couldn't tell which direction the sun was, so I didn't know if it was morning or not. Did I sleep, or had I passed out again? I could drag my hands around, but I couldn't lift them. My legs wouldn't move, no matter how much I willed them to. I felt like I was breathing water. My ears were filled with cotton. Everything sounded muffled, except the pounding of my heart, nearly drowning out everything else. The tree bark was darker than ever, and I couldn't even move my eyes to see if there was anything else around me.

I closed my eyes. I felt lightheaded. I wasn't breathing. I forced my chest to rise and fall. Soon, I was taking it on faith that I was still breathing. I couldn't feel the muscles moving anymore. My heart was quiet. Was it that I couldn't feel it as well, or had it actually stopped? The world around me shrunk. In that moment, I felt relief. It was almost over. I felt myself falling away, down a dark well and the light of the world becoming a pinpoint.

And then, it was gone.

I bubbled.

That's the only way I can describe it.

There was a moment of complete nothingness, when even the relief I felt had ceased.

And then, I felt myself starting to drift up. And the blackness started to change. It was becoming blue. A very dark, almost black blue, but definitely blue. I felt the outer edges of myself shimmering a bit, like they should be pulling off and drifting away, but they didn't. My body rippled gently. It didn't shake, it just rippled as it slowly and gently rose up, the blue around me getting lighter and an awareness that I was moving towards the top of something. Like a bubble from the bottom of a lake.

I couldn't really see anything. I couldn't really move, either. I wanted to move my arms, my head, just my eyes, but nothing happened. The peace I felt was no match for the panic setting in. What happened to me? What was going to happen to me?

The blue got lighter until it started to look white. And I thought I saw some sort of surface. Strange shapes on the other side, wobbling and rippling just like I was. I couldn't hold my breath, so I braced myself. I was about float to the surface, and whatever was on the other side.

I felt the surface touch me. It started to move past me. I felt it outlining me, but I still couldn't see whatever was past it. Then, I felt the surface move behind me, get smaller, and vanish.

Pop!

I didn't know when I had closed my eyes. I didn't know I had eyes to close. But I instinctively opened them. Well, they didn't open so much as sprang open. As wide as the blue sky above me.

I sat bolt upright. I gasped. It was like my muscles were only capable of fast movements. I felt like a bug held before someone's eyes, no refuge. I shot to my feet, slowly circling backwards while looking around. I couldn't think the bubbling was a dream. I wasn't in the forest anymore. I was standing in a rocky area, almost like a mountain gully. Very little vegetation, rough dirt on the ground, towering walls of rock with plenty of crevices.

It seemed innocent enough, until I got a really close look around. The colors around me weren't normal. They seemed too perfect. The next shock came when I saw the small tree, barely bigger than me, with all the leaves its few tiny branches could hold. It was remarkably full and hardy. In fact, in this rocky environment, no tree should be that full and hardy.

But the biggest shock was when I looked at the ground, hoping the dirt would give me some idea where I might be. Different areas had different dirt. But it wasn't that the dirt was so noticeable. It was the footprints.

Or the lack of them.

All I saw were my footprints, made after I came around. There were no other footprints leading to where I was or away from it. No one else had been around. Did I just appear here out of thin air? I then got a really good look at where I had been laying. I could see impressions from my lower body when I started moving around. I saw the impressions my hands made as I pushed myself up. But nothing where my upper body had been. I knew the position my hands and arms were in because I had to move them to push myself up. But there was nothing where they should have been when my eyes first opened. And just moving, I was leaving impressions in the dirt with every step.

The bubbling wasn't just my senses leaving me as the sickness attacked. Something had happened. For a brief moment, I thought, maybe this is Heaven.

I slapped my face. Get serious, Hannah. There's no such thing.

I gave myself a quick pat down. No broken bones, no injuries. No lesions or marks from the plague, either. The scars on my hands from working in the field and the calluses on my feet were gone. And then I felt something else. My tongue was touching teeth. I had lost some of my teeth, but they seemed to be back. I dove my fingers into my mouth to feel, not caring that I didn't know where they'd been. Sure enough, I had a full set of teeth in my head again.

I thought for a minute about the ramifications of this. Then I carefully started to untie the rope around my waist. I looked down and pulled up the bottom of my peasant dress, fighting to move the extra fabric out of my field of vision. When I got the dress around my chest and bunched aside, I took a good look at my stomach. The cross that had been branded there was gone.

I dropped the dress and tied the rope back on, carefully watching around me for any sign of movement. Once I was back to being presentable, I moved to one of the rocky side walls. I wanted to be able to move for cover in an instant. I climbed up a bit and carefully moved from one bunker to the next, progressing through the gully. I felt better than ever. Good thing, too. I wasn't used to moving so easily, and a few times, I slipped. I actually fell down the rock face onto the ground. The first time, I bounced up and dashed behind some rocks in case the noise had alerted anyone. While back there, I noticed that I had simply moved. Despite falling from a height like that of a castle wall and rolling like dice out of a drunk's hand, I wasn't injured. I was absolutely none the worse for wear. I went back up the rock side. The second time it happened, I didn't bother taking cover, I just sat listening for anything before climbing back up. The third time, I was actually getting upset with myself for being so clumsy.

After the third time, I moved some distance when I heard it.

"Singer? Hannah Singer?"

A man's voice. Sounded pleasant enough, but that meant nothing to me. I ducked into a crevice and willed myself to hold my breath. Pressed up against the wall, I heard the voice down below. It was moving past me.

"Are you here? I want to help you."

I'd heard that one before.

I kept listening close as the voice moved on and faded away. I didn't even try to see who it might have been. This wasn't someone just hoping to run into victims. He knew I was there. He knew who I was. And I didn't trust that he really had my best interests at heart. I don't know how long I held up, but I made sure it was long enough for him to leave.

I eventually made it to the edge of the gully. A gigantic plain spread out in front of me. There was blue sky as far as I could see with brilliant white clouds dotting it. The clouds moved gently, but stayed out of the way of the brilliant sun shining down on everything. Maybe I had just been exposed to it for too long, but the vibrancy of the colors no longer felt so strange. It was simply there.

I stayed in the gully a little longer. The wide open space made me nervous. There was nowhere to duck or take cover if whoever was looking for me came around again. I decided to wait until nightfall. My clothes were darker colors – vibrant now, but still dark. It would provide me with a little more cover than just darting out now like a frightened field mouse. I moved back into one of the crevices to wait.

As I sat, low against the wall and inside the shadow of the cave to minimize my chances of being spotted, I thought about taking a nap. After all, there was no telling how long I'd need be awake to make it across the plain. Part of the reason people travel as a group is to help watch each other's backs. But I was alone. And there wasn't a random threat, there was someone looking for me. If whoever it was came along with me in this cave, I'd be trapped. I felt pretty good, completely rested and not the least bit tired, regardless of how far I'd traveled. I decided to wait and take my chances that I'd make it through the night.

I sat there, waiting and thinking, turning everything over in my mind. I was fighting to keep thoughts of the supernatural from intruding. I didn't want to be wrong about there being nothing on the other side of life. I had made my peace with becoming nothing. The idea of there being a whole new world, one that not even Bible study could prepare you for, was too much for me. I actually started shaking, but I willed myself to pull it together.

I started remembering what I could from the Bible, just to do it. It's a lot of information, I figured that would take long enough. But when I got done, it still wasn't dark. I started remembering other things. Songs I had sung. The names of people I knew. Conversations I'd had. I tried making some stuff up.

I eventually poked my head out and crept to the edge of the gully. If the sun had changed position, I couldn't tell. I sagged against the rock. This was going to take forever.

I couldn't stay here. I had to move on, see what else was out there, figure out what I was going to do next. I carefully moved down the side of the rock face, watching and listening for anything. When I got to ground level, I looked at the horizon. There seemed to be a patch of trees off in the distance to my left. That became my destination. I steeled my will. I took a deep breath. And I started running.

I ran normally at first. Then I made it far enough onto the plain that I knew there was no turning back. If I spotted a threat, I'd never make it back to the cover of the gully before I was noticed. I pushed myself to run faster, panic reinforcing my speed. I just kept pushing, knowing that I was running faster than ever.

It was after a while that I noticed I wasn't getting tired. My legs weren't burning. I wasn't breathing hard. I wasn't sweating. I literally felt like I could run forever. I pushed myself to run faster. I could. It wasn't by much, but it was faster than I ever had. And I felt something.

Joy.

I finally felt something other than fear and intimidation. And I didn't want it to end. So I kept running as best I could.

I finally made it to the wooded area I saw from the gully. It was just thick enough. Strangely, I wasn't worried about marauders lying in wait. That made me nervous. I was becoming too complacent. I decided I needed a little time to gather my wits again. I climbed up a tree, watching for anyone else. I kept going, more interested in getting up than how I would get back down. I figured I'd simply jump. After all, I seemed to be invulnerable now. I got to a point I was happy with – near enough to the top to see the sky, but still with enough cover to hide me. I sat in the crook of the tree, my back against the trunk, and relaxed.

I thought about where I was and what had happened to me. I wanted to be left alone, and I apparently got my wish. Well, sort of. Whoever that other guy was. But there was really nothing else around. I heard birds singing, but I didn't see them.

Then I saw them flying overhead, way up in the sky. I envied them for a moment, how high they were, how untouchable by threat. As they flapped their majestic wings, a couple of them left the flock and started flying around like they were searching for something on the ground.

On the plains I had just left behind.

One of them got even lower, and I saw I wasn't watching birds.

The wings came out of the back of a human figure.

An angel.

I caught myself before I slid off my perch.

The angel flew past the tree I was hiding in. He was still a distance away, but I still felt lucky he didn't notice me. I stopped paying attention for a moment, locked in the shock of my thoughts. Angels were real. I saw one, plain as day. And this wasn't like the occasional wisps I saw when the plague was destroying me. I knew this was no trick of the mind. And in that moment, every thought I was fighting, shoving down from my mind, simply slipped around and came up. Like a bubble from the bottom of a lake.

I was dead.

Pop!

I covered my face with my hands. Oh no, oh no, oh no! Now, what was I going to do?!? I saw angels! The priests had been right! And if they were right about death and what lay beyond, did that mean Hell was also real? And was that where I was bound?

I didn't move. I didn't dare. I occasionally saw actual birds fly by, but I couldn't admire their beauty anymore. I was in big trouble, and I had no idea how to get out of it. Could I stay hidden in that tree forever? I was ready to find out. It beat the alternative.

It had to have been a couple of days. Night never fell, so I couldn't be sure. I was starting to get antsy. Frustrated. I was sick of sitting still. There had to be something else to do, somewhere else to go. I mean, the angels hadn't found me. Whoever that was in the gully hadn't found me. Maybe there was more to this place.

It was after a while that I saw something out by the horizon. It appeared to be a person walking. He seemed older than me, maybe by twenty years. He was grizzled. He looked like a ship captain of some kind. He wore a white shirt under a jerkin with beige leggings and leather boots over his shins. He hobbled when he walked, which seemed odd to me.

He was some distance away and looked to be moving past the forest I was hiding in when an angel dropped down out of nowhere. It still caught me by surprise, I thought I could see them coming. The angel engaged him in conversation. It seemed pretty cordial, and the captain shook his head a few times, once even held up his hand in a "no" gesture, and the angel shrugged. The angel then spread his wings and flew straight up into the air.

I quickly slid off the limb and dropped to the ground. I landed perfectly on my feet and bent, like a cat. I quickly forced how neat what just happened was out of my head and carefully came out of the forest. I started peeking out from around the tree when the captain saw me. He stopped, turned to face me full, and gave me a gentlemanly bow. "Greetings, m'lady," he said. He straightened with a smile, turned and resumed walking.

I don't know why, but I dashed out of the woods and caught up to him. Maybe the fact that he was content to leave me be did it. "Um...excuse me, sire...."

"Hawthorne," he said, stopping, spinning to me, and bowing gentlemanly without missing a beat. "Arthur Hawthorne, at your service."

At my service? I wasn't going to ask for that much. "Uh...I saw you talking with that angel...."

"Aye," he said, looking to the sky in the direction the angel had left in. "They're still trying, even after all this time."

"All this time?"

"Do you have any idea where you are?"

I just stood where I was. I moved my mouth, but no sounds came out.

He smiled reassuringly at me. "You're in no danger." He was about to say more, then closed his mouth. He eyed me up and down. "You seem pretty smart. Why don't you tell me what you've figured out?"

I thought it over. I told him the most important thing, hoping he would correct me. Please, let him correct me. "I'm dead."

"Very good. You're off to a flying start."

My body felt limp. My shoulders sagged. Nothing else really mattered now. "What do I do now?"

"It's entirely up to you. You can always take your chances with the courts."

"What courts?"

"Where you're judged and they determine if you go to Heaven or not."

Something in what he said struck me odd. "I don't have to be judged?"

"Nope. You're encouraged to, but if you would rather stay here, they won't force you."

I needed to know more. And Hawthorne seemed to have the answers I needed.

Hawthorne made the first move. "Look, you clearly need something to do. What do you say to a partnership? You accompany me as I wander. You can be my friend. And I can be your protector. Well, sort of. There are no dangers here, but I can act like there are. It's not like I have anything else to do. What do you say?" He extended his hand for me to shake.

I thought it over. Something that wasn't so transitory. Someone I could talk with.

I stepped forward and shook his hand. "Pleased to meet you. I'm Hannah Singer."

He bowed deeply and kissed my hand. "The pleasure is all mine, m'lady."

Artie, as he insisted I call him, truly was a gentleman. Well, a rogue. He served on a pirate ship.

"Want to find a different partner?" he asked, his jovial tone not completely covering the worry in his voice.

"Don't be silly," I smiled. By this point, I liked him too much to judge him for that.

They took what they wanted when they wanted. They weren't interested in being murderers, and would usually leave the people on the ships they raided somewhere. But things went wrong when they came across a navy that ran them down. Artie died during the boarding, the speed and skill that served him so well in his youth having gone away.

Artie had a peg leg in the later half of his life. When he died, his spirit reformed with the leg intact, but he still had the habit of walking with the peg. He also used to wear an eye patch, but had both eyes again. His tattoos were gone, too. He figured out pretty quick that he was dead.

Artie's knowledge of the Afterlife came from encounters with the angels and other beings called "Advocates." According to him, they argued over the fate of your soul when you went on trial. The two sides were the Churches and the Celestials. He figured whoever was looking for me back in the gully was an Advocate, but he had no idea which side they were on.

When Artie was alive, he didn't pay much attention to the Bible or what constituted living a Christian life. So, he simply opted not to file a petition and wander around the Valley Of Death. It was lonely, sure, but it beat going to Hell. Well, for the most part. He didn't run into many Advocates anymore, but angels still checked in on him from time to time in case he changed his mind about petitioning. He hadn't, and they left him alone until next time.

I don't know how long the two of us wandered around the Valley Of Death. But I can honestly say I had more fun than when I was alive. We formed our own little pirate duo. We were the Salty Dogs – not very impressive, but who else was going to know to complain? Like my name suggests, I could sing a little bit. He wasn't so good, but I brought him around, and soon we were creating our own little "scourge dirge." We traveled far and wide, learning lots about the Valley Of Death and how it was laid out and arranged.

One day, we were by a pond, watching ducks swim on top and fish swim underneath. I had been telling him more about my life in my original village.

He cocked a smile at me and said, "You know what your problem was?"

"I didn't know when to keep quiet?"

"Nah, that would have served you well on my ship. You should have been a pirate!"

"Oh, wake up, will you?"

"I'm serious. You would have been able to learn to read. You could have been boisterous and as long as you could back it up...."

"If I could back it up...."

"Oh, I know you could have. I met some lady pirates. And let me tell you, the guys treated them with respect. On land, if you wanted to learn to read or be involved, you had to be a courtesan. But at sea? Your ship was your country, and you lived by whatever rules you chose."

It was a seductive thought. What kind of life could I have had, had I gone to the seaboard instead of further in the forest to another village? Well, I probably would have died in a bloody battle like Artie. But it would have been worth it.

Our wanderings soon took us to another area we weren't familiar with. We entered the woods surrounding it and ventured deeper. As we went, Artie walked casually until I stopped him. I heard something. It sounded like singing. Flat and mournful. When Artie heard it, he was as uncertain as I was.

"I say we check it out," I told him.

Artie looked at me like I was nuts. "What if it's dangerous?"

"So here's what we do. I go first. I'm spry and limber. If someone gives chase, I'll lead them past you and you blindside them."

Artie wasn't kidding anymore. "What if something happens to you?"

It was strange how much we'd switched personalities. His friendship made me more bold, while mine made him more afraid. I guess he was worried about going back to being alone. I knew the feeling. "Look, you said nothing can hurt us here, so I'll be fine."

"But what if it is something that can hurt you?"

"That's why you have my back, Artie. Will you be okay without a weapon?" There wasn't a loose stone or fallen tree limb anywhere.

Artie held up his fists to me. "What do you mean, 'without a weapon?'"

We did our secret Salty Dogs handshake (no, I won't tell) and he went behind a tree as I crept forward.

We were close enough that it didn't take me long to get to the source. There was a clearing in the forest, next to a giant rocky hill. A waterfall poured down it into a pond. The clearing had a place for a fire and some people milling around. Just a few, three total. They seemed bored.

I stepped into the clearing and said, "Hello."

I was ready for any reaction, from running and screaming to a frontal assault. Neither happened. One of the three simply said, "Oh. Hi. You must be a straggler, too."

"A straggler?"

"Delaying going to trial as long as possible."

I examined them. They all had a look of dread in their eyes. The same look I saw in Artie's every once in a while. The one I could tell was in mine.

I called out, "Artie? I think we're okay."

The one who spoke asked, "Who's Artie?"

Artie came out of the woods. "I'm Artie."

The speaker stood up and shuffled his way over. He couldn't have been more than thirty, but he moved like he was twice that age. "Hello, Artie. I'm Joseph."

"I'm Hannah." I moved to shake Joseph's hand. His grip was weak, his hand just kind of there. He didn't tighten his fingers or lift at his elbow.

42

It turned out there were seven stragglers total there. Artie and I decided to make the number nine. The stragglers had actually done some pretty clever stuff. By the waterfall, they had fashioned a spout that would drip water into a crude clay pot. When it filled, they emptied it and put a mark on the rock wall. It was a way of keeping time. They had already gone over their original marks once before and were starting to again. They had been there a long time, although exactly how long, no one really knew.

All the stragglers had one thing in common – they had lived lives that guaranteed them a place in Hell. No one knew what to do, all they knew was they didn't want to burn for all Eternity. They formed their own little group. Celestial Advocates would occasionally come around to remind them that they could go to trial, but without guarantees, no one was interested. They also put up with Church Advocates coming around, not so much to remind them of trial as to twist the knife. One showed up after Artie and I joined the group. We were off to the side in the forest, practicing the grappling skills all pirates should have, when we heard someone shouting.

"Still putting off the inevitable, huh? Why don't you just end your suffering and get it over with?" boomed the man's voice.

Artie and I crept through the forest, watching for any allies the shouter had. We got close enough to see without being seen.

The man who stood there was maybe halfway between Artie's age and mine. He was short, but his attitude made up for it. He held a Bible in his arm and was pointing in judgment to everyone else with his free hand. The stragglers just went about their business, ignoring him.

The guy gave a whale of a fire and brimstone speech, reminding everyone how unworthy of forgiveness they were and expressing disbelief that they didn't want to take their chances at trial. After criticizing them for not being man enough to face the punishment they'd earned, he stalked off into the woods. When we were sure he was gone, Artie and I looked at each other.

"Let me guess," I said, "Church Advocate, right?"

"Right you are. Not a very loving God, is He?"

"Not if that's who represents him." I thought for a moment, remembering the voice that called to me in the gully. "What are the Celestial Advocates like? I don't think I've ever seen one."

"They're a lot nicer. And they like to say you have a fighting chance in the courts."

"Do you?"

"Don't know. If anyone is Cast Down, they never come back. And if they get into Heaven, they can't come back. All you have is faith."

That wasn't enough for either of us.

It had been three "clay pots" later that I was sitting by the fish pond, listening to the waterfall and just meditating. Everyone was pretty much in their own little groups at the moment. As I sat, another straggler came up next to me. Nathan was a nice guy who served as a knight. Under orders of his lord, he seized things from the church that the lord felt were rightfully his. The priest responded to this by saying Nathan was going to Hell. Not the lord who gave the orders, Nathan. Nathan had died of the plague like I had.

Nathan sat next to me. He carefully took off his boots and rolled up his pant legs. He put his feet in the water, wiggling his toes at the passing fish as if he was saying, "hi". He was silent for a long time. At first, I thought he was just looking to commune with someone. Then he spoke. It was so soft, no one else would hear.

"I'm going to petition."

My head snapped around. I fought the urge to grab him by the shoulders and shake him while screaming, "ARE YOU MAD?!?" I kept my voice down, but I couldn't hide the panic. "You can't do that! You'll go to Hell!"

"I can't take this anymore," he said. He pointed to the clay pot, filling with the slow but steady drip of water.

"An eternity of pain and suffering?!?"

"This is also an eternity of pain and suffering. It's just more subtle about it."

"No! Don't do this! There has to be something else! We can find it! You and me and Artie! We'll head out! We'll find an answer!"

"No," he said, standing up. "I was never afraid when I was alive. I don't like being afraid now." He gently pulled me up and gave me a big hug. I wrapped my arms around him, like I was hoping that would keep him from leaving. "Whatever happens, I promise I'll find a way to let you know." He then stepped from my arms, gently slipping away. Like a bubble from the bottom of a lake.

I stared as he went to the other stragglers still around and informed them of his decision. It was the most activity I had ever seen them do. They also begged him not to go. I stood, rooted to my spot, hoping that maybe numbers would succeed where I didn't. But no. Nathan pulled himself from the group and entered the forest, heading for where everyone knew the Celestial Courts were.

Artie was off somewhere, and I was glad. I went into the forest, off to the little clearing where Artie and I practiced combat. I sat in the middle of it. And I did something I had never done in my life.

I cried.

The clay pot had filled with water and no one bothered to empty it. No one made further marks on the wall. Artie tried to lift my spirits, but I could tell he was upset as well. Everyone liked Nathan. He was a good guy. He didn't even make a mistake, he was part of a mistake his lord had made. He did not deserve to burn in Hell.

Artie and I continued to practice grappling, but it wasn't much. Our hearts just weren't in it. We would go through basic motions for a while, then we'd give up and just sit.

"Do you think we'll know? I mean, do you think Nathan will find a way to tell us what happened?" I asked.

Artie just looked at the ground. "I don't know. I've never known anyone who had."

We both laid back, looking at the sky, watching for any clouds so we could talk about what they looked like. I squeezed my eyes shut, trying to keep the tears at bay. Suddenly, we heard a strange noise that made us sit bolt upright in shock.

It was a cheer. A joyous cheer.

We looked at each other. That didn't happen out here. We leaped to our feet and raced back to the stragglers' camp.

As we came out of the forest, we saw the stragglers gathered in a tight light group around someone. And we saw enough flashes through the gaps to see who was the center of attention. It was Nathan. He had returned.

I couldn't believe it. Nathan was back. And no one was upset. Something must have gone right.

Somehow, Nathan saw me through the gaps. His face lit up like the sun and his hand shot over the top of the crowd, waving wildly. "Hannah!"

He politely but firmly pushed himself out of the crowd, running for me. He wasn't wearing the clothes he left in. He was now wearing white robes with a blue tint to them. He didn't seem to notice Artie at all. His gaze was focused on me, calling my name the entire time.

Nathan scooped me up in a big hug that I couldn't wait to return. He was really back. He wasn't in Hell. He put me down, and his voice was still loud. "Hannah! You have to petition!"

"It went that well, huh? I'll take it under advisement."

He straightened, quirking his head to the side, examining what I said. "No, you aren't getting this. You need to petition." He then put his hands on my shoulders and looked me dead in the eye. "They're waiting for you!"

I felt myself go pale. "Who's waiting for me?"

"The Celestials!" he beamed. "They know about you! They've been looking for you! When I told them I knew you, they asked me to tell you!" His voice returned to normal volume. "They want you to get into Heaven."

"That's impossible! I was an Atheist!"

"That doesn't mean anything! I watched some trials!"

"Wait, you watched trials?"

"Yeah. They have a gallery where you can watch the trials. I had time while waiting for mine. I saw three trials involving Atheists, and all of them got in!"

I looked at Artie. Artie was looking back at me. I shifted my eyes to Nathan. "What about that stuff about believing in Jesus and that?"

"They have some way of taking care of that!"

This was too much for me to process. I quickly pushed his hands from my shoulders. "I...I need to think. I'll think it over."

Nathan smiled at me and nodded his head. "You don't have to be afraid, Hannah." He started walking back to the other stragglers. As he did, he looked at me over his shoulder and said, "They're waiting for you."

45

The Apocalypse could have happened in front of me and I wouldn't have moved, blinked, or acknowledged it. Every thought in my head was replaying what Nathan had just told me. One of the sides in the Celestial Courts knew about me, and felt I deserved to get into Heaven anyway. That guy back at the gully. Had he been one of them? Was Nathan right? Could they really pull off a miracle?

I vaguely heard Artie saying something about stripping naked and jumping into a poison oak patch.

"What?" I asked, twisting my face to him.

"I thought that would snap you out of it." He wasn't smiling. He looked scared. I remembered the last time I'd seen him look like that. It was the day Nathan left us. He asked, "You're thinking about petitioning, aren't you?"

"No...yes...maybe...I don't know...."

"Well, that about covers everything, doesn't it?"

I shook my head, trying to clear it. My thoughts were such a jumbled mess. I could only walk over to the group, Artie following.

Nathan was telling everyone about his whole process. He had gone to the court building, and was directed to the clerks' offices. He filled out a petition, and was escorted to a place called the Interim, where he waited. If neither side contested his petition, he was on his way to Heaven. The Church opposed it, the Celestials did not, so the Celestials became his personal Advocates. He met his Celestial, who guided him through some things that took care of his past sins. He went to court. The Churches said he shouldn't get into Heaven, the Celestials said he should, and in a short time, the Tribunal agreed with the Celestials. Nathan was on his way to Heaven. All he had to do was go to see St. Peter, and he would cross over.

"So why didn't you?" asked Artie.

"Once you cross over, you don't come back. I promised to let you know what happened. And then, there was her." And Nathan pointed to me.

All their eyes were upon me. Nathan continued speaking while looking right at me. "Well, I think it's time for me to get going. Unless there's anything else happening here."

The fear I felt was powerful. I thought about Nathan, and everything he said. How I was already facing an eternity of pain and suffering. The Valley Of Death was just as terrible as what I imagined Hell to be. Nothing happened, nothing could ever happen. And for the rest of my time here, there would be this uncertainty, day in and day out. I understood why Nathan couldn't live like this forever. There were times when it got to me, too. And fear was the only thing that kept me from trying to change anything.

I closed my eyes. And I heard myself say, "I'll petition."

Nathan let out a whoop that probably could have been heard back at the gully. He scooped me up in a hug and twirled me around. When he set me down, he smiled at me. "You're not going to regret this, Hannah! When do you want to go?"

No point in putting things off. "Can you take me there now?"

"Absolutely."

Artie stepped forward. "I'll come with."

I held up my hand. "No. Stay here. I'll come back and let you know."

"He can come with," Nathan said. "They won't do anything to him unless there is a trial for him. He can watch your trial."

In short order, some of the other stragglers opted to come with, too. They wanted to watch the trial and see what would happen. But Artie was looking to watch my back. And I wanted to have a friend with me to keep me strong. And with that, our little group set off for the Celestial Courts.

I hated that there was no way to really measure time. I was curious how long we traveled. It seemed long, and it didn't seem long. We eventually got to a ridge. As we went up, Nathan said, "Get ready. What you're going to see will take your breath away."

No sooner had my eyes gotten over the top of the ridge than I saw the Celestial Court building. It was beautiful. Kings would fight wars to live there. It was bigger than any castle, so clean and white, it seemed to have its own light. And yet, for all the columns and steps and everything, it remained a thing of beauty, not a testimonial to how wonderful its occupants were.

Everyone had stopped and was looking at it. Except Nathan. He had already seen it, nothing new to him. "Come on, they're waiting for her!" he called. Everyone snapped to and we continued on our way.

We got to the main building. We got some looks from people, but that was all. "Okay, Hannah. The clerks' offices are right over there," Nathan said while pointing. "You go in there and fill out your petition. I'm going to find Michael and let him know you've arrived."

I started walking, Artie falling in step with me. Nathan put a hand on Artie's shoulder. Artie gave him a look that could have melted stone. Nathan wasn't phased. "She has to go alone," he said.

"She will not be alone. Not with me around," Artie rumbled.

"Artie," I said, "I'll be fine. Remember. Nothing can hurt us here."

"Unless you petition," Artie said.

"Until after the trial," I countered. "I'll be fine. Really."

Artie weighed his options, then relented. "Please be careful," he said. We did our secret handshake, and I went to face my fear.

The clerks' office was a little way inside the Court grounds. There were lots of buildings and courtyards and all kinds of places. It was amazing. I searched for the correct building, wondering how I would find it. Then I noticed the sign above the door of one particular building. Somehow, I understood it to say, "Clerks," but don't ask me how. I went to it and stepped inside.

There was a small line of people, probably others looking to petition like I was. There were several tables, each of which had someone sitting there with scrolls, parchment, feathers, and ink wells. Each table was occupied, so there was nothing to do but wait. Eventually, I was at the front of the line, and was sent to see a clerk called Abraham.

Abraham was writing something on a roll of parchment. He looked up and smiled at me as I approached. I stood in front of him, and he motioned for me to sit on the stool in front of the table. "I just need a moment," he said. When he finished, he rolled up the parchment and held it up above his head. A childlike angel flew in out of nowhere and took it without stopping, heading out of the building.

"Welcome to the Celestial Courts," Abraham said. "You are looking to petition, yes?"

"Uh...yes."

He handed me a blank piece of parchment with a dotted line at the very bottom and his quill pen. "Please sign your name."

I took the parchment and the quill. I turned the quill around a couple of times, unsure what to do with it. "Uh...I never learned to write."

Abraham didn't miss a beat. "Just put an 'X' there and kiss it."

I carefully scratched out an "X" with the quill and then kissed it. Suddenly, words started forming on the parchment, starting at the top and going down, like an invisible hand was filling it out. It didn't look like the words used when I was alive, but somehow, I could read them. I understood them. And I smiled when I knew that my name was at the top of the page.

I read the words as they appeared. There wasn't much to it, just a request to get into Heaven. But I was reading. I didn't want this to end. But Abraham snapped me out of it. "I can assure you there are no hidden clauses in there, m'lady."

"Oh, I wasn't...well, I was just...."

"Oh, right. You don't know how to read. You'll have plenty to read in a little bit. But I need this in order to start the process."

I smiled sheepishly. "Oh. Of course."

I handed him the parchment. He turned it so he could take a quick look at it. He saw my name at the top and his jaw dropped. When he spoke, his voice was a whisper. "...you're Hannah Singer?"

I would have bolted from the building if he hadn't been smiling when he said it. "I'm not that big a deal, am I?"

"Depends on who you ask," Abraham responded. He held up his hand, two fingers extended. Two of the child angels zipped up. He addressed the first one. "Please inform Michael that Hannah Singer has arrived." He then addressed the second. "Please tell Holman that Hannah Singer has arrived." The angels zipped out, and he turned back to me. "Lady Singer, if you would please go to over to the Grand Fountain at the center of the courtyard, your Celestial Advocate will be along shortly."

"Don't I get a say in who my Advocate is?" I wasn't sure I wanted just anyone thrown at me.

"Yes, but I think you'll like the one Michael assigned to you. Just give him a chance." He then rolled up the parchment and held it up. Another child angel flew by and grabbed it.

I really didn't know what else to do, so I got up and wandered out of the clerks' offices. I wasn't sure where I was supposed to go, so I asked someone passing by where the fountain was. They pointed me in the right direction.

I couldn't believe how beautiful the fountain was. It was gigantic, with water streams shooting everywhere and intricate designs. I went up to it and leaned on the wall, watching bubbles from the bottom rise up and pop. It gave me an uneasy feeling, so I focused on the water streams instead. It couldn't have been long when I heard a familiar voice ask, "Hannah Singer?"

It was the voice from the gully. It haunted my thoughts, I would never forget it. I turned around to face the man who followed me without being there.

The man was actually a little older than Artie, maybe by ten years. He was a bit pudgy, with a fringe of gray hair hanging off his bald head. He wore a brown robe over his white ones. His smile made his face more circular, and he radiated calm. He had to have been a monk. He held a scroll that was tied shut in his right hand.

I pulled myself up straight. "I'm Hannah Singer."

He pulled his hand with the scroll up and tapped his left shoulder with his fist. "Noah Holman, your Celestial Advocate. It is a delight to meet you."

"You don't know me very well, do you?"

He held up the scroll and waggled it in front of me. "Quite the contrary. I'm very familiar with your life. You're not as bad as you think."

"That's not what everyone in my village thought."

"Oh, believe me, if they knew what they were in store for, they wouldn't have done half the things they did."

I ignored that last bit. "So, I'm guessing we confer or something?"

"We will. But Michael would like to sit in as well. I'm afraid we have to wait for him."

I shrugged and turned, leaning on the fountain wall again. "I got nothing better to do."

I focused on the fountain so I could ignore the guy. But he wasn't letting that happen. He came up, staying a respectful distance away, and leaned on the wall with me. "Beautiful, isn't it?"

Idle chitchat. "They'd love something like this back in the kingdom."

"They'd never have one in the kingdom. You have to know and understand true beauty to create something like this. Frankly, no one with the resources or ability to create something like this has that knowledge."

"How nice of God to keep it from those who would really appreciate it."

"God doesn't keep it from people. People keep it from people."

"It's God's world, right? He can just give it to us."

"God made the world for you. It's yours, not His. The whole point of life is to live. How can you live if God is doing everything for you?" Holman let out a sigh. "So many people don't want God. They want a servant, someone who takes care of things for them. Or grants them things they shouldn't have. Riches, extended life, they want God to make them something other than human."

"I never wanted anything from God."

"Well, technically, you never thought to ask. It's easy to ignore something you don't think is real."

I looked at him. "Are you suggesting I would have been praying for things that would treat God as my servant?"

He continued looking at the fountain. "Had you believed, sure. Everyone does. And you know what? It's okay. You're only human. God understands that. He did make you, after all. It's a part of ambition. If people didn't at least occasionally ask for and strive for things beyond their grasp, they'd never advance, and God would think something was wrong."

I had said the things I did to shut him up. Instead, he not only kept talking, he got me to talk. A flower breaking a stone. "What a messed up way to make humans."

"Well, it does have its moments," he smiled.

We just stood there, leaning against the wall and watching the fountain. Whether it was the fountain or Holman's company, I felt myself relaxing. And I didn't want to. I was surrounded by enemies looking to make an example of me. Right?

Eventually, a voice rang out. "Holman?"

Holman spun to attention. "Over here, sire."

I had seen plenty of big men. This guy was bigger than any of them in every aspect. He had to be at least half a head taller than anyone alive. His muscles were huge. He didn't look like he could push a mountain, he looked like he could shove it. Medium brown hair erupted from his head, flowing in wavy patterns into a short cut. Looking into his eyes, you could almost see the wheels turning in his head. This guy was no dummy. Sharp angles and a square jaw formed his face. Powerful arms bursting from his robes wore bracers the same color as his hair, a single gold cross imprinted on each. This guy was a fighter, one you wanted on your side. He walked with strength, turning his shoulders into every step. And despite how intimidating he was, the friendly, excited smile didn't seem the least bit out of place. "Holman! That's her, huh?"

I took a step back. Holman whispered to me, "Relax. You're on our side." He then said aloud to the approacher, "Yes, it is!"

The guy quickened his pace. He was up to me before I knew it. "Hannah Singer! Welcome!" He then scooped me up in a giant hug. If I wasn't invulnerable, I thought for sure he'd crush me.

I peeked out of the crux of one arm to look at Holman. Holman smiled. "See? Nothing to worry about." I couldn't speak, so I couldn't say what I wanted to at that moment.

He eventually released me. "It's great to finally meet you!"

I managed to straighten my spine. "And you are?"

"Oh, sorry, forgot. I'm St. Michael. Just excited. You aren't the easiest person to find."

I rolled my eyes. "What's with all the excitement? I wasn't a Queen! I wasn't some fierce warrior! I wasn't a healer or anything! I'm just some stupid

Atheist who got everything wrong!" The last time I lashed out, I ended up getting a cross branded on my stomach. But I didn't care. I couldn't take any more of this.

Holman looked like he wanted to reassure me somehow, but didn't know what to say. Michael, however, didn't flinch in the least. "You weren't a stupid Atheist. You were a smart, good person who got a raw deal. Everyone deserves a Heavenly reward."

"Everyone who believes."

"Everyone," he corrected me. "Let me ask you this – if God is so mean and merciless, if He can't wait to send people who mess up to Hell, why are there so many ways to earn forgiveness?"

Michael had said something that I couldn't just ignore or nullify or anything. I couldn't argue his point. He continued, "The world is harsh. He knows it. We all know it. Living in strict compliance with the Bible there just isn't possible. So you do the best you can. It's not the what of your actions that determines your fate, but the why. You're supposed to forgive your enemies. But you don't. Is it because you just didn't want to, or because forgiving them means they'd take advantage of you again? You think God is going to be mad at you because you survived?"

Michael held his hand out to me, reaching for me, inviting me to come with him. I was too stunned to put up a fight. I walked up, Holman following behind me. Michael put his arm around my shoulder and held me to him as we went. "Relax, kiddo. I know this is a lot for you. It's going to be fine. I'll make sure of that." I heard the smile in his voice, and I reminded myself not to believe.

We went to Michael's office. Once we were seated, we went over my life in minute detail. Lots of stuff in there I didn't remember, which figures. Just some really basic sins. Oh, and the Atheism. Had to take care of that. I was told to go to Penance Hall, and that should fix everything. Holman offered to walk me there. But something was bugging me, and I needed an answer. "Actually, Michael, would you mind taking me instead?"

"Not at all," he shrugged. Everything was finished, so Holman excused himself to check on his other cases. Michael and I headed out.

As we walked, Michael smiled at me. "Ask away."

He was sharp, I had to give him that. "Is there something special about me?"

"Well, uh, everyone is special...."

"Don't sugarcoat it. You haven't yet, don't start now."

He looked at me and his smile changed. It wasn't the comforting, reassuring smile. It was the kind you get when you recognize a kindred spirit. "Well...no. You are a very ordinary, everyday person."

"So why are you involved in my case? You're an archangel. I can't believe you have nothing better to do than watch out for some very ordinary, everyday person."

We were walking past one of the gardens. "Let's go in here. Take a load off your feet." I didn't feel the least bit tired, but I knew this was going to take a while.

We got inside the garden area. Flowering shrubs were blooming everywhere, with carved stone benches at strategic places. A few others were here, meditating. Michael lead me to the furthest bench, away from everyone. We both sat down. After a moment, Michael scratched his nose and looked at me.

"You see, Hannah, I'm in charge of the Celestials. I help coordinate things. And I tend to take a special interest in the really tough cases. The ones where I feel the person deserves to get into Heaven, but getting a ruling that way is going to be difficult."

"So what's so difficult about my case? You guys seem to think it's pretty basic. I mean, all I have to do is repent?"

"It should be simple. Under normal circumstances, I wouldn't have sent Holman to look for you. You wouldn't have even had an Advocate assigned to you until you petitioned. We deal with so many Atheist cases, they don't even concern me. I don't usually get involved in them."

"So what's different about mine?"

Michael looked out at the blooms. "I don't know. We weren't really aware of you until relatively recently. About the time your old village tried to save your soul." I involuntarily touched my stomach. "Apparently, there were a lot of prayers and the Churches here heard about you. They are really worked up about you and have made it clear that they will not allow you into Heaven. Basically, I have an acute interest in your case because they have an acute interest in your case."

I knew enough about St. Michael to know he faced the devil. So his being serious like this gave me a sinking feeling. I mean, I'm just supposed to be some run-of-the-mill Atheist case. In, out, and over. "What exactly are they up to?"

"I don't know. Neither side has to disclose their trial strategy beforehand. I honestly can't see what is so different about you."

"And that's why you're involved in my case."

"Not just involved," he smiled at me. "I've decided to make Holman a junior. I'll be leading the defense."

I wrapped my arms around my stomach. "That doesn't make me feel any better."

Michael leaped up from the bench and went behind me. He started working my shoulders, trying to loosen me up. "Don't worry. I've led plenty of defenses. I'm not green, I can do this."

I knew he was sidestepping the point. It wasn't a question of inexperience. It was a question bringing out the big guns. The Church was being secretive, and their behavior was enough to get Michael to take them seriously. This was no ordinary case. I was looking at going to Hell.

I leaned forward and started heaving. I didn't care if I made a mess on myself, I felt sick and didn't know what to do. But nothing came up. My body just behaved as it would have back in the world, so there was no getting rid of the sickly feeling.

Michael came around and knelt in front of me. He carefully lifted my head up. He saw I was crying. He started wiping my tears away with his thumbs. "I knew I shouldn't have done this," I sniffled.

Michael wrapped me in a hug. "Listen, you're going to be okay. Don't let them scare you. They have to come up with something really special to surprise ol' Michael."

I hugged him back. Tightly. I made a huge mistake. Artie probably would have been all right. Nathan was fine. But the Churches were looking to make an example of me. Or maybe just to deliver the finishing stroke I denied the village. This wasn't an ordinary trial. They were out to get me. And there was no way of telling how.

"What if I ran?" I asked.

Michael reeled back. "Guardians will be dispatched to bring you back. Your petition has been filed."

He didn't need to say anything else. Running would be my certain doom, since it would make it look like I really had something to hide. The Churches would have a field day with it. "Can we delay the trial?"

"Only for so long. Sooner or later, they'll know you're stalling and force the trial to proceed."

I broke down. I just wanted out of there. I wanted to go back to the clerks and rip my petition up in front of them. I wanted to yell at Nathan for talking me into this. I wanted to scream into the face of every last Church that they'd never get me. I wanted to just drain away into nothingness, where I would never be victimized again. I was crying, and my eyes weren't hurting. Just what I needed, another reminder of my situation. I couldn't handle this anymore.

Michael just kept me in that hug until I finally ran out of tears. When I was finally done, he pulled back a little. He held my face in his hands, forcing me to look into his eyes. Eyes that seemed to go on forever, like the sky above me. "Now, you listen to me, Singer. No one who deserved to get into Heaven has EVER been denied. And I'm not going to let that happen now. I've argued trickier cases than some Atheist. God's will is for you to get into Heaven. You can't fight God's will. There is ALWAYS a way. I promise I'll protect you. The Churches won't lay a finger on you."

I sniffled a little and nodded my head. Michael then released me and took his seat next to me again.

"I hate what I've become," I told him.

"That's kind of general. Can you be more specific?"

"When I was alive, I was never like this. I was bold, strong, unafraid. I bet I've cried more since I got here than the entire time I was a baby."

Michael put his arm around my shoulder again. "Don't be so hard on yourself. You're in a situation beyond anything you could have prepared for, your beliefs are being rewritten as you go, you're facing a horrible fate...only someone heartless wouldn't understand." He gave me a squeeze. "The key thing is, do you let the situation get the best of you, or do you move on?"

I thought it over. My life in the village, when I was being branded, I'd figured out a way to get out of there. I'd bested a bunch of church people blinded by their own self-righteousness. Surely, I could do it again.

"I think I'm okay now," I told him.

He gave me a couple of thumps on the back. If it weren't for my invulnerability, he probably would have knocked the wind out of me. "You know, penance is good for the soul. Not only that, but it makes it harder for the Churches to stick it to you. What do you say we get you repented?"

I nodded my head. We stood up and resumed walking. We soon arrived at the Penance Hall. Michael bowed and swung his arms like he was presenting it. I did a quick curtsey and went inside.

The place was huge and long, like a banquet hall. Several tables were neatly arranged. There was only one other door, against the far wall. I walked up to the first desk. The lady behind it smiled at me. "Can I help you?"

"Uh...hi. I'm here to repent."

"Absolutely." She turned around and looked over the room. "Why don't you talk to Richard. Right behind me, seven tables back."

Richard looked like he'd been doing this a long time, both in appearance and attitude. Grey hair and wrinkles, and when I approached, he had his elbow on the table and chin on his fist, daydreaming about something else. I stood before him and cautiously cleared my throat. He didn't even look. "Go ahead and have a seat," he said in the most bland way possible.

I sat in front of him as he pulled out a blank roll of parchment. At the bottom was a dotted line. "Please sign at the bottom."

"But I already filed a petition."

"This isn't a petition. It's just a list of your sins."

I looked at the size of the parchment. You could have put one of the books of the Bible on it. Just how many sins did I have in my past?!? No wonder the Churches were after me! I nervously made an "X" on the dotted line and kissed it.

Suddenly, the parchment shrank. It was maybe the size of a royal proclamation now. I saw my name at the top and a list of some of the things I had done in my life. Some of them, I didn't even know were considered sins.

Richard turned the parchment so he could read it. If he thought it was exciting to meet Hannah Singer, he didn't act it. He looked over the list and said, "Hmph. I don't see what you're so nervous about."

Yeah, I've been hearing that a lot lately, I thought.

He spread out the parchment. All the entries were in glowing red letters. He started in the middle. "Oh, here's a good one. Blasphemy against the church. Why'd you do it?"

His lack of reaction threw me. "...uh, I didn't believe?"

"So, the church had no authority over you. Without that authority, you weren't defying them, you were disagreeing with them. Technically, it's difference of opinion, not blasphemy. Disallowed." He touched the entry, and it stopped glowing, turning brownish-black.

I was still blinking and processing that when he got to the next entry. "Clothing and food taken before you left your original village."

I snapped out of it. "They gave me that stuff. I was free to do what I wanted with it."

He looked at me, still bland. "And that cloak?"

I had grabbed a cloak off a wagon as I snuck out that night. I didn't really need it, but I took it anyway. "...yeah. I stole it."

"Are you sorry?"

"Yes."

Without missing a beat, Richard said, "Congratulations, you repented."

"That's it? Shouldn't I at least say an 'Our Father' or 'Hail Mary?'"

He looked at me with a mischievous smile. "Do you even remember how they go?"

I searched my memory. "...I'm not sure."

"Say you're sorry."

"Pardon?"

"In a minute. First, say you're sorry."

"Uh...I'm sorry?"

"Congratulations, you repented." Richard touched the entry on the scroll, and the glow turned to blue.

I blinked in confusion. "What if I'd done something really wrong?"

Richard looked at me. "You misunderstand the point of this. This doesn't absolve everything. Just the really basic sins, ones against yourself or that are relatively harmless. Lustful thoughts, swearing, losing your virginity, getting in a drunken brawl, things like that." Richard pointed across the way behind me. "See that guy over there?"

I twisted to my right. At one table sat two people. One I figured was doing the same job Richard did. The other was probably a Petitioner like me. The scroll was long enough that the ends fell off the table and curled up on the floor. There was a smattering of blacked out letters and glowing blue, but they were few. There were so many glowing red entries, it tinted the appearances of the people sitting there. The guy I figured to be a Petitioner had that look on his face. The look of the damned.

"I know who that is," Richard told me, his voice lowered conspiratorially. "He was a thief in the woods. Stole, killed, and was proud of the evil he'd done. Those things don't get forgiven. We don't have that authority. You have to own up to them at trial."

I shivered as I looked back at Richard. He smiled at me. "Relax, you were one of the good ones. What say we continue?"

I could only nod my head. We started going over the entries. Things were disallowed. Things were forgiven. It was going pretty well. Eventually, there was only one entry that still glowed red. It was near the top, directly under my name. It read, "Atheist."

Richard leaned forward and folded his hands on the tabletop. "Well, we have just this one little entry here. This is really the biggest problem. See, one of the prerequisites for getting into Heaven is you have to believe in God and Jesus." He jerked his thumb towards the door at the far end of the hall. "So go on in there and say hi."

My eyes shot wide. I stared at the door. "God and Jesus are behind that door?"

"Yes. You Atheists demand proof before you believe. They figure actually meeting Them is as definitive proof as it will ever get. So, until you go in there and believe those two in there waiting for you are real, any Heavenly reward you earn will be suspended."

"I wouldn't lose it?"

"No, you just wouldn't get in until you believe in Them. I mean, you want to wait, that's up to you. I just don't see the point."

I kept staring at the door. It felt a lot further away than it really was. "What do I say to Them?"

"Whatever you want. Some people talk to Them. Some yell at Them. Everyone does what they want."

"They're going to hate me...."

"They're not going to hate you," Richard said with a wave of his hand. He picked up his quill and another piece of parchment.

"I denied Them...."

He looked down at the parchment and started writing. "You know, this would be a whole lot easier if people read the Bible less."

I wasn't going to get anywhere with Richard. It seemed the only real option I had was to go through the door. I got up and started walking between the tables.

Every once in a while, someone would look up and see me. They had to know what was happening. After all, if you already believe, they aren't going to send you to meet God and Jesus to repent. Everyone that looked at me gave me a knowing smile and an occasional thumbs up.

I got to the door. I gently wrapped my hand around the handle, took a deep breath, and pushed it open a bit. I didn't see anything inside except blackness. I found my nerve, and then I went through the door. The blackness was everywhere, the light from the hall illuminated nothing. I stood, and heard the door close behind me.

It was strange. Pitch black, but I could still see myself. I could apparently walk. I caught a little glimmer out of the corner of my eye. A small, blue pinpoint of light arced gently above me, then around me, then under me. I was standing on nothing! But I never felt afraid that I would fall. Eventually, other blue pinpoints started drifting in. When they got closer, they would veer from their course and come to me. More appeared, like they were pouring in from the sides, slowly swirling around me, lighting my darkness.

I was nearly cocooned in the lights when the darkness just beyond me lit up. The pinpoints eventually were engulfed by the light. Then a pair of distinct lights appeared in front of me. They had no human shape, but I knew who They were.

I just stood rigid, staring at God and Jesus. I felt nothing but love and acceptance from Them. I felt so horrible for all the things I'd said and believed about them. I moved my mouth, but no words came out. All I could manage was to croak, "I'm sorry...."

Suddenly, my mind expanded. I saw myself standing there, like an outsider. My awareness expanded to include everything in the Valley Of Death. Everything from the world. The stars in the sky. The universe. In that moment, I knew everything. I was everything. The frailties and strengths of the human spirit. The sheer power and fragile existence of love. The true depth of wisdom. It was part of me, and I was part of it. And I understood why, no matter what I had done, God would never turn me away.

Then, it was over. I was standing in the room on the other side of the door. It had a stone floor, the same brilliant white as the the court building itself. There were candles around, too few to provide light, but there wasn't a single wisp of darkness anywhere. I fell to my knees, my arms holding me up from the floor. Everything I had just experienced was slipping away. I just couldn't contain the knowledge of the universe. Like a waterfall pouring into a pint glass. I mentally wrapped around what I could, willing myself to hold on to it. But it drifted away. Like a bubble from the bottom of a lake. I was helpless as it went...

Pop!

I don't remember getting up. Or walking to the door. Or opening it, stepping through it, then just standing there dazed as it closed behind me. Some of the people in the hall saw me come out. They just smiled and nodded at me, then went back to their duties. Except Richard. He was watching me the entire time.

All I could do was mouth to him, "I had no idea...."

Without taking his eyes off of me, Richard reached over to my parchment. He touched the word "Atheist," and it turned bright blue.

By the time I came out from Penance Hall, the Churches had filed their formal objection to my petition. The Celestials had already filed "No contest", so they would be advocating for me at trial. Michael had picked out a blue ribbon panel of juniors to assist him. Advocate teams typically have one lead and one or two juniors. Michael had four. He was determined to squash the Churches like grapes.

"All that's left is to determine when the trial is," he told me.

"Don't I still have to meet the Church Advocate?"

"Not if you don't want to. And frankly, I think you're spooked enough."

Actually, I felt a lot better. Meeting God will do that to you. "So, when does the trial start?"

"Churches say they're ready any time. I just have to let the clerks know we're ready, and they'll set up a hearing."

"How soon can it start?"

This caught Michael by surprise. "Most people want a little more time before trial."

"The Churches think they have a winner. I want to catch them before they see anything they've overlooked."

The smile on Michael's face changed again. That kindred spirit thing. "We can probably have the trial start in a matter of moments. You sure you're ready?"

"You're the Advocate. I think the question is, are *you* ready?"

Michael let out a hearty laugh. "Your friends are by the Grand Fountain. I'll meet you there."

I went to the Grand Fountain, where I had met Holman and first met Michael. Artie, Nathan, Joseph, the rest of my personal cheering squad. I started giving them a quick rundown of everything, minus the more fraught-with-portent sections like the Churches wanting my head on a platter. But before I could finish, Michael appeared, two Guardians in tow. The Guardians already had their wings out and looked mean.

"Don't mind them," he smiled. "They're just here out of procedure. If you're ready, trial can start now."

I thought it over. This was it. There was nothing more to be learned, nothing more to be anticipated. The cards had been dealt, it was time to play. "I'm ready."

"Then let's go!" Michael declared. A Guardian took their place on either side of me, and Michael led us to the court building.

We got to one of the courtrooms. The ivory doors had a gold relief pattern. Michael held one door for me, Artie held the other.

The courtroom was actually pretty sizable. Certainly bigger than I expected. As I walked through the Gallery, I looked at the two tables on the other side of the low dividing wall. The table to the right had Holman and three others, pouring over scrolls and talking amongst themselves. Holman was facing back, presumably to watch for our arrival. The table to the left had three people. They sat, their backs to me, straight as boards with their hands folded. Those had to be the Churches.

Holman noticed us as soon as we came in the door. He quickly gestured to the others and they all turned around. They stood straight and proud, like knights ready to fight for the fair maiden's honor. The Churches didn't budge.

Michael went past the table and came around to Holman's side. The Guardians brought me up. Michael motioned to a seat on the other side of the table from him, second one in from the left. "Have a seat, Lady Singer."

I sat down, and the Guardians went to stand in front of the judge's bench. I tried to ignore the rising fear I felt. I snuck a look at the Church table. They only had a couple of scrolls out, not much. No discussion, no activity.

I waited for Michael to get up to speed. He sat down next to me in the seat furthest left, right by the aisle. Holman took the seat to my right. One of the other Celestials took the last seat, the other two stood behind us. I leaned up to Michael and whispered. "This could be an easy victory if you play your cards right."

He turned to me, genuinely interested. "What makes you say that?"

"Did you see the Church table?"

Michael took a quick look to the side. The three Churches waved at him with the biggest phony smiles ever. Michael looked back at me and arched an eyebrow. "What do you see?"

"It looks like they only prepared one argument. They are wagering everything on one horse. Give them some time to build their arguments up, knock the horse out from under them, and they won't have anything to get back in the game with."

There was that smile again. The kindred spirit smile. The one that made me feel proud. "You would make a good Advocate, Singer."

I turned behind me to look at the Gallery. It had filled in a little, some other regular souls. They gave off a different vibe from the angels. You could tell who was who. There were actually quite a few of them now, and a smattering of angels here and there. My own little cheering section was in the front row on the Celestials side, with Artie sitting directly behind me.

"Hannah?" Artie said, more a plea than a question. "Look, you know I'm a pessimist. It's taking everything to keep from saying good-bye to you. Please prove me wrong." I smiled at him, and we did our secret handshake.

Suddenly, chimes sounded. Everybody stood up. I was just a second behind. Suddenly, angel wings sprouted everywhere. Some in the Gallery had wings that didn't look quite right and floated behind them instead of protruding from their backs. Once again, you could tell who was an angel and who wasn't. The only ones without wings were my cheering section and I. I noted the Churches and all the Celestials except for Michael also had the ceremonial wings.

To the right was what I presumed to be the jury box. There was a door behind it. The door opened, and twelve angels, wings already out, entered. This was the Tribunal, who would decide if there was a good reason to grant my petition. In that moment, I forgot about everything. The power, the wisdom, the beauty, it all just overwhelmed me. For the first time I could remember, I felt jealous. I would be honored to be one of them. But for now, I'd settle for just coming out of this trial in one piece.

The door at the back opened, and another angel came in, also with his wings already out and carrying a scroll. His name was Pahaliah. I didn't find out until later that he was the angel invoked by those trying to convert people to Christianity. Basically, Michael had stacked the deck as much as he was able to. If the Churches wanted to send me to Hell, they'd have to earn it.

Pahaliah took his place at the judge's bench. He sat, set the scroll off to the side, and surveyed the court. He paused a little as he examined me. I

59

couldn't read his expression, and I refused to flinch. The corner of his mouth quirked up for just a split second. He banged the gavel, signaling court was in session. Everyone in court except the Guardians, the Advocates, and I sat down.

"Who is the Petitioner?"

Michael had already warned me not to say or do anything unless asked. I kept my mouth locked up as Michael declared, "The Petitioner is Hannah Singer."

"And who are her Advocates?"

"Noah Holman, Thelonius Minton, Jack Pidgeon, Gideon Forrester, and St. Michael, acting as lead."

Pahaliah arched his eyebrows. "Did I review the correct case file? I thought Singer was just an Atheist."

"Singer is a good woman and deserves the best chance at getting into Heaven," Michael said with a shrug.

Pahaliah looked at the Churches with a bit of skepticism. They just stood where they were, arms straight, waiting patiently. "And who advocates for the Church?"

The one furthest to the right at the table, closest to the aisle, spoke. "Byron Bell, Mark Freedman, and Victor Spire, acting as lead."

Pahaliah returned his gaze to me. Was he nervous for me? "Will the Petitioner please take the stand?"

Instinctively, I bowed. I heard a snort from one of the Churches, but ignored it. I wanted to limit their options to attack me as much as possible. I strode out from behind the Celestials' table and walked with head held high to the dock. It was a small area about a yard square, ringed with banisters except for the entrance. I went to the exact middle, stood in something similar to what is now called "parade rest", and looked out at the court.

The junior Advocates sat down, leaving only Michael and Spire standing. Pahaliah faced Michael, but his eyes were on me. "Advocate for the Petitioner goes first. Michael?"

"Singer was an Atheist when she was alive. However, that is her only crime. It is a well-established precedent that Atheism is not sufficient to bar someone from a Heavenly reward. She has repented her sins and renounced her Atheism. With other petitions being granted with far greater sins than hers, Casting Down is not only ridiculous, it is overkill. There is nothing in her history to warrant opposition from the Church. And that, simply put, is it."

I had been expecting a longer opening argument from Michael, so his "simply put" threw me a little. Then I realized what he was doing. He couldn't argue until he knew what he was arguing against. The Celestials were representing me, so they had to go first. Michael was throwing his turn, giving nothing and forcing the Churches to lay out their case.

Pahaliah kept facing Michael, but shifted his eyes to Spire. "What are the grounds for opposition?"

Spire looked like he had been given the greatest gift. "Petitioner should be Cast Down due to being an Atheist."

Pahaliah was unconvinced. "She repented."

"Her penance is moot."

This got everyone's attention, especially Michael's. "Her penance was just like all other penances you have not objected to," Michael said.

"It's not the penance that the Church objects to. It's who is repenting. The other Atheists that have been through here, they have always had some sort of doubt about their beliefs. Even if they didn't realize it, deep inside, they hoped they were wrong or still held out hope that maybe God was out there. They were still Christian, even if they were making a decision to be Atheists. So God's mercy still extends to them. But Singer never believed. Not once. As such, there is no core of Christianity that entitles her to representation in this court."

Michael's face darkened. The jovial, friendly guy was falling away, and a wrathful archangel was taking his place. I was more frightened of that than the Churches. "Everyone is entitled to a chance at Heaven, regardless of their beliefs."

"You are going to continue to represent her?"

"I promised I'd watch out for her."

"But you can't represent her. She is beyond the purview of the court."

"No one is beyond the purview of the court."

I suddenly tensed, my head tilting low and to the side. A thought had just struck me about how Spire was arguing. The more I turned it over in my mind, the more convinced I was that I knew what he was doing.

To Hell with the rules. I screamed from the dock, "It's a trap!"

I didn't even realize I was leaning on the banister. Everyone was looking at me in confusion. Except the Churches. All of them, especially Spire, looked like great thieves finally caught in the act.

Michael and Pahaliah quickly looked at Spire. His look was disguised in a flash, but not fast enough.

Pahaliah looked at me. "Young lady, I'm afraid I can't allow you to talk out of turn. You may only speak if an Advocate asks you to."

Michael actually stepped on Pahaliah's last couple of words. "I would like to question the Petitioner!"

Pahaliah nodded without taking his gaze off of me. "Granted."

Spire's words shot from his mouth like a cannon. "It is too early in the trial to question the Petitioner!"

"There are no gag orders or mandated time for questioning, she is free to answer anything put to her at any time." Pahaliah spoke forcefully, letting Spire know he better not try to challenge him right now. "Go ahead with your questions, Michael."

Michael pulled himself together enough that his voice was normal volume, but you could hear it wouldn't take much for him to go over the edge. "You said, 'It's a trap.' What, exactly, is this trap, and what is it set up to do?"

Michael was putting a lot of faith in me that I knew what I was talking about. I hoped I would prove him right. "It's a trap to destroy the Celestial

Courts, and I'm the tool they're using."

Michael and I just looked at each other for a moment. "Go on," he said.

"The courts are for the protection of Christians, not non-believers," I explained. "If you extend mercy to me, you are in violation of the covenant God made. The court will have to be dismantled. And the only ones who will determine who gets into Heaven will be the only ones with authority under the covenant."

Michael darkened like a thunderstorm. The Guardians actually flinched. Michael slowly turned his head to Spire. Spire was smiling, full of righteousness and smugness. When Michael spoke, it was a deep rumble. "You snake."

"One way or another, she's going to Hell. The question is, who will be going after her?"

"BURN!!!" Michael's yell shook the entire courtroom. He and Spire had thrown out the pleasantries and were in each others' faces, yelling at top volume.

I started running through options in my mind. There had to be something. Anything. Not only was I unwilling to let the Celestials get rooked, I was unwilling to let these devious Churches succeed. I looked at Pahaliah. His attention was riveted to the scene in front of him. When I talked to him, his head snapped around as if he was coming out of a trance. "This is my choice, right? I decide what happens to me?"

Pahaliah looked frightened for me. "Don't do this. You don't have to. There has to be a way. Michael and his juniors will think of something."

"I wish to confer with them, please."

Pahaliah looked at the two fighters before him. He made a decision. He banged the gavel three times. It was enough to get their attention.

Pahaliah folded his hands, closed his eyes, and tilted his head. "Does council wish for a recess so they may confer?"

"Sounds good to me," Michael said. He glared at Spire, who weathered it expertly.

"Court is in recess." He banged the gavel, and Michael was out the doors in a flash, his juniors racing after him.

Pahaliah addressed the Guardians. "Please take Lady Singer to Michael's chambers so she can join the consultation." Then he looked at me. "Don't give anything. There has to be a way. This isn't over."

The Guardians came around to the dock to escort me. I walked carefully and easily, not even casting a glance at the Churches I could hear snickering and talking excitedly amongst themselves. As I approached the aisle, my cheering section was looking at me with outright fear. Artie was terrified. He started to talk, struggling to say anything. Nathan was also frightened. "Hannah...I didn't know...."

As I walked past them, I kept my head straight. But I shifted my eyes to them, put my finger to my lips in a "shush" gesture, and smiled. Michael had said, when it is God's will, there is always a way. I was about to put that to the test.

The Guardians walked me down the halls. They weren't bothering to be threatening anymore. Word had gotten out about what happened in the courtroom. As we passed people in the halls, they either frowned worriedly at me or smirked at me. Pretty easy to tell who was a Celestial and who was a Church.

We got to Michael's chambers. One of the Guardians rapped on the door.

"Who is it?!?" thundered Michael's voice.

"Hannah Singer, here to consult with you," he responded.

The door opened a crack. I simply pushed it open and went inside.

As I closed the door behind me, I took in the chaos. There was barely room for me in there. Angels and Advocates were everywhere, yelling back and forth and gesturing like crazy. Lot of hubbub over little ol' me.

No one was really paying attention to me, least of all Michael, wherever he was in all of this. I took a deep breath and boomed at the top of my voice, "Whose fate is this, anyway?!?"

That brought everyone up short. I finally spotted Michael, standing on the far side of his desk, a giant scroll unfurled in his hands. "We just need some time, Hannah. We're going to get you out of this."

"You can't get me out of this."

He threw the scroll down on his desktop. No one jumped. "You are NOT going to Hell!"

I walked further in. "You will be in violation of the covenant."

"I promised you! And I keep my promises!"

"Michael, you can't Advocate my case." I took a deep breath and said, "I have to."

The whole room burst into cries ranging from, "You can't do that!" to "You're insane!" Michael had to raise his voice just to be heard saying, "Everybody shut up!"

Once quiet had returned, he looked at me. "You can't be your own Advocate!"

"Why not? What qualifications do I need?"

This caught him by surprise. "Well, none, really."

"Then I am fully qualified, aren't I?"

"You don't know what to expect!"

"Listen. If you represent me, you violate the covenant and the Churches will control everyone's fates. If I represent myself, there is no violation of the covenant."

"Not good enough," he countered. "It is still extending God's mercy to someone outside of Christianity."

I smirked at him. "Not exactly."

You could have heard a feather fall in those chambers. Everyone was leaning in, hanging on every word I said. I stated simply, "I will not just go into

Heaven. I will earn my place or I won't go."

Michael came around from the desk. He stood in front of me, staring down at me. I tilted my head to the side as I angled it up so I could look Michael in the eyes. He studied me for a moment, then he finally spoke. "What, exactly, is your defense?"

I explained it to him.

There was dead silence.

Then riotous laughter burst forth.

There was a lot riding on this. Not only my fate, but the fates of many others the Church could say didn't qualify as real Christians. Some time was spent holding a fast mock trial, with Michael and everyone else in his chambers arguing against me, trying to knock me down. I weathered them all. Eventually, the only question left was, would it work with the Tribunal? There was only one way to find out.

Michael informed me that Advocates were required to have wings. As I wasn't a real angel, I would get ceremonial wings like I had seen. I was allowed to choose my own design. I didn't feel comfortable wearing wings with details that approached looking like angel wings. I opted for the most basic design. Each wing looked like teardrop with the point going down, with a smaller upside down teardrop on the outer edge and a flat top. Good enough for me. The wings were granted to me. I could deploy and rescind them at will. I said I wanted a couple of minutes to make sure I had my head straight. Michael said he understood, and he headed off to sit in the Gallery.

I found out later that the rest of Michael's team and lots of angels and Advocates had already taken places in the Gallery while I was getting my wings. My personal cheering section had grown. No one breathed a word for fear of tipping my hand. The Churches tried to ambush me. I was going to return the favor.

Michael came into court and headed for the front of the Gallery. Artie was still sitting directly behind where I had been, leaving the aisle seat open. Michael took it. He sat down and sagged.

Artie looked at him in shock. The trial was about to resume, and there were no Advocates at the Celestial table. And, most significantly, no Michael there.

He didn't hide his fury. "You promised you'd protect her!" he hissed.

Michael made no movement other than arching his eyebrows. "Just watch. You're never going to believe this."

I strode down the hall, the Guardians actually working to keep up with me. At the courtroom, I pushed both doors open from the center. Everyone turned to look at me. I ignored their gazes. I was strong. I was confident. I was invulnerable.

At my table, the Guardians stopped and looked at each other. They were supposed to hand the Petitioner over to their Advocate. This time, they were one and the same, so they simply shrugged and headed over by the judge's bench. I sat down, folded my hands, and closed my eyes. Spire was going to flip his wig. I kept my smile down by reminding myself this might not work.

It took a moment, but the Churches eventually noticed that I was sitting alone, and in the seat for the lead Advocate. Spire eyed me carefully, wondering what I was up to. He came up next to me and tried talking. I opened my eyes as he said, "Hello, Singer. Going to be your own Advocate?"

I said nothing.

"I hope you have a good plan. Otherwise, you're going to Hell."

Still nothing.

"Well, you'll be going to Hell, anyway. With Michael or without him."

Still nothing.

"Hey, I'm talking to you."

I kept staring straight ahead. I heard his voice rising a little bit. He was getting angry. That was what I wanted. I was sure of what I had in mind, but that didn't mean I didn't want as much in my favor as I could get. Him being angry and not thinking clearly was one of the most important things.

He came around to the other side of the table. He leaned on it, putting his nose practically up against mine. "What are you doing, Singer?"

I let my eyes unfocus and stayed locked in my own little world.

Spire straightened, looking at the Gallery. He advanced towards Michael. "What are you two up to?" he demanded.

Spire stopped short when Michael looked at him. Well, glared at him. No one plays St. Michael for a sucker, and the fact that Spire nearly succeeded in using him enraged him. And trust me, whatever you can imagine about the wrath of angels, it's nothing compared to what Michael was radiating at that moment.

Spire looked past Michael to Artie. "You're Singer's friend, right? She told you what's happening. What is she up to?"

Artie didn't stop facing the front. "She told me nothing. But knowing her, it's something that will blow you out of the water."

"Come on," he said patronizingly. "What is she doing?"

Artie closed his eyes and started singing softly. "Yo ho, all together...."

Each person Spire tried to pump for information would face the front, close their eyes, and sing along with Artie. Everyone in the Gallery was with me. The Guardians didn't sing, but they were smiling at me. I let a smile creep onto my face as I swayed to the music. Yo ho, all together....

The chimes sounded. Everyone stood and the sea shanty stopped. Spire dashed back to his seat where his two juniors were getting nervous. The suspense was killing them. They could dish it out, but they couldn't take it. Everyone with wings deployed them, including me. I felt quietly proud to have those wings behind me.

The Tribunal came back in. The first angels looked over at me and tripped. No one was expecting the sight of Hannah Singer, alone with Advocate wings. They took their places and faced me, waiting.

The back door opened and Pahaliah entered. He casually looked at the

Advocates, saw me, and stopped dead in his tracks. He made no effort to disguise the look on his face. After a moment, he nodded his head and said, just barely loud enough for the Advocates to hear, "This ought to be good."

Pahaliah took his place at the bench. He looked right at me. From behind me, over my head and between my wings, he saw Michael. With all attention riveted to Pahaliah, no one saw Michael give him a smile and a wink. Pahaliah sat down and banged the gavel. The Guardians, Churches, and I were the only ones left standing.

Pahaliah sounded like the question was being dragged out of him. "Who is the Petitioner?"

I answered with confidence. "The Petitioner is Hannah Singer."

There was a pause. Pahaliah knew what was coming, and he clearly didn't like the thought of helping me become a sitting duck. Finally, he asked, "And who are her Advocates?"

I steeled myself. This would test if this crazy scheme would work, and would set up the big reveal. "Hannah Singer, acting alone."

The Churches started laughing. Spire looked right at me. "Are you serious?!?"

Pahaliah banged the gavel. "Need I remind you there is still procedure to follow at the moment?"

"I am remembering procedure," Spire said respectfully to the bench while folding his hands. "She's not a Celestial Advocate. She hasn't been trained."

I wasted no time in firing back. "An Advocate is a position in this court. A Celestial Advocate is a position appointed by St. Michael. I am not here as a Celestial, I am here as an Advocate."

Spire was addressing me like I was a very slow child. "The other side is supposed to be represented by a Celestial."

I kept my gaze focused on the bench. "Exceptions can and have been allowed for a Petitioner who feels that someone not officially a Church or a Celestial can better represent him or her at trial. For example, such arrangements have been made for cases where both sides have contested the petition."

Spire looked a little disappointed. "So the Celestials are no longer supporting the petition."

Michael stood up. "May I address the bench?"

Pahaliah looked at him. "You may."

Michael stepped into the aisle so he could be seen. "The official position of the Celestials is and has always been 'no contest'. 'No contest' does not support the petition, it just stays uninvolved. Petitioners do not have to accept our advocacies, they can decline. We've just never had anyone do so before."

Pahaliah took out a scroll and started rolling through it. I figured it was the rules of the court. Pahaliah looked up. "Singer is within her rights to decline Celestial representation."

"But she needs a Celestial!" Spire protested. "She cannot argue without knowledge of Christianity, something that she, as an Atheist, is not qualified for!"

This was the crux. Spire was arguing to force a situation where he could either destroy the Celestial Courts or become the first Church to Cast someone on grounds of Atheism. My arguments, if they worked, would nullify this for all future cases. But I had to get to a point where I could make my arguments first.

But I knew I had it in the bag. Spire was so focused on getting his way, he wasn't paying attention. He was not hiding his self-righteousness and overconfidence. They were open targets, and I knew I could exploit them.

I aimed a shot right for his vanity. I tilted my head up and closed my eyes. "I don't need knowledge of Christianity!" I declared with as much pomp as I could. "I'm not afraid of him! I have facts on my side! Spire could have beaten St. Michael, but he's not smart enough to beat me!" I was trying to make it personal. It wasn't just an Atheist telling off a Christian, but a woman was telling off a man instead of being subservient. Not only was this an affront to social order, but also to his interpretation of the Bible.

That did it. "The Churches have no objection to Singer acting as her own Advocate!" he declared. He stuck his neck in the snare, and I was now waiting for the right time to pull it.

Michael sat down. Pahaliah looked like he couldn't believe the metamorphosis occurring in front of his eyes. Was I the same person from a short time ago? He focused on the task at hand. "And who advocates for the Church?"

"Byron Bell, Mark Freedman, and Victor Spire, acting as lead!" Spire made sure to give a flourish to his own name and being lead. Good. The fire was still burning.

"I guess there's no point in asking you to take the dock, Singer. You can't speak in there, so you might as well stay where you are." He sighed. "Advocate for the Petitioner goes first. Singer? Your opening arguments."

I needed to keep Spire wound tightly for just a little longer. I decided to smack his sense of order. "Heaven is a reward for leading a good, Christian life in accordance with God's wishes. And that I have done. When others in my village were falling to the plague, I continued to bring them food and comfort, even when everyone else had turned their backs on them. I helped work the fields so that the community could survive. And I sought to co-exist peacefully with them. And that was just towards the end of my life. That alone proves I led a good Christian life and deserve to get into Heaven."

I knew Spire was like a knight, ready for the signal so he could joust and ram his spear into his enemy. I simply tilted my head to him and smiled, indicating I had said what I wanted to say.

"The rules for Heavenly admission are simple!" Spire declared. "They have to believe. At no point while she was doing those acts did she believe! It wasn't doubt, she did not believe God existed! She ignored Him! That alone means she did not lead a Christian life! By not worshiping Him, she defied God's will!"

Pahaliah simply looked at me. Opening remarks were officially over. He folded his hands and sat patiently. Any questions as to whether or not this was the time were erased when I heard the whispers of Michael behind me, saying, "Go! Gogogogogo!"

I returned my attention to Pahaliah and twisted the spring. "I didn't defy God's will. I upheld it."

Spire's voice had dropped to a rumble, like approaching thunder. "What are you talking about?"

One more twist. "God wanted me to be an Atheist."

Snap.

Spire's "WHAT?!?" was probably heard outside the courtroom. I acted as if he'd said nothing and reiterated my point. "By being an Atheist, I was doing what God wished. If following God's wishes makes a Christian life, then I have earned a place in Heaven."

I saw Pahaliah pick up the gavel and place it aside, out of his immediate reach. The message was subtle, but clear – you two hash this out.

Spire couldn't wait to argue. "By your own admission, you should be Cast Down!"

I decided to go with passive arguments. Instead of volunteering my own deeds, I would let Spire make points and I would nullify them. It put the burden on him, and meant I wouldn't be volunteering anything he could use. What's more, he was so riled up, he'd likely forget some things here and there, making my defense easier. "I heard nothing in my admission advocating such a fate."

I stole a quick look at the Church table. The juniors were as far over as they could get and hunched a little bit. Spire's behavior made it clear they were to stay out of his way. They would be no help to their lead. There was only Spire and me. A duel to the death.

"How does acting as if God doesn't exist constitute upholding His will?!?"

I kept my calm. "Atheism is part of God's plan."

"Prove it!"

"Do you accept, as fact, that God made the world and humanity?"

"Yes!"

"And God made us beings capable of love and other attributes?"

"Are you saying Atheism is Free Will?!?"

"No, I'm saying Atheism is part of the human make-up. If Atheism was so bad, God could have eliminated it from human nature, like being able to fly. I mean, He doesn't have to put up with it. It exists, it continues to exist, so it is somehow a part of God's plan. A part that involved me."

"No! That is Free Will! You are choosing to ignore God, it is not part of your nature, it is a conscious choice!"

I knew the Churches would switch between Predestination and Free

68

Will in a heartbeat if it would help them win. The best bet was an argument that ignored either option and forced things in a direction Spire wasn't prepared for. "So, you're saying God, in His infinite wisdom, intentionally created beings as part of His plan that He wouldn't know if they would cooperate?"

"He doesn't know that they'll turn away!"

"Does that constitute a mistake?"

"God doesn't make mistakes!"

"Then allowing people to be Atheists is not a mistake, Atheism is not a mistake, it serves a purpose."

"What possible value can being an Atheist provide?!?"

"Atheists believe in focusing on the now. On what needs to be done to make things right. There are no second chances, there might not be a tomorrow, so do all you can now. It encourages critical thinking. Especially of religious theology."

"Like what?!?"

"People interpret Scripture to suit their ends. It's very easy to validate hatred and injustice with it. An Atheist, because she is not focused on Scripture, will consider the human element more readily. Something easy to forget if you only follow Scripture. Just ask the people the church ignored in my village as they died while I gave them sustenance and companionship."

He played an ace. "That's absurd! Why would God create people that ignore him?!?"

I trumped it. "God's plans are frequently unknowable. He works in mysterious ways. Are you saying God has to explain Himself to His creation before He does anything?"

He tried to salvage it. "You have no understanding of God! I have studied the Bible, in life and for the past hundred years! You can't know His plan!"

"I know it as well as you do."

"Based on what teaching?!?"

"Based on the same thought process you have. The covenant states that, what you hold true on Earth, He will hold true in Heaven. That means that you are free to use your best guess as to His intent, His plan, everything, and it will not be held against you if you get it wrong. Neither of us could know when we were alive what was really happening. My interpretation of how the world worked was no less valid than yours."

"Mine is based on study!"

"Yours is based on repeated lessons, not individual conclusions. But they had to start somewhere, as someone's individual conclusion."

"History has validated them!"

"How?"

That stopped him for a second, then he was off again. "Time has validated them!"

"How? Longevity doesn't mean correct. Otherwise, why would Jesus have been needed?"

"Because of faith!" Spire had found his second wind. "It's not a question of belief, but faith! You had no faith!"

Nice try. I shrugged and said, "God didn't think it was necessary for me to have faith."

"The Bible says you are to have faith!"

"Then why does God hide so much and enable Atheism to exist?"

"Proof denies faith! Without faith, God is nothing! He has to hide or He will cease to exist!"

"So how did God exist before the people He created to worship him? What faith existed then?"

Spire moved his mouth, but no words came out. I wanted to keep him from closing the argument, to have its lack of resolution hanging out there like a sword above his head. "Besides, if proof denies faith, why does God reveal Himself? He could have shown Himself to me to stop me from being an Atheist. He's done it before."

"Name one person God revealed Himself to!"

"Moses." I was focused on the trial so I wouldn't be distracted, but in the back of my mind, I wondered, did I just hear Michael stifle a laugh?

Spire's face actually turned red with rage. "That was Moses! He lead the Israelites out of Egypt! He was part of God's plan!"

"So was I, I just didn't know it at the time."

"You weren't a leader! You were just some woman!"

"How was I to know if I was just an Atheist or an Atheist for a reason? How do you know?"

"What else could you be?!?"

"I think I know what I was, and what else could I be. So we have different interpretations of God's will...."

"WILL YOU SHUT UP ABOUT THAT?!?"

There was a noise from the bench, making Spire look to it. I knew what it was. Pahaliah had just dragged the gavel noisily over. It was within reach. Spire was teetering over the line.

Spire readjusted quickly. "So, what we hold true on Earth is held true in Heaven, right?"

I knew a leading question when I heard one, but was confident I could handle whatever he threw at me. "Correct."

"So, if an Atheist holds that there is no Afterlife, shouldn't the fate you seek be eternal nothingness and to cease to exist instead of Heaven?"

I had to hand it to him, that was a good one. I thought quickly. "No, because interpretation does not equal fact."

"What?"

"The fact is God exists and there is a Heaven. Had I known that, I would have adjusted my beliefs accordingly. I did not know that, so my conclusions are based on erroneous assumptions. I should be punished for not knowing?"

"You aren't being punished, you are getting what you believe you should have."

"What's the point of the Celestial Courts, then? Everyone coming through here believes they deserve Heaven, so they should get it? Why should the church bother with absolution and the forgiveness of sins? If people feel they have done enough, shouldn't that be all that matters?"

Spire was getting angry again. Good. His capacity for lucid thought threw a scare into me. "You couldn't just believe just in case you were wrong?"

Oh, this was familiar ground for me. How many times did I have this argument in my village? "That isn't belief, then."

"You could have still gone to church and studied the Bible. Just in case you were wrong as an Atheist."

"God sees all and knows all, does He not?"

"He does."

"Then He would have to know that I don't really believe and I'm not doing it out of respect for Him, but to buy my way in. My deeds and actions will have nothing to do with it."

"You would be living a good Christian life."

"I WAS living a good Christian life."

"You didn't believe. You ignored part of a good Christian life."

"So being false is part of a Christian life?" I took advantage of the pause. "The only ones who would be impressed with that would be the church. God would regard me as a liar. God's displeasure in me can be overridden by you because I made you happy with me? Are you suggesting that making the church happy is preferable to making God happy?"

Spire suddenly smiled. His suggestion had been to stall for time, enabling him to think of something else. He looked like he found gold. "So, being an Atheist is part of God's plan."

I wanted to make sure he gave me enough rope to hang him with. "That is correct."

"So, by being an Atheist, you are doing what God created you for?"

"That is correct."

"Then you shouldn't get into Heaven."

"How so?"

"You did what you were created for, just like the sun, the rivers, the animals, the stone that makes the knives. You are just another element and not a true living being."

I was no longer nervous or afraid. I was running. "That can't be true."

"But you said yourself you are part of God's plan. God created you for a purpose. If you aren't a Christian, you don't get into Heaven. So you are just another thing from the world who served its purpose and now should be gone."

"If that's true, then why am I here?"

"That's what we're deciding. Whether or not you have a right to be here."

"But I must. I died, I clearly have a soul. Therefore, I am entitled to a Heavenly reward."

"A construct of God to facilitate a purpose has no soul. Does water have a soul?"

"If I'm just water, why did you allow me to be my own Advocate or to even stand trial instead of opposing me for not being a living being?"

I yanked the line, and the snare dug into Spire's neck. His eyes bulged out and the red tint returned to his face. I continued, "You have acknowledged that I am a living soul, so your argument is irrelevant." It was time to put this away. "Weren't you paying attention? No wonder you're losing the case."

I thought he was mad before. Turns out there was a whole other level left to go. *"BURN!!!"*

The gavel sounded like thunder rolling from the Heavens. Even I looked. Pahaliah had reached his limit. "Guardians, escort Spire from the Courts. He is barred from Advocating any cases until he repents and apologizes to me."

The Guardians advanced. I kept still. I felt I had the Tribunal on my side, and I didn't want to ruin it by gloating.

I noted Spire didn't even try apologizing there on the spot. He simply turned around and started stalking out of the courtroom. The Guardians had to catch up with him. He shoved the doors open and stormed outside.

Better see how I stand with the court. "Are we in recess until the Guardians return?"

Pahaliah looked out to the Gallery. "Michael? You available to fill in?"

"It would an honor, sire." Michael had raced out of the Gallery and stood in front of the bench before he finished his sentence. He stood straight with his arms folded across his chest. He was intimidating to everybody. Except me. I just knew.

Pahaliah then looked to the Church table. "So, would you like to continue redress of arguments?"

The junior Churches looked at each other in confusion. They had no preparation and being out of the loop meant they had no plan of attack. They both stood, and Mark Freedman stated, "The official position of the Churches is that Singer should be Cast Down for being an Atheist."

I remembered this from the mock trial in Michael's chambers. Closing arguments. I had nothing more to add. "The official position of the Advocate is that I have lived a life in accordance with God's will and I should be allowed into Heaven."

Pahaliah looked to the Tribunal. "You have heard the Advocates for Hannah Singer state their recommended fates. You may now make your decision. You wish to confer?"

This was a bit scary. The Tribunal didn't have to take either recommendation. They could disregard what we said and determine some other fate. Reincarnation seemed most likely to me, giving me another lifetime to be a Christian. I didn't particularly want to go around again, but it beat going to Hell.

The Tribunal had looked to each other and whispered a little bit, then the lead Tribunal stood up. "We are ready to rule."

I felt all the attention pull from me and settle on the Tribunal. I bit my lip. "And what is your decision?" Pahaliah asked.

"Petition for entry into Heaven is granted."

My eyes shot wide. It worked! It actually worked!

I was on my way to Heaven!

I fought with everything in me to keep completely still. The Gallery was silent, like they were afraid any noise would shatter the ruling. Pahaliah stood up, a quiet smile on his face, and bowed to me. "Congratulations, Lady Singer. So be it!" He banged the gavel. And the courtroom went nuts.

Everyone was cheering, but I barely heard it. I was still in shock. I couldn't believe it! I had actually pulled it off! I didn't even notice Michael had dashed up and enclosed me in a bear hug. Slowly, my awareness expanded to include what was around me. I hadn't even realized I'd willed my wings away. I felt everyone patting me on the back, whether to congratulate me or to prove I was still there, I couldn't say. I caught sight of Artie. "Any chance you can be my Advocate?" he asked. I managed to reach out to him, and we did our secret handshake.

Michael finally released me. He put his hand on top of my head and tousled my hair. "You did it you did it you did it! I knew you could, kiddo!"

"So what now? What happens next?"

Michael pointed to the side, and everyone got quiet. There was a door on the left side of the court. "That is the Petitioner's exit," he said. "It'll take you to where you go next."

I looked at my cheering section. Artie was actually misty eyed. "Go on, Hannah. You've earned it."

I stood there, my shoulders drooping a little. "What about the others?"

Joseph smiled. "We'll tell them. Chances are, you'll be seeing us before too long."

I smiled weakly. But I forced myself to move. I didn't want Spire to get another chance at me. I looked over my shoulder the entire time. Everyone was smiling and waving. All except Michael, who had his back to me and was talking to them. I turned my head, so no one would see my face, and strode up to and through the door.

When the door closed behind me, I was in the center of a chamber of some sort. It was like it was covered in purple velvet, black wrinkles flowing along. The only flat spot was where I was standing. The material spread out and curved up around me, like I was inside some sort of cloth ball. There was no trace of the door that just closed. My peasant clothes were gone. I was now wearing white with a rich blue overrobe. I stood for a moment, then the room started to shift. The wrinkles moved and the room stretched into a sort of tunnel, with an opening at the end. A white light was there.

I walked towards it. I stepped through the opening, and saw the Pearly Gates. Huge, with gold and white everywhere. I could vaguely see what was on the other side.

Standing in front of the gates was a man. He was pretty solidly built, and smiled at me happily. "I am St. Peter. Welcome to Heaven."

Suddenly, another man materialized. I had met Him before as a being of light. Now, I saw Jesus as a regular person. They both beamed at me.

I couldn't wait any longer. I dashed up to the gates and stood in front of them. "My petition was approved."

"We know," St. Peter said. "You just have one more choice to make."

My face fell. Jesus laughed. "You don't have another trial. You have your judgment. This is yours. The decision has more to do with him." And Jesus pointed behind me.

I turned and looked. Michael came running up, only starting to slow down when he got close. "You didn't really think I wouldn't see you off, did you?" he said with a smile.

I rushed up to him and gave him the biggest hug I could. He returned it happily. When we finally separated, I told him. "That was really something back there, wasn't it?"

"You know, Singer," he said, eying the Pearly Gates, "you have a judgment in your favor. You can enter Heaven any time. Nothing says you have to go right now."

I was about to ask why I would want to do that when I answered my own question. "You want me to be an Advocate."

"I want you to be a Celestial," he corrected. "Even without your arguments, you are a Christian now, so you are fully qualified."

I thought it over carefully. Well, I tried to. I wanted to jump at it, but I wasn't sure it was a good idea. "Can I think about it?"

"Just promise me you won't cross over until you tell me what you decide."

"You got it."

He smiled and walked away. I looked to St. Peter and Jesus. "How would I get back?"

"Just pray to us. We'll bring you over," Jesus said.

After a moment, I said, "I need some time."

"Take all you need," Jesus said. The area was bathed in a brilliant light that kept getting brighter and brighter. When it finally faded, I was in the main courtyard for the Celestial Courts, near the Grand Fountain where this all began.

I leaned against the fountain and looked at the water. There were still little bubbles forming from the water pouring in, rising gently to the surface where they burst into nothingness. Well, most of them. I don't know why I didn't notice before, but there were a few other bubbles. They didn't burst, not right away. They sat on top of the water, riding proudly and seeming to give up only when they were ready. A few of them stayed for a long time. And kept staying. They just wouldn't go away.

I felt myself really relaxing. I really had nothing to lose. If it wasn't working, I could simply go on to Heaven. But if I could make it work, I could help the next Hannah Singer, someone with almost impossible odds and being used for machinations, and save her from a horrible fate.

I walked into the court building and went to Michael's chambers. I knocked on his door, and heard him say, "Come in."

I went in. Michael was seated at his desk, with two others in front of him. They were wearing robes, so I wasn't interrupting a case conference. I stood away from the door and said, "I want to be a Celestial."

Michael jumped up with his hand extended to me. "Welcome aboard!"

We clasped hands, and my face fell. When he removed his hand, the inside of mine was covered with a thick brown substance I was hoping was a brownie. I looked at the other two Celestials. One of them shrugged at me. "Congratulations. You're officially one of us now."

And I wondered if this was really such a good idea....

And that was how it started. The first Advocate to argue for themselves and win. And one of the periodic attempts by the Church to eliminate the Celestial Courts reduced to ashes.

Michael clearly didn't want me going anywhere for a while. He made the other Celestials introduce my arguments into their trials and get them upheld. Had I gone to Heaven, it would be over. But with me not there yet, there was the possibility the Churches would go for a retrial. By the time Michael agreed to a hearing, the precedents had been set and the Churches just couldn't win. That's my big brother, always has my back.

Artie and the others had gone back to the stragglers, thinking that me going through the door was the last they would see of me. When I showed up to say hello, they flipped. Especially Nathan. He still hadn't gone, he wanted to tell everyone about what had happened. He went to Heaven at peace. The other stragglers were not only thrilled to see me, but when I told them I was going to be a Celestial, they all wanted to know when I was ready so they could petition. Yes, Artie, too.

I was a quick learner, and went from junior to lead in no time. Word shot around the Valley Of Death about a Celestial who defended herself from getting Cast Down, and if you were scared of what might happen to you at trial, she's the one you wanted on your side. I thought it was unfair, there were other Celestials who could handle specialized cases better than me and I would get them appointed when I could. But there was a gradual increase in stragglers petitioning, and all because they had hope now.

Michael and I went back to my old village one day. The plague was over, and the village was having one of its festivals. We had gone after I made sure that even the grandchildren of the people who remembered me were dead. We saw jesters and heard lute players and enjoyed roasted apples. We got several and went out of the village to the countryside. Sitting beside each other on the ground, we ate in silence for a while.

"You know, when you think about it, the Churches made a bigger mistake than they ever realized," I said.

"Oh, really, Hannah?" By this point, Michael was calling me by my first name instead of my formal last. "How's that?"

"If they hadn't fought my petition, they could have still tried their scheme to dismantle the Court." I took another bite and chewed thoughtfully. "I thought my whole argument was a bluff. Was it really?"

Michael looked at me. "What do mean?"

"That couldn't have been coincidence. Did I live the way I did because I actually WAS a part of God's plan? To eventually protect the Celestial Court and to advocate for stragglers?"

Michael carefully looked at me. "You want to know the truth?"

I nodded.

Michael looked back to the sky. "There is no plan. Humans are too unpredictable. You give some people every advantage in the world, and they do nothing with it. And some, you give them nothing but suffering, and they rise up and change the world."

I wasn't sure if I felt relieved or disappointed. "So I really was a very ordinary, everyday person."

"You are far from ordinary and everyday, Hannah," Michael said, looking at me. "God doesn't have a plan. He's just very good at taking advantage of situations."

We smiled at each other. We "clinked" our apples together, and enjoyed the rest of the day.

IN THE NAME OF THE FATHER

There is an automatic assumption that Celestials are the defenders of all souls, that anyone that asks for God's mercy gets it, and we make sure they get it.

Wrong. Wrong. Wrong.

Strictly speaking, we defend God's mercy first. God loves. God forgives. God understands. But that's only with those who are genuinely good souls. There are people who must atone for their misdeeds, to right the wrongs they've committed, or that their evil simply cannot be undone. We do not defend those. We oppose them. With everything we have.

A lot of people, when they first become Advocates, are shocked to find out that Celestials can and do block petitions. Generally, the Churches are saying people don't deserve a Heavenly reward and we're trying to establish they do. So when the dynamic flips, when the roles reverse, when the Churches are trying to get someone through the Pearly Gates and we're trying to stop them, it gets interesting.

One of the duties of Advocates is to travel the Valley Of Death. There are always new souls who have died and don't know what to do next. When they realize they didn't automatically drift to Heaven, they get understandably scared. Others are stragglers, people who are aware of what has happened and that they have to petition with the Celestial Courts, but for whatever reason, they aren't doing it. Usually, they think they are guaranteed a place in Hell if they do.

Advocates for both sides go out to look for them and let them know what their options are. Maybe even give them a pep talk. At least, that's what we Celestials do. The Churches are just the opposite. If they get the slightest hint that you haven't lived a life in strict accordance with their beliefs, they will start preaching fire and brimstone like you wouldn't believe, scaring people into straggling even longer. Or, if it is someone they really think is righteous, they will do everything they can to rush them to the Celestial Courts to start the process....

...well, that's how it usually goes.

Stragglers spoke of The Legend Of Hannah Singer, a woman who somehow pulled off a miracle. She had been guaranteed to go to Hell and the Celestials couldn't save her. She represented herself, alone and without a leader, completely outfoxed the Churches, and now had a Heavenly reward waiting for her. The only reason she wasn't in Heaven was because she volunteered to become a Celestial Advocate and help those in deep trouble like she had been. This was in the relatively early years after all that happened. Nowadays, it's history that everyone knows is true. But back then, it was folklore everyone was hoping was true.

I became a near constant on the Celestial tours in those early centuries. Many stragglers would petition, hoping to be represented by me, feeling I was their best hope (most of the time, they would get other Celestials because what they had done really wasn't that bad and my caseload was high, but make no mistake -- without me, they never would have set foot in the Celestial Courts). But other stragglers would think The Legend was just a legend. Coming face to face with me in the Valley Of Death, often brainstorming winning defenses on the spot for them, made me very real to them and eliminated their doubts.

It was about the middle of the 16th Century. I had just finished another defense. I sort of lost -- didn't get a Heavenly reward, but the penance was easy. If days existed here, he'd be in by nightfall. I walked down the halls when I heard St. Michael's footsteps approaching. There was lightness in his step, which meant he was friendly and I didn't have to watch out for his pranks at the moment. I turned to greet my surrogate big brother. "Well met, Michael. Looking for me?"

He stopped in front of me. "Yes. Any pending cases?"

"No, just finished up. I was just about to return my case scrolls."

"I'm heading for the Valley Of Death. I'd like you to come with me."

"Looking for stragglers again?"

"I'm thinking it could be an intervention."

An intervention happened when the Churches were working stragglers over constantly, using fear and intimidation to keep them from even trying to petition. We would then try to undo the damage they'd done. Usually, we were there after the fact, but sometimes, the Churches would be in the middle of their little spiel when the Celestials would show up. We'd basically throw down with them, on the spot and in front of the straggler. The whole point was to make the Churches look like the bullies they are and that there wasn't as much to fear as the stragglers had been led to believe.

I immediately noticed something odd. Interventions are spur of the moment. Because there is no omniscience in the Afterlife, no one really knows if the Churches have cornered some poor soul at that moment and are gleefully putting him through the wringer. Usually, we stumble across them on our tours. The fact that there might be some advance notice caught my attention.

I tucked my scrolls into my robes and said, "Well, no point in wasting time."

Michael smiled at me. He touched my shoulder, and with the speed of angels, we wound up in the Valley Of Death.

We were on the edge of a wooded area. Lots of expansive hilly areas around us. Michael took a last look around and said, "Some of the tours coming back say they've been running into a group of Churches around here. They've been sticking to the same general area and being very defensive. They're hiding someone."

"Going to sneak up on them?"

"Yeah. No unnecessary talking. We need to find out what they are doing and who they are doing it to."

"Which is why I'm here."

"Yes. You're proof that whoever it is has nothing to fear."

I took in my surroundings. "It's a Spaniard."

Michael looked at me strange. "How do you know?"

"They've been staying in this general area, right? Feel it. The air. The humidity. The light. The landscape. It's probably a Spaniard."

Michael just stared at me, blinking. Finally, he faced me, pulling himself up to his full height and poking his head down at me. "Three songs says you're wrong."

Angels wager songs. I rose up on my tiptoes and put my nose as close to his as I could. "I raise you two."

"You're on," he smirked. We clasped hands, each of us trying to crush the other's fingers as we shook. Neither of us yielded until we separated.

We turned to march out of the forest, and got maybe five paces when Michael stopped cold. I wasn't sure what the problem was. After all, nothing can hurt anyone out here, not even throwing yourself from the top of a mountain (I tried it. Blame Michael. He dared me). I came around in front of Michael to see his face. His eyes were wide, like some universal truth had just been revealed to him. "Michael? You okay?"

"Spaniard, you said?"

I looked around carefully. "Yeeeaaaaaaah...."

Michael took in his surroundings. He then squeezed his eyes shut and pinched the bridge of his nose. "I know who it is. I still need to confirm it, but I know who it is."

"Is it really that bad?"

"We've been preparing for trial for him for over seventy years."

"Who is it?"

Michael just held his finger up. "Do not spar with him. At all. Just keep your mouth shut, act respectful, keep it together."

"Okay...."

We wandered out until we came to another forest area. Michael was sneaking around trees. It was amazing how someone so large and powerful could move effortlessly and silently, like a feather on the breeze. He would motion for me to move certain ways, occasionally going back. I caught glimpses of Churches at various parts of the forest. I knew they were lookouts.

Eventually, we made it to a point where we could see a clearing. There were some Churches milling around, talking amongst themselves. Seated in the exact center of the clearing was an older Spaniard. He was dressed as a Catholic holy man, and the regional differences in the clothing confirmed he lived and died in Spain.

Suddenly, something clicked in my head. I knew exactly who it was. I turned to look at Michael and whispered, "So, that's the mighty Torquemada, huh?"

Michael looked furious. "Yes."

I examined our subject of focus. Tomas de Torquemada had the arrogance of a self-made leader. He simply sat, content within himself, not caring what existed around him. He looked like he could wait there forever, his round face and flat nose like a sheer mountainside. He looked annoyed, like this delay was the ultimate indignity for someone of his import.

I whispered to Michael, "Do we leave, or do we introduce ourselves?"

"Introducing ourselves is too subtle for me right now."

"Who said anything about subtle?"

Michael looked at me and smirked. We whispered between ourselves and a plan was formed. It would have to happen fast.

In a flash, Michael willed his flaming sword to appear. I grabbed it in one hand and willed my ceremonial wings to appear. Michael then grabbed my free hand and its corresponding ankle and swung me around like a modern kid playing airplane. Three spins, and Michael launched me into the air. He had aimed me so that I dropped directly in front of Torquemada, facing him. I raised the sword high above my head in a chopping position and screamed, "DIE, HERETIC!"

And in that moment, I knew what it felt like to be Michael.

Torquemada cowered in front of me, shielding his face with his arms and cringing while pleading for his life. Meanwhile, two Churches screamed, "We'll save you!" and charged at me. Three other Churches saw this and panicked. Because I was on a tour, I was technically on duty. Physically attacking an on-duty officer of the court is grounds to automatically Cast Down. But the Churches rushing me were on duty, too, so the three would-be white knights couldn't tackle them. Two raced out, grabbed the rushers, and spun them off balance. Meanwhile, the third grabbed me by my waist, lifted me up, and started hauling me away from the point of impact. A couple of other Churches were screaming, "We've been found! We've been found!" Who they were calling to, I have no idea, because everyone there pretty much knew at that point.

Before I could be released, I was starting to convulse with laughter. The Church put me down, and I promptly dropped to my knees, barely holding the flaming sword up. I didn't want it to touch the ground, I had no idea what would happen, but the more you hold laughter back, the worse it gets. Suddenly, the sword vanished. Michael had willed it away. I immediately leaned over until my head almost touched the ground, my wings shaking as I laughed uncontrollably.

I heard familiar footsteps approach. I knew the stride, and I knew the irritated demeanor. It was Victor Spire, the most senior Church. He led the opposition to my petition about two centuries earlier, trying to use me to destroy the Celestial Courts. My continued presence was an affront to him, which made each victory in the Celestial Courts that much sweeter. I heard him stop in front of me. "Great. Just what we need. Another Michael."

Michael came out of the forest at that moment. "Can't get too much of a good thing."

I had somehow managed to will my wings away and roll onto my back. I was recovering my breath and taking everything in. Torquemada was full-blown insulted arrogance. He was standing now, looking down on me and saying, "So, you're the infamous Hannah Singer."

I simply folded my hands on my stomach and smiled at him. After all, I did promise Michael I wouldn't be confrontational. What's more, I'd already had my fun.

Michael was now standing next to me, on my opposite side from Spire. Michael was keeping his fury with Spire pretty well under control, considering Spire tried to play him like a puppet. "So, this is why Torquemada hasn't turned up on the court dockets yet. You're keeping him out here."

"Just protecting him from prying eyes," Spire responded. "We know how you Celestials can't wait to put the screws to him."

Michael smirked. "Insisting he atone for his misdeeds is putting the screws to him?"

"They weren't misdeeds. He believed he was doing right for the good of Christianity. He's protected by the covenant."

Already my mind was working. God made a covenant with His people that, whatever was held true on Earth, He would hold true in Heaven. It was to help ease worry about misunderstanding God's will. The Churches, though, loved to use it as a trump card to override the Celestials' arguments. Trials usually boiled down to creating exceptions to the covenant or reasons it didn't apply.

I bounced to my feet. "You really think the covenant will protect you in the Celestial Courts?"

I noticed Michael wasn't trying to stop me. He had to be wondering what I was up to. Spire focused his ire on me. "The covenant is simple and clear."

"Like your head."

"Personal insults are a sign of the small minded."

"And your small mind is betrayed by wagering everything on the covenant. We Celestials get that disregarded quite often."

Spire looked furious. "Well, maybe we need a different venue for trial."

I made my face look surprised. "No! You don't mean...."

Spire was nose to nose with me. "Yes! Trial by God! Unlike angels, He has to rule according to the covenant! All your arguing will be for naught!"

"No! That's not fair! That's not...."

"Michael? Get your pet Atheist out of here."

I felt Michael get a rough grip on my shoulder and everything around us shifted. We were back in his chambers. Almost immediately, his grip relaxed.

I turned to look at Michael. His face was proof that he had been acting. He tilted his head to the side. "What was that about?"

"Just doing you all a favor. They go for trial by God, God will have to rule according to the covenant. That also means hitting Torquemada for all the sins he was too arrogant to repent."

Michael just shook his head as he released my shoulder. "I'm glad you're on our side."

"That makes two of us," I smiled.

81

Michael gestured to the chairs in front of his desk. I went to one, checking for a tack before I sat down as Michael went behind the desk. He plopped down in the chair and looked at me. "They're stalling."

"They think they can eventually hit on a winning defense," I shrugged. "I mean, they had to know they weren't hiding him from you."

Michael nodded. "They know they need their best. We started preparing for Torquemada before he became Inquisitor General. It didn't take omniscience to tell how he was going to go."

I didn't know Torquemada personally. Not only was I from England, but my death and his birth were separated by about a hundred years. I started learning of him because of the wave of excommunication trials and victims of the autos-de-fe that we were getting. Torquemada was acquiring legend status among the living on Earth. Many Christians feared him more than they did Lucifer, which is a pretty amazing feat.

I leaned back and folded my hands under my chin. "They won't use the covenant," I said with certainty.

Michael leaned in. "What makes you so sure?"

"How long has Torquemada been dead?"

"About fifty years now."

"They haven't gone to trial. The covenant is worthless. Torquemada's crimes are too great. A green junior could pot the guy if that was their only defense."

"How would you nullify it?"

"Assuming we could only argue church doctrine instead of philosophical points? Easy. The Bible says, 'Thou shalt not commit murder.' His autos-de-fe violated the very laws of God he sought to enforce. He didn't modify existing doctrine, he ignored it. Poof! Gone! Huzzah!"

Michael just nodded and smiled. He leaned back. "Good idea to keep in mind if it comes up."

"I'm guessing the opposition is going to be situational instead of direct." "Situational" meant it was based on how the person was living in relation to their religion rather than anything personal, such as contradictions in their personal philosophies. If that sounds like a lousy defense, it is. Neither side relies on situationals, they only use them as a starting point or an emergency fallback. If an Advocate actually uses it, it means the trial is lost and they're just hoping to say they gave their all.

"Well, in this case, situational looks pretty good," Michael said. He didn't sound convinced. Since neither side has to disclose their trial strategy beforehand, cases are won and lost on the spur of the moment. This is the reason for mock trials and brainstorming, to try and anticipate what might happen. And when you have every religious zealot on one side scheming, that becomes nearly impossible.

"What kind of situational defense are you looking at?" I asked.

"How he selected his victims. There's a lot of debate about why he chose who he did. If we can make his reign of terror into a political power play that used religion instead of being about religion, we may have a good shot."

Not bad, but not good enough. It put the Celestials in a reactive position, relying on the Churches to feed them something they could use. There had to be something more. I started turning things over in my mind. The covenant was out as a defense. Sure loser. Trial by God was out. Also a sure loser. And there was no way Torquemada would be kept there forever, there had to be some potential avenue....

I declared, "Your situational is dead in the water. They're going for Divine Right." Divine Right was when a person took the whole "God's representative on Earth" thing way too seriously. Excessive behavior was the result of zealousness and eagerness to serve their master, not maliciousness. In other words, temporary insanity. Divine Right wasn't much good for getting into Heaven, but it was great for keeping out of Hell.

Michael blanched. "If they do that, Privacy Of Mind applies." God knows our thoughts, but others aren't supposed to know them. Any behavioral factors must be demonstrated by action, looking into someone's mind is not allowed. And if someone talks fast enough and acts sincere enough, they can redress their behavior as insecurity or ignorance instead of malice.

"Which means you can't use anything about the circumstances of his appointment or the victims he chose unless you can clearly demonstrate malice on his part. On the bright side, they'll never call for a mistrial." During a mistrial consideration, God looks into your private thoughts and reasoning. Torquemada would drop into Hell like a stone if they tried that.

"Sounds good," Michael nodded. "Not guaranteed, of course, but it does have a good chance of success. Forces the trial away from where we can influence it."

We talked for a few more minutes about where it would lead and what else they might try when Michael stopped me. "Hannah? Would you mind sitting in on a brainstorming session right now?"

"Sure," I said. I could feel myself blushing. I'd never been asked to brainstorm a case I wasn't involved in before.

Michael held up his hand with one finger extended and a putto, David, appeared. "Please ask Noah Holman to come to my chambers."

Holman turned up soon. Holman was a great guy. He was my original defender at my trial and my primary teacher when I decided to become an Advocate. The three of us threw ideas back and forth. When all was said and done, the possible oppositions were a lot more solid and Holman would be better prepared for surprises at trial. I still needed to return my scrolls, so I politely excused myself and went on my way, thinking I'd done pretty good there.

I would soon find out I did better than I realized.

Occasionally, when writing these memoirs, I have to rely on the skills of a fiction writer. Some things happen when I'm not around. There are times when I can learn what happened, like a transcript, if you will, and other times I have to sort of recreate the scene based on what I know of the participants. This part that follows is a blend of the two. Michael told me most of it later on, but I know both participants well enough to fill in any blanks.

After I had left to return my scrolls, Michael and Holman talked a little more. Holman noticed there was a slightly distracted air to Michael. Holman simply sat quietly, waiting for Michael to break the silence. When it kept dragging on and on, Holman simply asked, "You're thinking it, too, aren't you?"

Michael's head snapped up to him. "Thinking what?"

"Michael, don't play coy with me. Not after all our years and cases together."

Michael leaned forward, putting his elbows on his desk and holding his chin up with his folded hands. "I'm trying to find a reason not to."

"Why? We both know Singer can handle this. She's proven herself many times."

"She's handled tricky cases, yes. But those are still relatively simple. This isn't just some grey area case, this is Torquemada. He has the Churches' entire collective brain trust working for him. She's never led something of this scale before."

"In a way, she has. When she defended herself."

Michael leaned back. "I want to. I really want to. I mean, she's always been a great Advocate. She's a natural. And she's just advancing by leaps and bounds. She's one of the best I've ever seen, and she's only been doing this for about two hundred years. She's got the smarts, but...."

"She just hasn't had the experience yet?"

Michael looked at him. "Humans are so unpredictable. What if it's too much?"

"I say we play off of her mentality. We've seen the Celestial Courts are more important to her than her sense of self. She will step aside if it means winning the case. There's no way she'll let pride get in the way of blocking Torquemada. I don't think we have anything to lose."

Michael thought it over. "How about we see how Hannah chooses her juniors and how she divides responsibilities? She does good enough, we let her lead this opposition."

"How about we give her a group to choose from, and explain to her that this is in case the trial gets out of hand and we have to take over?"

Michael closed his eyes. "I can't believe I'm this nervous for her."

"Well, it is understandable," Holman said. "However, not only do you have no reason to be afraid, but you have to let her try. You're losing us."

Michael looked sadly at Holman. Celestials generally start to burn out at about three hundred years. Making it to four hundred is amazing. Longer than that is a miracle. Holman had been going for about four hundred twenty-five years, and everyone noticed the change happening. Most of the other grey Celestials were vacating and claiming their Heavenly reward. In fact, Holman was the only Celestial left from my original trial.

Michael was looking at a vacuum among the greys. There were plenty of Celestials to handle the basic cases, but the really tricky ones? Not many of them. They both knew their horse had the pedigree, they just weren't certain she could run.

"Okay," Michael said. "She leads, and is to step aside if the trial moves outside of her."

"I don't think you'll have to convince her," Holman smiled.

I was sitting in the Water Gardens, going over scrolls and making notes for future defenses when David, the putto, raced up. "St. Michael wants to see you in his chambers immediately."

I shot to my feet. "Tell him I'm on my way." I was already walking before David left.

When I got to Michael's chambers, I politely rapped on the door. I heard Michael and Holman chorus, "Come in!"

Okay, that's odd. I opened the door and stepped inside. They were both smiling at me. If it was only Michael smiling, I would have looked for a bucket of water above my head or some other prank. Holman's matching expression reinforced that it wouldn't be a prank. Which wouldn't necessarily be better.

"Have a seat, Hannah," Michael smiled, gesturing to the chair I left a short time ago.

I closed the door and went to the chair, checking for a tack just in case. Michael flicked his hand at his door, and it vanished into the wall. As I sat, I realized I was about to be offered something really really big. And there was only one thing I could think it would be.

"I think you know what this is all about, Hannah," Michael said.

I threw my dart. "You want me to junior on Torquemada's case."

Close, but not a bull's eye. "No. I want you to lead."

I couldn't hide my surprise. "Are you sure that's a good idea?"

"I'm going to be blunt with you, Hannah," Michael said. "First, you've been doing really well with grey area cases. Sooner or later, you're going to be taking the really tough ones. I'd rather find out now while there are still experienced Celestials to back you up whether or not you can handle it."

I nodded. "Got it."

Michael sighed. "It's more than that, Hannah. The second point is how this trial has to go. We don't know what the Churches are planning. You said yourself this can't turn on church doctrine, there are too many ways to undermine it or use it against them. They are going to rely on some philosophical stance and hope they catch us napping. You are one of the best I've ever seen at thinking on their feet. They've never been able to ambush you, even at your own trial. I'd like a team of juniors that can handle the doctrine angles and you dealing with the Churches' trickery. Understand, if you are in over your head or they do focus on doctrine, I expect you to step aside and let Holman lead."

"Why not just make me a junior, then? I'd still be able to speak and argue."

"I want to see if you can lead a trial like this."

I understood. It was a test, to see if I could live up to my potential.

I stood up, arms straight at my sides, and said, "I accept."

I saw Michael smile warmly at me. I looked at Holman. He was smiling the same way. Michael asked, "Well, Hannah, you are now lead. What do you do first?"

Out of habit, I checked the chair again for a tack before I sat down. I leaned back and folded my hands under my chin. "Let's start with a list of Celestials so I can pick my juniors."

"Greys?"

"Everyone. Greys, yes, but also Catholic Celestials, someone to keep the discussions of doctrine focused. And there might be another diamond in the rough that we can use. I don't want to overlook anything that will help."

I did catch Michael and Holman smile at each other. Beyond that, I don't know. From that moment on, I was lost in thought.

I began with my junior selection. Lots to choose from. Holman was my first choice. He showed me the ropes, he nearly kept me out of Hell, and he was the most experienced grey. I wanted him there. My second choice was George Burkeshire. He was the resident Celestial expert on Catholic doctrine. My third choice was Ferdinand Vasquez. He was a newly minted Celestial, only juniored three cases so far. But, he was born and raised in Spain at roughly the same period as Torquemada's reign. He could provide valuable insight into life at the time, and might even help in interpreting Torquemada's actions if Divine Right really was in the cards. My last choice was George McCreedy. McCreedy knew Christian history and how doctrine had changed and evolved over time. He was a walking encyclopedia, and I wanted his knowledge if Scriptural intent came up.

Holman expressed surprise at my choices. When he was lead, he had chosen three juniors, all greys like himself. He wasn't going to say much, since this was now my case. But I knew he was having trouble biting his tongue.

On the other hand, Michael was very impressed with the direction I was going in. "An excellent team, Hannah. It should get significant results."

"We'll need them," I said. "Spire's going to lead this." Church officials were automatically entitled to the best defense the Churches could provide, and that meant the senior leading.

We had numerous sessions and mock trials, readying for anything they could hit us with. There was only one problem – Torquemada hadn't petitioned yet. Neither side could request a trial until Torquemada made his intentions clear.

"They want to make sure they'll win," Michael explained.

"I know. I'm just getting impatient here," I grumbled.

"We can't force them to make him petition."

"No, but we can encourage it."

"How?"

"Let word get around that I'm going to lead."

Michael's face quirked. Spire had been itching for payback ever since I foiled his plot and made him look like a fool at my trial. With an untested-at-that-level Hannah Singer as lead, it would be a chance to rebuild his ego and teach me a harsh lesson.

Michael let it out in casual conversation that I was lead. Some Celestials asked me if it was true, and I said it was. Then, a Church asked. I knew that was it. He ran off, and a short time later, Torquemada appeared at the clerks' office. Spire filed "No Contest" and requested a trial as soon as the petition hit his desk. I knew he couldn't resist. Michael immediately filed his opposition and trial request, and everything was set.

I didn't bother trying to interview Torquemada before trial. I could have, I knew where he was. Most Petitioners stay at the Interim until their trial. Torquemada stayed on the Church Campus so that he wouldn't have to mix with the commoners. That only steeled my resolve. I was going to teach this clown a lesson he would never forget.

Just before the trial was to occur, Spire got sneaky. I was consulting with another soul I was going to defend when Holman came dashing up. I could tell from the look on his face it was something important. I went over, and he whispered urgently, "Your trial has been moved."

"Moved? To where?"

"Grand Courtroom."

That made me arch my eyebrows. "I've never argued in the Grand Courtroom before. Not even as a junior."

"I know. Spire's trying to intimidate you."

I smiled evilly. "Let him."

Holman's face fell. "Let him?"

"Trust me." And I dashed away from Holman to finish my consultation.

It was strange. The more Spire's machinations emboldened me, the more nervous Michael and Holman got. Michael made sure I remembered my signals – Advocates have little signals they can use to communicate to their bosses in the Gallery that they are in trouble and need help. I mostly did it to humor Michael. The more arrogant Spire got, the easier he was to defeat. It would still be a fight, but the resolution was less and less in doubt.

The time of trial came. I marched down the hallways to the Grand Courtroom. Two Guardians stood outside of the doors. They saw me and nodded as they stepped aside, as if they knew what I was in for and I didn't. I pushed open the right door and strode through.

Inside, it was bedlam. I knew the Grand Courtroom was the only court with a Gallery that occupied two floors. Cases of great import were heard there. It was standing room only. Angels and Advocates talked amongst themselves, discussing trial strategy, what they would do, and whether or not I was insane. Even the two court Guardians in front of the judge's bench were whispering back and forth. I was a little worried. I mean, I always am. The day you no longer worry about the outcome, it's time to vacate. But the Gallery was buzzing with activity. It was exactly what I wanted.

My team of juniors were already at the Celestial table. They looked nervous. I took the lead Advocate spot with the stool furthest left and greeted them. They greeted me back. Holman asked, "Are you sure about this?"

I just nodded.

I stole a quick look at the Church table. Torquemada was already here, sitting in the Petitioner's chair, second in from the aisle. Spire was already looking over documents with his team of three juniors. Unlike my trial, he was taking this very seriously. He looked at me and held his hand up in a fist, acting like he was crushing something in his grip. I widened my eyes, formed my mouth into an "O", and slapped my hands to my cheeks. "Oh, the big bad man is scary!"

"I've been waiting for this for a long time, Singer."

"Go burn." I turned back to my juniors, continuing my review and organizing scrolls so I knew exactly where to find things the instant I thought I needed them.

I had noticed the seat behind me on the first floor of the Gallery was empty. I knew it was being held for Michael. He wouldn't miss this. Sure enough, he turned up, dashing down the aisle and taking the seat. He was clearly worried about me.

The chimes sounded. The time for preparation was over. Everyone stood and we deployed our wings. I faced the front, letting my eyes drift to the Tribunal box on the right. Twelve angels entered from the door next to it, wings already out, radiating integrity, power, and grace. Maybe someday, I thought. Maybe someday....

The door at the back opened and the presiding angel entered. This was a Catholic trial, and the Catholic church doesn't really acknowledge individual angels. There were only three officially recognized angels, giving them jurisdiction to sit at Catholic trials, and only two available to choose from, Gabriel and Raphael (Michael can't because it would be a conflict of interest). Gabriel was God's herald and only rarely sat. Typically, these trials were handled by Raphael. Raphael entered, and I breathed a sigh of relief. Gabriel sat so rarely, no one really had a good read on how he would go. Raphael was a known quantity. I readied myself.

I needed to fight a perfect fight. My biggest threats in this trial were my own allies. Between Michael's (to be honest, perfectly justified) uncertainty and Holman's outright fear, I had to make sure I kept everything under control or they wouldn't hesitate to yank me out – blocking Torquemada was more important than seeing how capable I was.

That actually was another concern. Frankly, based on the prep work I saw Michael and Holman had done, I didn't think their case was strong enough to win. Not helping was their recommended fate – they were going for Casting Down. That meant the trial would have two extremes, and no guarantee what would happen. Shortly after I took over, I changed the recommended fate to lifetimes of servitude, families to be named later.

"Are you serious, Hannah?" Michael asked, sounding as if he wasn't certain he should relieve me right then and there.

I simply tapped him on the chest with the rolled up document and smiled. "Trust me. You're gonna love this."

If I wanted to pot Torquemada and prevent an insurrection, I had to take an early lead and not let up. The easiest way to do that was to keep the Churches focused on everything else. I was relying on a little misdirection. I would spring my surprise about my recommended fate at the right time, when it was sure to cause the greatest disruption to the Churches.

Raphael hit the gavel and sat. Everyone in the Tribunal and Gallery sat. "Who is the Petitioner?" he asked.

"The Petitioner is Tomas de Torquemada," Spire answered with authority.

"And who are his Advocates?"

"Mark Freedman, Richard Chapel, Hunwald Gire, and Victor Spire, acting as lead."

"And who advocates for the Celestials?"

I answered without hesitation. No sign of weakness. "Ferdinand Vasquez, George McCreedy, George Burkeshire, Noah Holman, and Hannah Singer, acting as lead."

"Will the Petitioner please take the stand?"

Torquemada left the Church table for the dock, carried by a purposeful stride. He stood facing me. His look said, how dare I waste his time. My look said, hold tight, you're in for a rough ride.

Once Torquemada was installed in the dock, most of the juniors sat down. McCreedy remained standing because there weren't enough chairs. I specifically wanted him to stand. Leads stand during trial, and of all my juniors, I figured any questions I had would most likely go to him. Vasquez was seated furthest away – I would only really need him for illustration. Holman was my procedural guide, so he was seated on my immediate right. I figured I'd consult with him, I wouldn't need his information immediately. Burkeshire was seated in the middle of them.

Raphael looked at Spire. "Defender goes first. Spire? Your opening statements, please."

I opened my ears as Spire began to talk. "Does anybody else recognize what is wrong with this situation? Allow me to spell it out for you – the Celestials are attempting to do an end run around justice. Torquemada served God. He sought to make the church stronger. He sought to stop corrupting influences that were leading humanity astray. And the proof that there is no good reason to deny Torquemada's petition is right there, in the lead spot for the Celestials!"

I felt every eye in the courtroom fall on me. I focused, keeping the attention from getting to me, resisting the pressure. Spire continued, "Hannah Singer is leading the Celestials! She has no background in Christianity, let alone Catholicism! Noah Holman is her junior! The best Celestial is sitting around, waiting to do something! Why? Because there is nothing he can do! There is nothing any of them can do! They know they have no argument on doctrinal grounds to block Torquemada! Desperate times call for desperate measures! So they put Singer in there, hoping for some point, ANY point, that will work!

"And that is not just a flaw, it is an admission of failure! They want something, anything, that will block Torquemada! The rules of procedure are quite clear – under the covenant, what is held true on Earth is held true in Heaven! There must be a good reason that the covenant doesn't apply, that an exception is to be made! And none can be made! Instead, they are going to try to convince you they have a good reason, that an exception could be made! Singer is brave, but she is in over her head! We already know she can't argue doctrine! And doctrine is the only important thing in this trial! If Singer does have any argument that can withstand scrutiny, it will be immaterial! End this farce and grant Torquemada's petition! Thank you!"

I felt a grudging admiration for Spire. His opening statements were intended to throw me off my game. And he was doing it by making me the center of attention. Everyone was already wondering how I could possibly win. Spire put the question foremost in their minds. What fate Torquemada deserved was less interesting than what Singer was going to do. And the attention had only become greater during Spire's opening statements. Intimidating? Oh, yeah. But at the same time, it was a perfect set-up. All that attention would become my greatest weapon.

Raphael looked to me with sadness in his eyes. It was the same look I was seeing on Michael and Holman. He was pinning his hopes on me blocking Torquemada's petition. I didn't look at anyone but Raphael. I didn't want my actions to be interpreted as panic. I did a quick adjustment to my trial strategy and my opening statements. I focused on keeping my voice even and reasoned. I didn't want to give Michael and Holman any reason to think I was shaken.

I didn't even take a deep breath as I started speaking. "Spire has overlooked an important detail." I felt a shift in the attention. Not a lot, I didn't want to dump the whole thing on Spire yet. But I did want to make sure he knew I could handle what he threw at me. "Spire says there are no doctrinal grounds to block Torquemada's petition.

"But there are.

"Doctrine from no less than Jesus Christ tells us to hate the sin, but love the sinner. We are to love and support our brothers and sisters in Christ. And yet, all these people subjected to the autos-de-fe? They were Christians. Some raised, others converted from other religions. But they were family, not enemies. And Torquemada tortured and killed them. Doctrine says, 'Thou shalt not murder.' Doctrine says, 'Love the sinner.' In fact, by leaving the heretics outside the faith alone, he showed more love for their public and unrepentant sins than he did those under his charge.

"Torquemada's actions have everything to do with doctrine. It is the doctrine of mercy, love, and understanding that Jesus came to teach. But most importantly, it is the doctrine of trust. Torquemada violated many doctrines in his time as Inquisitor General. To say this has nothing to do with doctrine says this has nothing to do with God. Torquemada willfully disregarded inconvenient doctrine, preferring doctrine that was dynamic and larger than life. And now proposes a trade-off. The effort he placed in applying doctrine is the same, he just focused it on certain areas instead of spreading it around generally. I will establish that his violations were so egregious, that even an Atheist with no background in Christianity, let alone Catholicism, can see the truth. Torquemada's petition should be denied, and he should be reincarnated into servitude to make up for it. Thank you."

Everyone relaxed a little. I didn't crack. And I wasn't about to. I was going to have more fun than I ever did when I was alive. And the only way to experience it was to keep myself in the game. The payoff was too big for me to risk doing anything stupid.

Opening arguments were over. Spire had put me in a pot of water and was trying to throw wood on the fire. "Mercy, love, and understanding?"

"You forgot trust."

"That was not forgotten. He did all those things. The autos-de-fe were for enemies of the church. That wasn't about sin, that was about subversion. It was war. Such people take advantage of mercy, love, understanding, and trust. In the name of preservation, it cannot factor in."

Nice try, Spire. He was trying to sucker me into arguing Torquemada's intent. If I went down that path, Spire would just have to declare Divine Right and all my arguments would be useless. Torquemada made his selection process clear, and arguing about whether it was unfairly applied or not would take too long with too uncertain a payoff.

The Tribunal was already on my side. They wanted to block Torquemada. They just needed a good reason. And the best place to start was with a recommended fate they agreed with. "Torquemada will still be showing all those qualities with my recommended fate."

"Lifetimes of servitude?"

"It's not the lifetimes that will prove his love of mankind, but the families I recommend he serve."

"So, you're going to name specific families for him to serve?"

"Yes."

"About time. So, who, Singer? Which families are you going to recommend he serve?"

I looked at Torquemada in the dock. "All of them."

Everyone looked at me like I was mad. Spire asked the obvious question. "How? How is he supposed to do that?"

I looked at the Tribunal. "By breaking the absolute power of his own Inquisition."

The face of every angel on the Tribunal lit up. They were liking this. From behind me, I heard Michael whisper to me, with unmistakable awe in his voice, "You are *good*!"

Spire was enraged. "You are suggesting he reincarnates until he overthrows his own office of power?!?"

"Or gets in a position to influence it towards mercy and away from the fear and intimidation it now employs."

I took a casual look around. I had just changed the focus from, "How can Singer pull this off?" to "How is Spire going to dig Torquemada out of this?" Now, all the attention was on him. And he was clearly feeling it. His ploy had backfired on him. He couldn't argue my fate was excessive, and he couldn't say it was unfair. Those making the final decision were already sold on it. His only hope was to prevent me from creating an exception, so that the Tribunal would have no choice but to grant petition.

Between the attention of the Gallery and the Tribunal on my side, Spire was starting to crack. I knew because he abandoned saying the Celestials had no standing with his next statement -- "He had Divine Right."

Paydirt! "Divine Right? God gives you the right to torture and murder people?"

"So he got a little carried away."

"So you admit his behavior was excessive."

Spire winced. He recovered, but not fast enough. "His behavior was not excessive! He took the measures he felt were needed to save the souls of his countrymen and destroy their enemies! Their corruptors! Those who presented themselves as Catholic to disguise their true motives! Can you come up with anything else that would have been effective?"

I didn't bother arguing. I had a better idea. I looked to Raphael and said, "Move to strike Spire's last argument."

"On what grounds?" Raphael asked.

"Privacy Of Mind," I smiled.

Raphael slammed the gavel and said, "Struck."

I heard Spire gasp. I just prevented him from arguing Torquemada's intent. He could only focus on what Torquemada had done. He had to validate his Divine Right argument somehow. And I knew what he would do.

"Divine Right is excused by the covenant."

Spire was worked up, but not too bad. He wasn't worried about losing just yet. He had to have one more trick up his sleeve. I needed to get it out of there. "Exceptions are created to the covenant for violations of humanity."

"Not in this case."

"This case is a very perfect reason why exceptions to the covenant exist."

"The covenant is to protect people who misinterpret God's will."

"Accidentally misinterpret. Willful is another matter."

"It was accidental. The chain of logic existed long before. Torquemada is being blamed for following false precedents."

"How can believing God's will is to torture and kill your fellow man anything but willful misinterpretation?"

"There are plenty of books of the Bible where major figures exhibit horrible behavior but it is excused. David's son died for David's affair, David did not."

Spire was getting desperate to point that out. Usually, that was my move. "So, such behavior should continue to be allowed?"

"No, just understood and excused. If understanding of what is allowed under the covenant comes from that, then Torquemada's actions are a reasonable conclusion based on history. Accidental misinterpretation."

I had to get rid of the shield the covenant provided and fast. When Spire had time to think, he was dangerous. "You actually condone the covenant being abused?"

"It is not abuse! It is human frailty!"

"Wisdom and understanding counter that."

"Wisdom and understanding take lifetimes. When the Israelites were wandering the desert, they didn't have time, they needed to survive. The covenant enabled them to take action without worry."

"Act in haste, repent in leisure?"

"It's not repenting. It's building a structure that can be added on to, expanding it and our awareness. It is from the covenant that God's laws spring forth. It gives us laws that transcend time. An Atheist like you doesn't understand all the concepts that exist thanks to the covenant. The myriad ways to atone for sins and earn forgiveness. Without the covenant, penance would just be talking to yourself and throwing your money away. Papal Infallibility enables those actions to have value and effect...."

I froze, paying only partial attention to Spire now. Papal Infallibility? Where did that come from? Was it something he hadn't meant to say, or was it just a ruse to throw me off? Papal Infallibility would not become official policy for centuries, but it was well established as being in effect. It could be a powerful turning point. Basically, it was the covenant with super powers. It had a more official vibe because someone other than the individual felt it was covered by church doctrine. It could succeed in places where the covenant failed.

I weighed my options. I could move to strike Papal Infallibility. But that was a risk. It would tip Spire off about the direction I thought he was heading in, and if I was wrong, he could relax, knowing I was going astray and unable to mount a credible challenge to his points. But the more I thought about what he had advanced so far, the more I thought I was on the scent. The covenant was worthless, meaning Spire's points were worthless. But if the covenant was replaced with Papal Infallibility, they had a new life. And a new level of threat. It shifted responsibility from the person who did wrong to whoever let him do wrong and made it nearly impossible to make sins and crimes stick.

That had to be it. It fit like a glove. His focus on the covenant smelled like misdirection. And Spire's reaction would tell me everything. I faced the bench, but shifted my eyes to Spire. I tilted my head up and called, "Move to strike Papal Infallibility from consideration!"

The effect was dramatic. Spire started to panic. And this wasn't manufactured, I'd seen his act often enough. I was close to the truth.

93

Spire screamed back to the bench, "Motion should be denied!"

I smiled. "It's that important, Spire?"

He calmed down. "No. It's just not necessary."

"Then you have nothing to lose by striking."

"Likewise, you have nothing to lose by leaving it in."

I focused my eyes on the bench. "Torquemada's appointment to Inquisitor General was at the behest of Queen Isabella. The Catholic church may have approved it, but the decision to appoint Torquemada to the position was hers. As such, it was not a papal decision, it was a royal proclamation. Papal Infallibility is beyond the scope of Torquemada's position."

"The origin of the office is immaterial, it was still a position of authority within the Catholic church! All offices are granted the protection of Papal Infallibility!" Spire shot back.

There were too many corrupt popes for me to argue worthiness of the protection. They all got it, Torquemada would, too. My best chance was to redress the office as a tool of the monarchy. "Which will extend Papal Infallibility to Queen Isabella and King Ferdinand, who judged him worthy based on familiarity, not any true qualifications!"

"They were followers of God! They wanted another whose faith was as strong as their own!"

I grabbed a scroll from the table in front of me, opened it, and started reading aloud. "'Without observing juridical prescriptions, have detained many persons in violation of justice, punishing them by severe tortures and imputing to them, without foundation, the crime of heresy, and despoiling of their wealth those sentenced to death, in such form that a great number of them have come to the Apostolic See, fleeing from such excessive rigor and protesting their orthodoxy!' Pope Sixtus IV, a year before Torquemada was appointed Inquisitor General! Papal Infallibility says Torquemada was wrong and it should not be extended to him!"

Raphael looked from Spire to me and back again. He then raised his gavel and slammed it as he declared, "Struck!"

"NO!" Spire screamed.

I had this in the bag.

Spire looked like he had just been stabbed in the chest with a spike. I gleefully aimed the hammer and swung. "No wonder you didn't go for trial by God."

Spire's expression was innocent. His tone was anything but. "I don't know what you're talking about."

"Torquemada had been installed, but his order had not been around long enough for precedents to be established granting him true authority. His order lacked legitimacy, and he could still be held accountable for his autos-de-fe. So you were going to use Papal Infallibility to grant that legitimacy and shield him from his crimes!"

It was on. We turned fully on each other, each stalking to close the space between us. "We are the church!" Spire boomed back. "We are the authority! We are appointed by God! Our positions put us above regular people!"

"You aren't supposed to be above them! You are to lead them, not rule them!"

"If everyone was equal, the world would be full of rulers!"

"It is the rulers' responsibility to do right by their followers!"

"The followers support the rulers! The rulers cannot exist without them!"

"THAT is peoples' only responsibility?!? Not to live and learn, but to support someone else?"

"They are taking care of others! They take care of the rulers, and the rulers take care of them!"

"They are treating people as a resource, not living beings! The rulers are not taking care of them, they are using them! The rulers are divorcing themselves from their brothers, sisters, from the humanity they are supposed to be a part of!"

"Few people get lives of note! Most people simply live and die, leaving nothing behind! Why not let their labors go towards a greater good that can transcend lifetimes?!?"

"Which just happens to be your chosen few! Easy for you to say when you control everything and don't have to share it!"

"Rulers deserve better! They are better! It is why they are rulers!"

"So, rulers have expectations of those they govern!"

"Yes!"

"Do the governed have expectations of their rulers?!?"

"They don't understand authority! If they understood, they would be rulers themselves!"

"Such authority is not about merit, but control! They either control others or control those who do!"

"Authority is earned and respected!"

"That is NOT how Torquemada became Inquisitor General, and NOT how he is viewed by people!"

We were literally nose to nose, the tips actually touching. Our breath warmed both our faces. Our eyes tried to pierce each other's. Neither of us blinked.

I growled to the bench without averting my gaze, "Move for closing arguments."

"I concur," Spire responded.

We walked backwards to our respective spots at our tables and forced our gazes back to Tribunal. I didn't have Privilege, so I had to go first.

"This is really simple," I stated. "Torquemada does not deserve Heaven. Everyone here knows it. The Tribunal, the presiding angel, the Gallery, the Churches themselves. The proof is in the Churches' own arguments. They have done NOTHING to address the litany of misdeeds and crimes Torquemada has presided over. Instead, they resorted to subterfuge. They came up with a chain of logic that admits no fault, no culpability, but followed link by link, will lead to Heaven.

"This chain, however, leads back upon itself, binding them. Despite egregious behavior, immoral acts, and insurmountable arrogance, Torquemada believes he deserves Heaven. And instead of admitting fault, offering to make right, to show even the slightest remorse, he and his Advocates are resorting to twisted logic and devious trickery. If he was truly so worthy, they would have something. There is no talk of people he helped. There is no talk of lives he saved. There is no talk of souls he redeemed. Just what he is entitled to and excuses for what he has done.

"Those who go to Heaven have humanity. They feel guilt and shame for their evil, never pride. Even if life forces them to live as opportunists, they still know there is a better way to live. Some still strive for it. Some simply dream of it. But they all know what they are doing is not how things are supposed to be. At no point has Torquemada acknowledged that the terror he subjected people to was wrong. He claims he was simply doing God's will. A man with the ear of the monarchy and riches to help people instead imprisoned, tortured, killed, and kept material possessions. He sought to destroy any thought he disagreed with, through burning books and eliminating ideas. God does not condone such things. He never orders books destroyed, people do. God does not fear people worshiping different gods and religions, people do. God does not fear people searching for their own truth, people do. And God does not force ideas and ways of life on others, people do.

"Religion is supposed to help people learn and understand their natures, their world, themselves. It is about us, about humanity reaching its potential, about becoming great. Religious leaders like Torquemada see humanity as flawed, unfixable, and worthless. The only use for humanity is to praise and prop up a God that existed long before them and will exist long after them. Torquemada's actions were not to make God glorious, they were to make himself glorious. We have seen numerous people subjected to the autos-de-fe gain entry into Heaven based on who they were as people. Allowing Torquemada entry despite how he lived while they were allowed entry for how they lived is not just a disservice, it's an insult to them and all that is fair and just. Do not allow this travesty to occur. Show that we will demand atonement, that the evil must fix what they have broken, that it is not someone else's job to clean up their mess. Torquemada's petition should be denied. Thank you."

Spire didn't waste any time. "Members of the Tribunal, Singer is using you. A bitter, vengeful Atheist, continuing her crusade against God and what He grants His children."

Oh, I thought he was low before. This was worse. He was trying to convince the Tribunal that this was something personal on my part, distracting them from Torquemada's crimes. I tried to get a read on the Tribunal. They didn't seem to be buying it. I'd know if I was right when Spire's speech finished and the ruling was made.

Spire continued. "Were Torquemada's actions excessive? No more so than any others. In fact, his autos-de-fe were not the result of misguided zealotry. He sought to preserve the rule of God over His creation, not deny its existence. Singer is trying to separate Torquemada from his station, to hold him to the same standards regular people are. Regular people are not faced with the responsibilities, duties, and other charges of someone in Torquemada's leadership position. Many try to use their power as a means to a glorious end, Torquemada is hardly unique. However, there was no selfishness in his actions, he sought to uphold the glory of God! Plenty of religious leaders, up to and including popes, have celebrated themselves and their achievements. They have gone to Heavenly rewards, and their behavior was worse. What is fair about holding Torquemada to a different standard?

"Torquemada has done nothing to apologize for. He was misguided, but not malicious. Do not allow this stupid Atheist to continue her vendetta against the earthly church. Approve Torquemada's petition. Allow him his eternal reward. Thank you."

If I had one more turn, I could have ground his statements to pulp, and that was just his few contradictions. But we had both said what we were allowed. It was out of our hands now.

Raphael looked to the Tribunal. "You have heard the Advocates for Tomas de Torquemada state their recommended fates. You may now make your decision. You wish to confer?"

The lead Tribunal immediately rose to his feet. "We are ready to rule."

"And what is your decision?"

The faces of every angel in the Tribunal box took on a fearsome look that frightened me, and the lead Tribunal stated forcefully, "The Petitioner is to be reincarnated in accordance with Singer's recommendation!"

Spire's jaw dropped and he screamed, "What?!?" I will remember it forever. My God, it was beautiful.

Raphael smiled at me. He raised the gavel, said, "So be it," and cracked it.

Spire threw his head back and screamed, "Call for a mistrial!"

Michael and I rolled our eyes and said in unison, "Oh my God...."

Suddenly, shafts of light streaked through the ceiling of the court and illuminated each member of the Tribunal, Raphael, Spire, and me. It was the light of God, examining us, determining what we had done. I actually winced for Spire. If you call for a mistrial, not because of a miscarriage of justice, but because you lost and want a do-over, you lose your post as an Advocate. I was pretty sure how this was going to go. Spire had just thrown his career away.

Suddenly, the voice of God was heard. "The trial has been fair and just. Spire's ego was its failure, and his own. The ruling stands. Spire is never to Advocate ever again." The lights vanished, and Spire's ceremonial wings vanished into blowing dust.

Spire just stood there, his righteous shock replaced with numb shock. He knew he couldn't explain it any other way. God knew the truth. Spire gambled. And lost. Everything.

I refused to feel sorry for him. After everything he had put me through, had put Petitioners through, after trying to dismantle the courts, he got what he deserved. Not only could he not Advocate anymore, but no one would even want to consult with him for fear of his name poisoning the Tribunal's verdict. Too many Celestials hated him, he'd find no refuge there. He had already had his trial. All he could do now was claim his Heavenly reward, knowing he failed God and himself.

The Guardians came to the dock. Torquemada was just in a daze. He shuffled to the Petitioner's exit to begin his next life, as a revolutionary against the very system he created. It was a tall order. I didn't envy him in the least.

I was starting to gather up scrolls when Michael came around the barrier and scooped me up in a celebratory hug. He was so proud of me. I caught a glimpse of Holman. He simply smiled and said, "I never should have doubted you."

Michael put me down and I straightened my spine. "Don't kid yourself," I told them. "You had every right to worry."

"Not anymore, we don't," Michael smiled.

Everyone else had filed out, leaving just us Celestials. Everybody was congratulating me and telling me what a great job I did. I ate it all up. It kept me from feeling sympathy for Spire.

Spire didn't bother saying goodbye to anyone, not even the other Churches. He didn't even go to his quarters. He simply prayed to Jesus and was escorted to the Pearly Gates.

Michael was surprised I didn't ask for Spire to be retried. "You could have, you know."

I thought about it. "Nah. He's already making himself suffer more than I ever could."

With Spire gone as senior Church, Alfred Smith took over. I'd faced him a few times in court. He wasn't that bad. I mean, we could at least tolerate each other. He wasn't interested in being confrontational. He was kind of aloof, however. Being senior wasn't his thing. I had a feeling he'd step down and let someone else be senior before too long.

And Torquemada? Did he ever repair his damage to the point where he could get to Heaven?

I'll let you know as soon as the Tribunal says he has.

As you read these memoirs, keep something in mind - I'm not telling you everything about the afterlife in general and the Celestial Courts in particular. There are some details I'm not allowed to share. They are kept secret for various reasons, and their knowledge among humanity is limited at best because, frankly, nothing good can come of it. There's enough holy wars among Christians, and they are in general agreement on a lot of Christian elements. Making everyone aware of the Big Picture is a disaster waiting to happen.

Now, some general things can be discussed, like some alternate religions besides Christianity. I can't tell how everything fits and interacts, but some of the older religions that predate Christianity are okay. For example, the Greeks. There are enough believers and those gods still exist, so I do have occasion, albeit extremely rare, to deal with them. Those courts are presided by the Oracle of Delphi. Those cases are far more civil and cordial, but they can be a bigger headache that the Celestial Courts. My most recent advocacy there was just a general property dispute - some land that was the site of a Greek temple was consecrated as holy, and the debate was which religion held sway over it. The Oracle heard my side and that of the Greek priest. We finished our arguments and waited.

Eventually, the Oracle said, "My judgment goes to the one with the purest heart."

The priest and I looked at each other. Finally, I said, "Uh...thanks?"

The priest looked at me like I was insane. "Not you, the Oracle meant me." He then looked at the Oracle and said, "Right?"

By that time, the Oracle had vanished. We went outside and hashed it out between ourselves.

One of the bright sides of my death was that I could read. Any language, any time, anywhere. And I really got into it. Which figures, I guess, as I am writing out my experiences. I was consuming books as quickly as I could - the Celestial Courts have a library that would put Alexandria to shame. As more books started appearing, the library itself grew. The size changed, but I remained their most frequent patron. Because there is so much to read (this may be Eternity, but there's still only so much time available), I have to prioritize. My favorite genre is fantasy and some sci-fi. Maybe it's because so many fantasy stories are set in an era similar to when I was alive.

It was about the middle of the 17th century. I was sitting one day, out on the steps facing the Eternal Sunrise. On the middle of the steps, back against the wall, the sunlight angles just perfect for reading. I was reading my collected works of Shakespeare. St. Michael came walking along and saw me. He climbed the stairs until he got next to me. He craned his head so he could see what I was reading. "'A Midsummer Night's Dream,' huh, Hannah?"

I smiled at him. "It's my favorite. 'My gentle Puck come hither. Thou rememberest since Once I sat upon a promontory. And heard a mermaid on a dolphin's back uttering such dulcet and harmonious breath that the rude sea grew civil at her song, and certain stars shot madly from their spheres, to hear the sea-maid's music?'"

Michael sat down next to me. He was on a lower step, so our heads were just about even. I went back to reading. He let me get a little further before he said, "Interesting passage you chose to quote there."

I just nodded my head and said, "Mm-hmm."

It was quiet for another beat before he spoke again. "Did you know mermaids are real?"

I lifted my head and just stared for a moment. I mean, I didn't know what to think. On the one hand, I found out about three hundred years earlier that God and Jesus and the angels and such were real, so you'd think something relatively mundane like mermaids would be an easy sell. On the other hand, I was being told this by St. Michael, the biggest prankster in the history of Creation. Had someone else told me mermaids were real, I'd be leaning towards believing it. But not with my big brother.

"Pull the other one, it's got bells on it," I said, putting my nose back in my book.

"You don't believe me." It was a statement, not a question.

"Do you blame me?"

Michael sounded dramatically pained. "What have I done to earn your distrust?"

"How about messing with the guy doing the abiogenesis experiment?" Michael had placed some field mice in a supposedly sealed container with grain in it. Admittedly, the container wasn't properly sealed, mice would have gotten in had they been in the area. Michael just kind of helped the results to occur.

"Oh, come on," he protested. "Would I prank you?"

I rolled my eyes. Disappearing ink. Tar on the seat of my bench before I sat down. Rolling my scrolls backwards so that I had to start from the bottom instead of the top. A fake snake that only saw use once, because I grabbed a chair and smashed it until it was kindling. I no longer jumped and yelped when Michael left a tack in the chair I was supposed to sit in. On the few times I didn't check, I would just get up, remove the tack, and sit, flicking the tack across the room from the palm of my hand. The only item he didn't use was the whoopee cushion. Michael is the actual inventor, creating the original from a pig's bladder. It didn't get the effect he wanted, though - people weren't reacting to the noise, but to sitting on a pig's bladder (lucky me, I was his first test subject). It would be centuries before he could acquire the definitive article.

"Shoo," I told him. "You're interrupting the good part."

"Shakespeare is nothing but good parts," Michael harrumphed. He got up and walked away, knowing his plot was working. He had planted a seed that would soon sprout into full grown curiosity. I didn't realize it at the time, but he was prepping me to advocate for a mermaid.

With no real concept of time, it's hard to tell how long it took me to crack. I mean, Michael was so casual in his revelation about mermaids, I couldn't decide for sure if I thought he was putting me on or if he was serious. It got to a point where every casual moment had the question intruding in my head. When I found myself sitting on my bench in my quarters and thinking about the existence of mermaids instead of reading my book, I decided this had gone on long enough. I stalked out of the Residencies and headed for the Ancient Forest. Usually, when I want to think, I head for the Water Gardens. But given the subject at hand, I didn't want to deal with that.

I found a fairly secluded spot and sat against the trunk of a huge tree, staring at the sky peeking around the full branches. I needed to find out if Michael was telling the truth or not, just so that my mind would let the subject drop. But how would I do that? Michael could easily convince the obvious choices to go along with the joke. Besides, it wasn't the best option. Clearly, regular souls weren't privy to this info. I'd been here three hundred years and this was the first I'd heard of it. Regular souls weren't granted omniscience.

But angels were....

I needed an angel. Somebody who knew lots but would be resistant to participating in a massive put-on orchestrated by Michael. Someone with almost no sense of humor.

I raised my hand and held up a single finger. Within moments, a putto, William, zipped up to me. "Yes, Lady Singer. How may I assist you?"

"Can you please ask Metatron if I may please have a fact-finding consultation with him?"

William gave me a smart salute and said, "Right away, Lady Singer!" and vanished. I wasn't sure how long it would take. Speed of angels is one thing, but if Metatron was busy with a consultation or a trial, I might be waiting a while. Or really, anything. Metatron did not like being interrupted.

I was about to try to signal a putto to cancel my request when Metatron appeared in front of me, standing tall, proud, arms folded and staring down at me like he was judging me. I jumped as well as I could from a sitting position. When I finally got to my feet, I saw the slightest hint of a smile on Metatron's face. I kept quiet about it - he doesn't like anyone thinking he isn't stoic. "You asked to see me?"

"Am I interrupting anything, sir?" I asked, a bit of worry creeping into my voice.

"I'm here now, so you might as well ask your question."

I recovered my wits. "Are mermaids real, sir?"

"Yes."

I looked to the side. "Oh."

"Let me guess - Michael's the one who told you?"

I snapped my head back. "Yes, sir."

Metatron narrowed his eyes. He was examining me. It was unnerving. He didn't unfold his arms. He simply lifted his right index finger slightly. In a flash, William appeared. "Please have my consultations delayed until further notice. I won't be long."

I watched the putto speed away. "I don't want to keep you...."

Metatron held his hand up to me, indicating I should stop. I did exactly as he wanted. When he spoke, his words surprised me. "There is something you need to see." He then reached out. "Come with me."

"You don't have to put things on hold for me, sir. I can venture to Earth."

"You won't know where to go or what to do. Come with me."

Metatron makes me nervous, but not as nervous as the thought that my stalling might make him angry. I carefully took his hand. Despite its pale and bony appearance, his touch was warm and comforting. It was the only thing that kept me from running away.

Suddenly, everything around me shifted and swirled like dust in a fierce wind. After a few seconds, everything poured back into recognizable forms. I was standing on a beach, pristine and beautiful. The sand seemed brighter than the sun shining down, not a cloud in the sky, and the water was a near perfect blue. I almost couldn't tell where the sky ended and the water began on the horizon.

Metatron released my hand and looked at me. "Do not materialize. Follow me." He put his hands behind his back and started walking into the water. He didn't float, he just kept getting lower, so he was just walking along the ground. I dashed to catch up to him, and kept walking behind him.

We walked down through the water. It was an amazing sight, I made a note to do this again on my own later. We got deeper, and the light faded, but I could still see perfectly well. Seeing the formations, the different fish swimming around, it was truly remarkable. A beauty no human would ever be able to see.

We walked up to a tall, expansive coral reef. Metatron was right at the bottom of it when he started talking, still facing forward. "When we get near the top, just peek out. Do not do any more than that, and keep your voice to a whisper. They can sense us." I nodded, then realized he wouldn't see me doing it. He just walked up the side. I was too intimidated to do the same, so I climbed the reef.

When I got near the top, I saw Metatron had stopped. His eyes were just over the top of the reef. He was still facing forward, not even casting a glance at me. My hands found purchase, and I slowly pulled myself up so that my eyes could see past the reef.

And there they were. Mermaids. Real live mermaids. Three of them. Nothing in my imagination prepared me for the actual sight. They were absolutely beautiful. And yes, they were nude. The scales on the fish halves of their bodies shimmered, as if light flowed through their veins instead of blood. Every color of the rainbow appeared at the slightest twitch of their tails. Manes of hair flowed from their heads. Had they been human, the hair would have reached their knees or lower. It trailed gracefully behind them or floated around them like their own personal cloud. They didn't sing, they were silent. And they actually looked a little sad. They were swimming around a sunken ship. I wouldn't have known it when I died, but now that I knew every language, I recognized it as a Chinese ship. One of the mermaids was swimming in and out of it, carrying objects out for them all to examine. The others just swam around, almost like they were pacing. I stifled a gasp, worried that I would be heard.

"Amazing creatures, aren't they?" Metatron's whisper commanded my attention. I couldn't believe it. He was actually smiling. I had never seen him smile ever.

I looked back and actually sank a little lower over the reef, to make sure I wouldn't be detected. I didn't want this to end. "Where did they come from? Did God make them? Like us humans?"

Metatron's voice got a little sad. "No. They are consciousness given form. They aren't actually alive. Not like you humans are. They don't exactly die. They just turn to sea foam. Eventually, it wills itself into the form of a mermaid again, and the process starts over."

My expression fell. "My God. Do they know all this?"

"Oh, yes, they are fully cognizant from the day they form. Eventually, they just lose the will to go on, and then they're gone."

I shuddered. Had I heard this when I was alive and still an Atheist, I wouldn't have given it any thought. But when you realize you have an immortal soul, the idea of living without one, that everything just stops, becomes horrible. "Those poor..." I struggled to find a word. "Things" was just condescending, and "souls" was inappropriate. I eventually said, "...mermaids."

"Not always," Metatron told me. "It's extremely rare, but a mermaid can become an actual soul. With the same characteristics as a human soul."

My eyes popped. I stared at Metatron. "That means that a mermaid soul...."

Metatron reached out for my shoulder. "I think you need to have a talk with Michael." He lightly touched me, and we were back in the Ancient Forest.

I raced through the Celestial Courts as fast as my feet would carry me. I was on a dead run for Michael's chambers, and nothing was going to slow me down. I even vaulted over a trio of Churches having a conversation rather than slowing down to go around them.

I got to Michael's door and knocked quickly. "Come in," came the response. I opened the door and entered. Michael was sitting behind his desk with two stacks of petitions, ones to read through and ones he had decided whether or not to contest. There was a mess of scrolls on his desk, all with ties, and no doubt each one had a corresponding petition.

I shut the door and leaned against it. Michael noticed the look on my face and smiled. "Who proved I wasn't lying about mermaids?"

"Metatron."

Michael rolled his eyes. "You asked Grumpus, huh? That figures."

I headed for one of the chairs in front of his desk. Michael flicked his hand at his door, vanishing it into the wall. Although I kept my eyes on Michael,

I did brush my hand across the seat to make sure there wasn't a tack there. "You have a mermaid that has petitioned, don't you?"

Michael stood up and walked across the room to one of his giant bookcases. One was jam packed with scrolls. They all had clasps, so they were court histories. From the middle of one group, he pulled out a scroll with a tie holding it closed. Best place to hide a tree is in a forest.

Michael gave me the scroll. I quit being defensive against his pranks. Times like this, Michael is all business. And so am I. "'Christina,' huh? Nice Christian name."

"Believe me, Hannah, she's earned it."

Reading the scroll had my eyes opening wide. Christina had been a mermaid who wasn't thrilled with simply turning into foam. She knew of the spiritual realm and wanted to become a real soul. She would pray every day, hoping to be heard. Eventually, an angel did hear and went to talk with her. Christina didn't have a soul, but she did have will. It was how she came to be in the first place and how her prayers were carried to the angels. If Christina's will was strong enough, she could eventually become a soul. But to do that, it would be three hundred years of work as a spirit. If her will faltered, she would vanish into nothingness. Christina was determined to make it happen. When her body became foam, her consciousness remained. She spent three hundred years doing everything she could. As a spirit, her influence was limited. She was best as a sort of muse, inspiring artists and people to create things to improve the quality of their lives, whether music or painting or even just storytelling, such as with one Mister William Shakespeare.

"There's a lot more to this if this sort of thing isn't general knowledge," I told Michael with finality.

"Right," he said. "Christina is what we classify as a 'shadow.'"

"Because of darkness?"

"No. That's demons. The 'shadow' thing is in keeping with the idea of God's light. All human souls have a light that shines within. Well, a shadow doesn't have their own light, they only exist because of someone else's light."

"Like God's."

"Exactly. And not only can a shadow not exist without light, but the stronger the light, the stronger the shadow."

"Or else it gets swallowed up by the darkness."

"You got it, Hannah. In order for a shadow to become a true soul, that light needs to be a part of them, to come from within, so that when the light that makes them is gone, they aren't gone."

I thought about that. "So the petition is not to get into Heaven."

"No. Usually, once shadows gain their souls, they go for reincarnation. They want to actually live life. They take their time getting to Heaven. The first petition is to make their soul complete and official, for that light of God to be given to them. And that's what Christina is doing right now."

"There's going to be a trial?"

"Yes."

104

"Is that unusual?"

"Yes, it is. In the past, when a shadow comes along, the Churches don't contest. It's a feelgood story, someone who has come around to Truth and Light and all that."

"Like an Atheist repenting her ways?" I smiled.

"I knew your trial was a bad sign," Michael said, his expression falling. "The Churches didn't start seriously opposing those outside the faith until relatively recently. Usually, it was, 'Hey, you've learned your lesson, we won't get in the way.' Christina started and is finishing her journey at the worst possible time."

"Isn't there someone more qualified to argue Christina's case?"

"There was. Abraham Lankshire. He'd been a Celestial for over seven hundred years."

I let out a whistle. I couldn't imagine advocating that long. How little did I know then. "What happened to him?"

"He vacated," Michael said. "I tried to talk to him about sticking around just a little longer so he could handle Christina's case, but he was burnt out."

"He was going to throw the case, wasn't he?"

"No, or at least, not intentionally. He was clearly losing his focus and drive. Shadow cases can't afford to have anyone at less than top form."

I considered that. Lankshire must have really gone downhill if inexperienced me could do a better job. "Shadow cases are that difficult?"

"They're becoming so. Like I said, we've never had this kind of resistance from the Churches before." Michael let out a sigh. "I'm not asking you to be a permanent member of the shadow courts. We have another candidate, Joshua Hunter, but he's still a little green. He's been here for a century and a half, but he's only been junioring in the shadow courts for the last forty years. The only one I can think of who might have a chance of staring down the Churches is you. I promise, it's only a temporary assignment. Nothing else is on the horizon. It will give Hunter a little more time to train and get ready. He'd be junior, I'd be making you lead."

I leaned back in the chair and lightly rapped my head against the wooden back. "Don't promise this is the only time."

Michael looked at me in surprise. "What do you mean?"

"I'm a Celestial Advocate. I became one specifically to help those facing impossible odds. I'd say a shadow qualifies for that."

"You want to be part of the shadow courts?"

"I want to be a part of them when you need me to. You are my boss, and you are my big brother. Don't promise me you won't ask for my help."

Michael smiled as relief poured onto his face. "Shadow court is a bit different from regular trials. I don't want to overwhelm you."

"I'll let you know if I'm overwhelmed," I said, standing up. "Why don't you show me around, introduce me to what I'll be facing?"

Michael led me outside the Celestial Court building. I wasn't surprised. After all, this "shadow" stuff clearly wasn't general knowledge. Wherever the shadow court was, it wasn't going to be where there were many people to notice anything.

We wandered around the Archives until we got to the Office Of Records. Michael kept walking past it, and his head started darting around, looking for others. I had a suspicion where we were going. The Records building has an outside wall at the back. There is one section of wall between stone supports that has nothing there. No windows, no decorations, no signs, no nothing. I always wondered why it was kept open and why Guardians discouraged anyone from loitering around there. I felt I was about to find out why.

Sure enough, we wound up by the wall. Strategic hedges blocked the view from a distance without looking like they were more than scenery. Michael got up to the wall and took one last look around. He smiled at me, then touched the wall. A set of black double doors appeared. They looked like wrought iron and were heavily reinforced. The black was so deep, it almost looked like another realm, one I was afraid I would fall into. On each door was a large cross, white and glowing over the background.

Michael put his hand on the door and muttered a couple of phrases. He then removed his hand. "The door will recognize you now."

I didn't see a handle on the door, so I figured it was a pass through. Angels can set doors so that they simply pull you through them to the other side without opening. It enables authorized visitors without letting anything else, from Advocates to sounds, in or out. I reached out and pressed my right palm on the door. I felt myself gently pour through to the other side. I turned to look behind me. I could see the faint outline of the doors' features over a view outside. Michael was looking very satisfied. He put his right palm to the door and shifted through next to me.

We were standing in a hallway. The effect was startling. The walls were the deepest black, but everything supporting them was gleaming white, a metaphor for the light that exists in even the darkest places. There were no decorations. The white of the floor and ceiling were one continuous color, not even the patterns of natural stone. It was like standing in an ink drawing, the only colors being on Michael and I. Down at the far side was another set of black wrought iron doors, once again without a handle. Michael placed his hand on it and muttered again. When he removed his hand, I place my right palm on it, and entered the shadow court.

Given the starkness of the hallway, the shadow court itself was jarring. The walls were transparent, showing what was going on outside the Office Of Records, although the interior of the building itself wasn't shown. The blue skies and green grass and ivory buildings almost made it feel like an open air court. There wasn't even an echo. Except for the faint outlines of the room's structures, you'd never know the difference. Well, that and no wind or scents.

The court itself was a lot like a regular Celestial courtroom. There were some aesthetic differences. The furniture in the room, like the benches in the Gallery and the Advocate tables and the banisters around the dock, were natural wood instead of clean white stone. It was the smallest courtroom I'd ever been in. With only a handful of exceptions, the Gallery and the court generally split the area in half. This was more like three parts to one in favor of the court. Clearly, not a lot of spectators came to these trials.

There was a woman sitting at the Celestial table. Well, she was actually sitting on the Celestial table. She was young and breathtakingly beautiful. Blonde hair poured from her head, curving and swaying in one motion. She was completely nude, her robes sitting in a pile to her right on the table. She sat with her legs tucked up next to her and absently stroked her hair. Three guesses who it was, and the first two don't count.

I looked at Michael. Michael looked at me, put his hands by his ears, and started flapping them to and fro like fish fins while sucking in his cheeks. I snickered. That was all it took to get Christina's attention. She twisted to look at us. "Oh, hello, Michael. Who's your friend?" Her expression quirked. "She is your friend, right?"

I smiled and started walking up to her. "Well, fake snake incident notwithstanding. You must be Christina." I got close enough to extend a hand to shake. "Hannah Singer, Celestial Advocate. I'll be leading your defense."

She shook my hand, although her grip was wrong. She was clearly new to the whole gesture. "Thank you, Lady Singer. Does my nudity bother you? Should I replace my robes?"

"Doesn't bother you, doesn't bother me."

Christina cocked her head to the side. "Forgive me, but it seems many humans have a problem with nudity."

"I'm a product of my times," I told her. "In my village, clothes were a luxury. Not everyone had them, and they had to work the fields naked. I don't see nudity as sexual or shameful. More like sympathetic."

Christina seemed to relax more. She was a mermaid, so clothes were a foreign concept to her. I wanted to keep her calm and relaxed, so even if her nudity did bother me, I would have toughed it out for her benefit. I also made a note - given how the Churches freak out about nudity, it would make a great distraction once trial was underway. If I could figure out how to incorporate it.

Michael came up and put a hand on each of our backs. "Well, I think you two are going to get along just fine, so I'll let you get acquainted. Anything else I can get you right away, Hannah?"

I looked at Michael. "Yeah. An audience with Hunter. And records for the last twenty cases the shadow courts have heard."

"They'll be at your quarters by the time you're done, and I'll find Hunter."

"My upcoming cases are standard stuff. No pressure, anyone can do them. If you can have them reassigned to so I can focus on this...."

"Say no more, it's done."

"How are the angels selected for the Tribunal and to preside at trial?"

"Standard Tribunal assignment, but only one angel has jurisdiction over the shadow courts. Pahaliah," Michael said.

I shook my head. You're slipping, Hannah. You should have guessed that. Pahaliah is the angel Christians pray to when converting non-Christians. Given the whole point of the court was to bring outsiders into the fold, so to speak, it figured he would preside. "Who's the specially trusted appointed guardian?"

Michael smiled. "You're looking at him."

No wonder he needed me to lead. He couldn't take this one no matter how much he wanted to. "If there are only certain Celestials and angels allowed here, there have to be only certain Churches. Who's my opposition?"

Michael beamed at me. I was asking the right questions. "Church by the name of Thomas Calvary. Name ring any bells?"

"A couple." Surprise registered on my face. "I've faced him a few times. Pretty straightforward. Pretty reasonable, too."

Michael picked up on the wheels turning in my head. "What's on your mind, Hannah?"

"Just thinking of strategy, I'll tell you later." Michael got that I didn't want to discuss it in front of Christina. Calvary was pretty sociable and decent to everyone. He got along well with all the Advocates. I'd even spent a little time in the Water Gardens meditating with him. He was calm, and wasn't obsessively focused on scoring a judgment in his favor. He never really went for the fire and brimstone like the other Churches did, and was gracious in defeat. He didn't take the cases personally....

...and yet, he was the Church for the shadow courts, and they'd been getting stricter and more discriminatory lately. I got the feeling I didn't know Calvary half as well as I thought I did.

"Where's Christina staying?" I asked.

"The Interim, like any other soul. Call me when you're done, Hannah, and I'll escort Christina back to where she's staying."

That struck me odd. "You're escorting her? Why can't I take her back?"

"I've put Christina under protective guard," he said. "The Churches that know about her have been teasing her, telling her she doesn't have a soul and to enjoy her last moments of awareness. Talking about the blackness that will envelop her."

"I'll get you," I told him. Something about what he said struck me as very significant, but I couldn't figure out exactly what. Michael turned and left the courtroom.

Christina seemed to have relaxed visibly. "Don't let Michael scare you," I smiled at her.

"Oh, he doesn't scare me. He's been very nice to me. It's just good to see him smiling."

I went to the Church table and sat on it, dangling my legs off of it. "He's been nervous?"

"Very. This is the happiest I've seen him." She smiled at me. "You don't really know how great your spirit is, do you?"

"That's not for me to judge."

"You're one of Michael's shining stars," she said. "He trusts you. He has faith in you. He's been worried for a while now. He wasn't sure you'd say yes. But there weren't a lot of options."

"Well, good thing the best option worked out."

She turned so she was facing me, leaning in and smiling. "So, what do you want to know about me?"

I reached into my robes and pulled out her scroll. I opened it and started reading. "I'm not sure you can say anything that will help."

I heard a gasp. I looked up and saw Christina staring at me like she'd been slapped. Her eyes were wide with shock. And there was something else -- something distant about her. Oops. Can't be so blunt with her, Hannah. "Let me rephrase that," I said hastily. "You didn't commit any sins, you inspired people, and you did everything the angels asked and that you could for three hundred years. Frankly, you're an afterthought in this case."

She seemed to recover a bit. She looked confused instead of hurt. "An afterthought?"

"There is nothing in your history that can be used as the basis for denying your petition. Whatever Calvary and his merry band are up to, it has nothing to do with you. You could not show up and it won't make any difference to the proceedings."

"Any idea what they'll say?"

I looked back at the scroll. "Not sure yet. I still need to talk with Hunter and read those case histories. The Churches didn't just suddenly start acting like this. They had to take some path to get where they are, and it should provide me with some clues. In the meantime, talk about yourself."

She blinked at me. "What do you mean, talk about myself?"

I rolled up the scroll and set it aside. "Tell me about yourself. It'll help me get to know you, plan your defense, and anticipate what the Churches will do."

She looked to the side. "I don't have much to talk about. I haven't even really lived. I don't have a soul."

"Don't be so harsh on yourself."

"It's what the Churches say. God never gave me a soul. They say it's the most important thing."

"So tell me what you think is important about you."

She thought for a moment. "Well, I love art."

I quirked a corner my mouth. "No kidding."

"Oh, yeah!" She shifted so her feet were hanging off the desk. Her pose was a mirror image of mine. That was a good sign, it meant she was comfortable around me. "It was what I was best at. Helping others create. I can't wait to be born! I'm going to create art, too!"

"What kind of art do you want to make?"

Her eyes tilted up. She seemed more in the moment. More tangible. More there. "I like painting. I mean, I could make a sky that will always be beautiful. Never threatening. You could see it anytime, day or night. Do you like art?"

"Sure do," I told her. "I love to read."

"What do you read?"

I shrugged. "Pretty much anything. I wasn't allowed to read when I was alive."

"So you couldn't write, either?"

"No."

"Do you want to write?"

"I never really thought about it."

"Maybe you should."

"I've read the plays of your buddy William Shakespeare. I can't write like that."

"You don't have to. Don't write like Shakespeare. Write what you enjoy."

"If no one else likes it, doesn't that defeat the point of art? To engage others?"

"Is the lute player with only one listener any less of an artist?"

I thought about it. "...no"

"Even if that listener is him?"

"I'm not a writer," I told her with finality.

"Not yet, but you could be. I can tell."

"Is that a fact now?"

"That was what I did. Inspire others to make things they enjoyed and enjoy what they made. You're a lot like them, Lady Singer. I can tell."

She was a real sweetheart. Her enthusiasm to help people and encourage was infectious. Those esoteric things that seemed so difficult seemed completely possible, that the desire to make something good and the willingness to figure out how to make it work were all it took. I pulled my mind back to the present. She was talking and engaged, and I wanted to keep her like that for a while. I asked her questions as she told me all about different kinds of art and artists and the wonders their hands created.

I don't know how long we talked, but she was an absolute delight. As she put her robes back on for when Michael arrived to take her back to the Interim, I felt my mind working involuntarily. It was already formulating arguments, anticipating opposition, figuring out ways to nullify, building several case scenarios and plotting how to handle each of them. Hunter could only be a guide, the whole case and Christina's fate rested on me.

And when she turned around, dressed, ready to go, and smiling, I vowed the Churches would never lay a finger on her.

I accompanied Michael and Christina back to the Interim. It was pretty uneventful. No one really knew the truth about Christina. The other Petitioners

110

thought she was just another soul like them. They were enthusiastic and delighted around her, many waving at her in welcome and calling her over to talk. If they allowed women in such positions, she'd make a great minister.

I walked back to the Residencies. Outside the main entrance was a man. He was younger than me. He wasn't a teenager, but not by much. That always made me a little sad -- he clearly didn't have a chance to live. And he looked like he could have lived. Death either got a sneak attack in or had help. His body was wiry and fit. His blond hair pulled back in a ponytail highlighted his face. Chiseled good looks, piercing blue eyes, and a well groomed mustache and beard adorned his face. His was sitting, arm on one knee, and looking around. There were several scrolls next to him. They had clasps, and unlike regular case histories, these were black. He saw me and stood. If he was going to be pushed over, it wouldn't be without a fight. "Hannah Singer?"

I offered my hand and a smile. "That's right. You are?"

He shook it. It was a very confident grip. "Joshua Hunter."

"You certainly look your name. Mind if I asked how you died?"

"Decapitation. King's orders."

"Really? What brought that on?"

"Stole and sold some of his horses to pay my taxes."

"That'll do it." Oh, yeah, we were going to get along just fine. "This way to my quarters."

We gathered up the scrolls. I counted twenty. Good ol' Michael. I led Hunter to my quarters and we went inside. I shut my door and touched it. It vanished into the wall. No one in or out or interrupting us. Only an angel could make it reappear from the outside.

"Won't that tip others off we are discussing something?" Hunter asked.

"Nope," I told him as I walked to my kitchen area. "I vanish the door enough, no one will think twice. Want some tea?"

"Some what?"

"Tea," I told him, holding up a small porcelain canister.

"Maybe another time."

I started steeping some jasmine tea (I made enough for two). "The bright side of the water here being drinkable is I can enjoy delicate flavors," I said with a smile.

"Must make a nice change of pace from ale all the time."

I pointed to the scrolls. "Let me guess...shadow court records, right?"

He nodded. "That's them. Last twenty cases, like you asked."

I picked one up, opened it, and started reading. "How much experience do you have in the regular Celestial Courts?"

"Fair amount," he said. "I was leading for a little bit before becoming part of the shadow court. It was partly what got me the position."

"This case is from almost six hundred years ago," I said, rolling up the scroll. "I figured the shadow court sits infrequently. Have you been part of an actual shadow trial?"

"Just one. Thirty years ago. It does meet infrequently."

111

I started tapping the side of my head with the rolled up scroll. "Just skimming this, it doesn't seem like the shadow court is all that different from the regular courts. Am I getting the wrong impression?"

"No, you've pretty much got it right. Same standard procedure. Churches opposed, we didn't, so we're the defenders. That gives us Privilege." That meant we would have the first and last word during trial. "Trials can turn on a variety of points ranging from doctrine to circumstances."

"So, same as a Celestial trial. Churches make their recommendation, and the covenant will automatically grant it unless we come up with a reason not to. The only difference is they don't grant a Heavenly reward but a soul."

"You got it."

I went back in my kitchen area and poured some jasmine tea into a pint. I came back and unrolled another scroll to look at it. I soon heard a quiet sniff from Hunter.

"What is that?" he asked.

"Jasmine tea." I offered him my pint. "Try it."

He held up his hands. "No no no. I couldn't."

"You're dead," I told him. "It's not like you're going to catch anything from me."

He carefully took the pint. He inhaled it and he smiled. He took a sip, and his eyebrows arched. Another convert. He offered the pint back to me, but I was already back in the kitchen pouring the rest into another pint. "Enjoy it," I told him.

He really enjoyed the tea, he asked me to make more. I was more than happy to. While he enjoyed the flavor and aroma, I examined the case histories in detail. Shadow trials didn't happen very often. And when they did, the Church case usually turned on one point.

"Not in God's image," I said.

Hunter snapped back. "Pardon?"

"Not in God's image," I repeated. "They don't seem to have any argument other than that. God made man in His own image. Beings He created have a soul. If someone is not created by Him, they have no soul. Therefore, they have no right to one."

Hunter nodded. "Which has never stood up when it's come up at trial. I don't get why the Churches are talking about it."

My head shot up. "They're talking about it?"

"Yeah. They've told Michael and I that they're going to use that line at trial."

I was already combing through another scroll. "Why is that?"

"No idea. I mean, you know something won't work and you do it anyway? Isn't that stupid?"

"It's not stupid. Whatever it is, it's very smart. The question is, what makes it smart?" I looked at Hunter. "I'm going to need to do some heavy thinking. I may have more questions later. You'll be available?"

"I have some very simple advocacies scheduled. They won't take me

112

long."

I walked over and made my door reappear. "I'll be in touch. I'll let you know when I get anything concrete."

He got up and looked around nervously. I rolled my eyes and asked, "What is it?"

"Can I take some of that tea stuff with me?"

After I had sent Hunter on his way (with a sizable canister of oolong), I went to the Celestial Courts. I checked, and Michael had most of my cases reassigned. There were just a couple that were ready for trial, real simple in-and-out stuff. I went and handled them myself. Won them both.

After I was finished, I took the scrolls to the Office Of Records. Russell gladly took them from me. I turned around to leave and found myself looking at Thomas Calvary. He was a respectful distance away, but not too far. It was like he was on the outer edge of my personal space. He stood there calmly, his short black hair dotted with greys and slightly pudgy appearance making him seem as friendly as usual. It made me suspicious then, and it made me really suspicious now.

"Hello, Calvary," I said casually. I was one of the few Celestials who called him by his last name. He told everyone they could call him by his first name, they were all pals. But people like that tortured me for being an Atheist when I was alive, so I maintained the formality with him.

He smiled and shook his head. "Still won't call me 'Thomas,' will you?"

"Give me time to warm up to you." I pointed to his empty hands. "No scrolls, so you're looking for me. What's on your mind?"

"Well, we don't have to talk here. We can go someplace more comfortable. How about my quarters?"

I thought it over. I didn't want Calvary to realize how seriously I was taking things. And if he saw the scrolls in my quarters and how I had organized them, he might change his strategy. And I didn't know if I'd be able to mine anything from his quarters, but it was worth a shot. Facing me in court is a known quantity - everyone knows my approach. "Sounds good to me," I smiled.

We walked in silence. Calvary seemed completely at ease. He wasn't worried about the trial. That was dangerous. It didn't mean he felt he had the case in the bag. It meant he made his peace with the judgment he was seeking. He had no qualms about making a sweet little thing like Christina vanish like she never existed. It took effort, but I kept my outrage under control.

We got to the Campus where the Churches reside and entered the Residencies. Calvary's quarters were on the third floor, close to the stairs. He held his door open for me. I gave him a curtsey and went inside.

I'd been inside a few Churches' quarters. I mean, we aren't all enemies. I noticed that the Churches that were generally nicer had normal quarters, like a tiny house, with furnishings, maybe some art pieces on the wall, some Christian items like a cross or a statue of the Virgin Mary, things like that. The more problematic Churches, the ones I was usually locking horns with, styled their quarters more like a miniature church. That was Calvary's. It was easily twice the size of my humble abode, with an altar and a bank of candles and other trappings. You could have probably held a service there. There was a stoup, a pedestal with a bowl of holy water, right by his door. Holy water looks a bit different here, you can differentiate between it and regular water. The bowl was pure gold and held by a golden statue of an angel swooping up towards the heavens. Very ornate. Very ostentatious. I was learning a lot about what Calvary was really like. And it wasn't very appealing.

I scanned for where we would actually sit and found it - tucked into the far corner were a couple of chairs with a small table between them. It was not lit by candlelight. We have special lights, sort of like light bulbs but with their own power. I have a few around my quarters, including by my bench to make it easier to read. The only such lights in here were behind mock-ups of stained glass windows. They were on all sides of the room, and there was no way a real sun would light all of them at once like that. The chairs were actually upholstered. Another difference from my quarters - I have a sack of straw on my bench to make it softer to sit there, I didn't yet feel that having a regular couch was okay. Over half the table was taken up by a statue of the Virgin Mary, like a kid sister version of the real thing. There was barely room for the smattering of Bibles there, including the one I detested most, the King James version. It had recently been completed, and I knew at the time that that particular version would be no end of trouble. Based on its position, it was the most frequently thumbed through here.

My focus came back to where I was standing, and I noticed something odd about the stoup - there was only one, and it was on the left side coming in, not the right. You're supposed to use your right hand. The stoup could be moved, so I figured there was another one and Calvary was testing me. I reached over with my right fingers, dipped them in the water, and made the sign of the cross on myself before going further. I continued to examine the room and build my profile as Calvary came in behind me. "The other Churches were wrong. You didn't catch fire for touching holy water."

Ha ha, very funny. I forced the subject to change. "Nice layout."

"Thank you," he said, moving another stoup out from behind a support that was hiding it and placing it on the other side of the door. "It was my dream to make a church like this on Earth, but I never got the chance. Parishioners would have loved it."

"I'm sure they would have," I said. No doubt, it would have been named after him.

Calvary vanished the door into his wall and gestured to the corner. "Why don't we have a seat over there?"

We walked over to the upholstered chairs. He waited for me to sit first. I will admit they felt good. Maybe I should have my bench...nah, better not. Calvary sat down in the other chair. We sat in silence for a few moments before I broke it. "So, what case are we going to discuss?"

"You tell me," he smiled.

I wasn't putting up with this. "You make the first move or I leave."

"You are willing to take a chance with no advance knowledge?"

He knew my court record better than that. Spur of the moment was my specialty, it was why no one had successfully ambushed me. I stood up. "Thank you, it's been a touch of Heaven, see you around."

I had turned to head for the door when his words rushed out. "It's about Christina's case. The mermaid."

I turned to look at him. I wasn't in the mood to be pleasant anymore. "I don't appreciate being tested."

"I apologize, but I think I deserve some reassurance," he said. "The shadow court is not general knowledge, and has to be kept secret. I wanted to know you wouldn't violate the trust."

"Michael's endorsement isn't enough for you?"

"Would it be for you?"

"Absolutely. Questioning Michael's sense of humor is one thing. Questioning his intelligence and his integrity is another."

Calvary got the message that he was walking on extremely thin ice. Word got around the Churches that the best chance of beating Hannah Singer in court was to keep me calm and relaxed. Hack me off, and I will go out of my way to obliterate your case instead of just going for a judgment. "I apologize," he said. "Such cases happen so rarely and the Advocates so seldom change, I just wanted to make sure."

I weighed my options. I could just tell him to suck mud and leave. But I felt he wasn't trying to be intimidating. In the cases I faced off with him, he was reasonable. I might get a peek at the logic he would apply to the case. The Churches were up to something very dangerous for Christina, and any knowledge would help.

I returned to the chair and looked at him levelly. I actually saw his Adam's apple move like a silent gulp. "Tell me something that'll make me want to stick around," I ordered.

"You shouldn't want Christina with a soul."

Good icebreaker. "And why is that?"

"You don't find that insulting? That someone not of God's creation can be rewarded with Eternal Life?"

"Speaking as someone who was nearly denied Eternal Life just because of her philosophy, I think it's a very beautiful thing that anyone can have Eternal Life."

"You weren't being denied Eternal Life, just Heaven."

"So, an Atheist has a right to Eternal Life, as long as that Eternal Life is endless pain. Yeah, that's much better."

"Let's leave the arguments used against you out of this," Calvary said. He was getting annoyed with me preventing him from making his point. "You have a soul. You earned a Heavenly reward. And unlike certain other Churches, I am glad you won your judgment. I think Atheism is just a point of view, not an act of defiance and a sin. Think about the cases we've faced each other on. Have I ever recommended anyone be Cast Down?"

I searched my memory, not only of my cases, but ones I knew he argued. Unless he was junioring, which meant he had no say in the recommended fate, I couldn't recall him ever moving for Casting. "So, clearly, Christina offends your sensibilities if you are asking for Casting now."

"I'm not asking for Casting."

"No. You're asking for something much worse -- for her to cease to be."

"And what's wrong with that?"

I looked at him enraged. He didn't flinch in the least. I focused on calming down so I wouldn't try putting my fist in his face. "How would you like it?"

"It's simply nature taking its course," he countered. "If she ceases, it's just what would have happened anyway. What you are seeking to do is what is causing problems because it's not supposed to happen."

"There is no good reason it shouldn't."

Calvary was leaning in now and holding his gaze with mine. "Yes, there is. God granted us souls. He did not grant anyone else souls. That is God's will. And the shadow court specifically dances around this and grants things God did not intend."

"So your stance is that the existence of the shadow court is wrong, period."

"Yes. That is exactly my stance."

"Even a sweet little thing like Christina who never did anything wrong and has done everything asked of her, just like any good Christian?"

Calvary gave me a sickly smile. "You're getting attached to her, aren't you, Singer?"

"She's a wonderful person."

"She's not a person. She could vanish at any moment. You wouldn't even get a chance to say good-bye to her. Blink your eye, and she's gone."

"And that's reason for me to refuse her? Because it will hurt emotionally if she dissipates?"

"Other trials you've lost hit you hard. They hit everyone hard. Christina's will be the worst because your best couldn't save her. All your prep work, everything you've invested, getting the Tribunal on your side, the perfect words in the perfect arguments? Poof! Gone like smoke on a windy day."

He hit on a very real fear of mine. Losing judgments was always bad, but those souls usually just had some fate that would eventually bring them around again for another trial. Christina would be gone, period. Losing this case would be the greatest heartbreak I ever knew. And I knew time would provide no refuge. I doubted Heaven itself would.

I stood up. "My feelings don't matter. I'm not Advocating for Christina to make myself feel good. I'm doing it because she has earned a soul and I can make it happen."

"You'll make a lot of Churches happy. You'll be so despondent, you won't want to advocate ever again. One mermaid gone, and it will rip you to pieces." Calvary leaned back in his chair and steepled his fingers. He was looking at them, not at me.

I was defiant. "She won't be gone. Not while I'm on the case."

"We shall see, Singer. Regular trials are just judgments. This is abuse of God's will. And it is not going to happen."

I could see my vision clouding, moving in from the fringes with only the middle, where Calvary was in my view, unaffected. There was a buzzing in my ears and I could feel the heat from them turning red. Calvary was dangerous. He genuinely saw no reason to think otherwise. Anything offered would be ignored as uninformed ramblings. He was going to wipe out a precious life before it had a chance to become one. My throat was constricting. Even if I could find the words to express my outrage, they'd never make it to my lips.

I turned carefully and strode to the door. I touched the wall, making it reappear. I dipped my fingers in the holy water and made the sign of the cross on myself. Then I dipped my hand in and flicked it at Calvary. Calvary just laughed. The laugh of someone who's already won and there's nothing anyone can do about it.

I stalked back to the Archives. I felt the knots my stomach would have been twisted into if I still had one. All the pain, all the fear, everything. And me, fighting to push it out of my mind. It didn't help that I could hear Christina. I poked my head around the corner of the building and saw her playing tag with some child souls. Despair descended on me like a waterfall, pushing me under and tossing me around. I ran for the Court Building and dashed inside.

The Court Building itself has a campanile, a sizable bell tower. Unauthorized people are to be kept out, but I'm friends with Dirk, the guy in charge of ringing the bells when needed. I found him and asked to be let inside. He didn't ask questions, just opened the door and told me he'd warn me if he had to ring them.

I went to the top and stepped outside, standing on the narrow ledge that jutted from the wall. The bells obscured my view of Christina, it was the whole reason I picked the position I did. I squeezed my eyes shut and fought back the tears. I couldn't afford to be distracted by my emotions. I had to think.

There was a golden thread I was missing, one that I could yank and make the whole thing unravel. But what was it? The Church argument that Christina was not made in God's image would never win. And yet Calvary and the Churches were acting like the case was in the bag. Why? There had to be some other argument they would use. But what was it? I started replaying everything in my mind. Everything I read in the scrolls. Every conversation I had. Hunter. Calvary. Christina. No answers. I dug deeper. I thought about how they responded. How they acted. What prompted their reactions. I had to go over them several times because the despair was just that powerful and I had to restart.

Eventually, I got myself under control. I was impassive as Christina's smiling face and enthusiasm went through my mind. I felt no comfort from

Hunter's words. The court records were cold facts, pieces of information like a royal proclamation. The Churches behavior was no longer infuriating....

My eyes popped. Suddenly, any urge to cry vanished. Everything the Churches did, everything Calvary said, crashed together into a single fused entity. I saw. I understood. I knew exactly what they were doing. I felt the corner of my mouth start to twitch up, like it wanted to smile in defiance of the rest of my mouth. I went back inside the campanile and simply dropped down the middle of the stairwell, landing expertly on my feet at the bottom. I came out and let Dirk know before dashing back to my quarters. I now knew exactly what I needed to do.

I grabbed every relevant case history, every relevant life scroll, everything I could think of, and bolted for Earth. I needed to think. I needed to plan. And my little quarters just didn't have the space for it. Any place with room was a public area where curious eyes could see what I was up to. I didn't want word spreading around, either from unknowing Celestials who didn't realize how important what they noticed was or Churches on the prowl. I went to Antarctica and into a deep ice cave, no way in or out. No light, but I was a spirit, so I didn't need it anyway.

There were sheer walls of ice everywhere, some higher than castle walls. I held my quill in my hand and started "writing" at the walls. Spiritual ink appeared, something no human would ever see. It was spelling out my words, drawing my images, giving form to my thoughts. Some walls held information about case histories. Others had precedents. Others had information from individuals who had been through their trials. Occasionally, I would point the quill at one wall and "draw" a line from one wall to another. A thread of light would appear, connecting the two points I commanded. Some wall sections looked like a spider had spun a glittering golden web between them.

I was so wrapped up in my activity that I didn't realize I wasn't alone anymore. Michael's booming voice was multiplied by the walls around us. "Hannah!"

When you think you are alone in a sealed cavern and suddenly realize you aren't, you only react one way. I jumped straight up in the air, my feet almost above Michael's head before I started coming back down. I put my hand to my chest, then remembered I didn't have a heart to check the beat of anyway. "Don't do that, Michael!"

Michael was staring around the cavern, taking everything in. "My God! All this is for Christina's case?"

"Yes," I said, rolling up a scroll and tying it closed again. "You were right about it being complicated. You just didn't realize how complicated."

"Yeah. By several factors, apparently."

"More like several orders of magnitude."

Michael looked at me, worry clearly on his face. "Are you up to this? I mean," and he spread his arms out around the cavern, "all of this?"

"Michael, not only am I the best chance of saving Christina, but I am the ONLY chance of saving Christina. You need me leading this defense."

Michael knew better than to question my conclusions. But he didn't like staying in the dark. "Okay. So what exactly are the Churches doing?"

"They don't want Christina with a soul. Plain and simple. Their argument is that, as a mermaid who willed herself into existence, she is not made in God's image and has no right to a soul. And they know it's a loser in the shadow court. Too many precedents, too easy to undermine their case. The trial itself is an afterthought. They won't get their way with it. So they are focusing on Christina. Christina is a child."

Michael arched his eyebrows at me. "Aren't you being a bit harsh?"

"It's not an insult, but a statement of fact. Christina is a child. She hasn't lived. She is emotionally underdeveloped. Any reaction she has is magnified. Joy, confidence, and despair. Remember, in order for her to gain a soul," I emphasized each word, "her will cannot falter."

Michael's eyes flew open. The Churches weren't after a judgment. They were trying to prevent one. If they could break Christina at any point before the ruling that would give her a soul, she would dissipate right then and there.

In a flash, Michael's face darkened and his flaming sword appeared in his hand. It started melting some of the ice walls around us, a thick fog appearing. "I'm gonna kill them!"

I pointed at Michael and commanded his attention. "No! Any of them can do this case! Cut off one head, another appears! The only way to pull this off is to build Christina up. Make her feel valued. Wanted. Loved. That she not only has every right to a soul, but there is nothing wrong with her gaining one. If she gets through the trial without her will faltering, it's over and there's nothing the Churches can do."

Michael willed his sword away. The fog quickly settled, condensed, and became ice again. I took a quick look. The spiritual ink simply shifted to other walls, nothing I wrote or drew had been lost. Michael noticed the changes. He looked uncharacteristically guilty. "Sorry, Hannah."

I came over and put my hand on his shoulder, giving it a little shake. "Hey, it's okay, big brother. If I had a flaming sword when I figured this out, I would have reacted the exact same way."

Michael looked at me. "And that's why you need to lead the defense."

"Right. Who better to reassure someone that there is hope against a bullying church than an Atheist who won her own trial, alone and without a leader?"

Michael started wandering around, taking in everything. The walls were basically my mind writ large, how I grouped information, how I made connections, everything. He could see the direction I was going in and the different attacks I was preparing for. I didn't have to play to Pahaliah and the Tribunal. That was a done deal. I had to communicate with Christina, keep her spirits up. She was the weak link in the chain, and I was going to build a fortress around it for protection.

Michael looked at me. He was clearly nervous. While he had faith in me, he never anticipated Christina's case becoming what it had. No trial I had faced had this much on the line. I smiled at him and asked, "You know what Christina told me the first time I talked with her?"

"No. What?"

"She said I was one of your shining stars."

Michael thought it over, then nodded his head. "She's right. You are."

"I'm not a shining star because I'm just that good. It's because I have to be that good. You're counting on me. Christina's counting on me. The shadow court, which doesn't grant mercy but grants life, is counting on me."

"That's a lot of pressure to handle," he said. There was nothing less than complete admiration in his eyes.

"That's what I do."

I told Michael I was ready for trial as soon as possible. I wanted to keep the time Christina could spend mulling over her situation and making herself feel bad to a minimum. Michael said he would put in the request soon, there was something he needed to do first. He took off, leaving me to finish my strategy.

Hunter showed up. Michael had told him where I was and suggested he stop by. Looking at the walls, he was impressed. "Not bad for my first shadow trial, huh, Hunter?"

He looked at me. "I have a lot to learn before I lead."

We went over everything, including what the Church was up to. Hunter's instructions were simple -- he was to focus on arguments dealing with shadow court procedure and to keep me from going overboard. The only way to keep Christina's spirits up were for me to hit the Churches with everything I had. I couldn't focus on their arguments. Those weren't important and wouldn't win anyway. What I had to do was discredit the Churches in Christina's eyes, to make her think they had no right to judge her. If I could do that, her will wouldn't falter and the whole thing was in the bag.

The time of trial was upon me. I walked casually towards the Office Of Records with my scrolls disguised in a picnic basket. No one was the wiser, and figured from my skipping that I was going to blow off some steam. After all, I hadn't had any trials lately, maybe I needed a break. At three hundreds years, Advocates began to feel the strain.

I got to the wall, making sure no one was around to watch. The door appeared as soon as I got close enough. I put my hand on it and poured through. Now, I could drop the act. I walked with purpose, fists clenched and swinging my arms a little. It wasn't an act for Christina's benefit. I was ready to fight tooth and nail.

I went through the other set of doors and was in the courtroom. The Gallery had a couple of others here, but no big turnout. They were actual angels, I could feel it. I nodded a polite hello to them as I went, and they returned the gesture.

120

Coming out of the Gallery, I saw Hunter was already at the Celestial table. He stood and bowed. "Well met, Lady Singer. Are you ready to seize the day?"

I looked at the Church table. Two juniors there. Giovanni Vasari was a Church from Italy, approaching his one hundredth year of Advocating. Also there was Mark Freedman. Freedman was the only Church from my own trial who was still around. He had never lead a single case. He was usually pulled in as a junior during grey area cases I handled because the Churches hoped Freedman could give them some insight into how I operated, enabling them to anticipate my actions and maybe get a jump on me. Hadn't worked yet, and it wouldn't work this time.

"'Seize the day?' More like a stranglehold." I sat down at the lead Advocate seat and started pulling scrolls out of my basket.

The two of us were reviewing scrolls and talking strategy. I snuck a look out of the corner of my eye at the Church table. Vasari and Freedman were just sitting there, looking bored. Most likely, they were there to provide information to Calvary, not to actually do anything at trial. I would still keep an eye on them in case they tried to get involved. There was too much on the line. But the odds were against it.

I heard the familiar sound of Michael's footsteps coming down the aisle, along with softer padding. As Michael was the Guardian of the shadow courts, he would bring the Petitioner to her Advocates. Michael brought Christina up. She smiled nervously at me. Hunter, ever the gentleman, shot to his feet and stepped down one chair, moving for Christina to take the now empty Petitioner's seat. She came around and prepared to sit. Hunter moved to scoot in her stool, and she froze. "What's he doing?"

I smiled. "He's being polite and pushing your chair in so you can sit."

"Oh. Is that how it's supposed to work?"

My jaw dropped and I shot Michael the most poison look I could. For once, he actually looked contrite. He hunched his shoulders and took his place in front of the judge's bench. Lord love a duck.

Hunter and I continued to talk, keeping the tone casual to keep Christina calm. Christina was nervously looking over her shoulder, watching the doorway to the court. Suddenly, I heard Christina let out a gasp and felt her getting smaller. Shot in the dark, Calvary had arrived. His stride had purpose. I could hear it.

I turned to look. Calvary was looking at Christina like a hungry wolf seeing an isolated sheep. Well, she wasn't isolated while I was around. I touched Christina's shoulder, getting her attention. I put my arm buddy-style over her shoulder. "Relax, kiddo. Don't let the Church scare you."

Calvary was up to us and could hear me talking. "He's not a monster. He's just a man. A man facing certain defeat."

Calvary focused his fury on Christina. "Oh, no. You're not getting a soul."

Christina scrunched down. I felt her dimming again. Her mouth was moving but no words were coming out. I gave her a squeeze. "You don't have to say anything. Remember, he doesn't have to beat you in court." I looked at Calvary and smiled. "He has to beat me."

I felt Christina relax and unfold beneath my arm a little. The change in Calvary was dramatic. He ratcheted up the intimidation. He pointed to me and said, "She's nothing. She shouldn't even be here. She's a stupid Atheist who got lucky and slipped through the cracks."

I couldn't believe it. I could feel Christina getting stronger. I knew what she was thinking and decided to reinforce her thoughts. "See, Christina? The Churches don't always get their way. They can lose. They do lose. They will lose."

"Not this time," Calvary hissed.

Christina looked him dead in the eye and pointed to me. "Talk to her."

Calvary gave me a look that could have drilled through the planet. "You won't win."

I kept smiling. "Watch me."

Calvary went to his table. I kept watching him out of the corner of my eye anytime Christina took a peek at him. He was very unsubtle. He looked at her, smiled, and pulled his finger across his throat. Christina grabbed my arm and put her head against my shoulder. I heard her muttering, "Save me. Please save me."

My gaze didn't shift away from Calvary. "You better believe I'll save you."

Christina straightened a little and looked at me. Her eyes were brimming with tears. "You really think you can?"

"You know what, Christina? I'm going to take your advice. I'm going to write this as a story."

That caught her interest. "Really?"

"Yes. But there's a catch."

"What's the catch?"

"You need to finish it. You're reading it as I write it, right now, in this moment. You can't close the book before the end of the story. You know the Greek plays, where the hero just suffers, and is vindicated at the end? You are that hero. You have to last to the end of the story."

"And God will save me at the end?"

"He's already saved you. He made me your Advocate."

She smiled. I felt her strength returning. I gave her a quick hug and whispered to her, "You have nothing to worry about. Once you get in the dock, you'll see that the Churches have no right, no business, and no clue."

I saw Hunter arch his eyebrows at me as if to say, "Really?" I just smiled and nodded at him.

The chimes sounded. Everyone stood up and we deployed our wings. Because Advocates aren't angels, we have ceremonial wings that float behind us and move as we move. Hunter's wings looked pretty decent next to my plain shapes. They had some definition, but were still humble. A definite reflection of their owner.

Christina's gasp caught my attention. She was looking at the Church table. I turned to look and see what I could do to reassure her this time when my jaw dropped. Calvary wasn't doing anything to intimidate her. His wings were not what I remembered. When I faced him in the Celestial Courts, his wings also had definition, looked pretty decent. This time, he had wings that were bold. They were thick and angled dramatically. Once again, a reflection of their owner.

I had to squeeze this in before the Tribunal entered and I could no longer speak at will. "Since when do Advocates get two sets of wings?"

"We don't," Calvary shrugged. "Technically, this is a separate court. Some choose different wings for it."

The Tribunal entered just before my hand could slap my forehead. I dropped my arm to my side. Two sets of wings. I'll teach him.

The twelve angels making up the Tribunal took their places in the Tribunal box. I was going to motion for Christina to notice them, but I didn't have to. She was staring at them in awe and wonder. I knew exactly what she was feeling. I felt it every time the Tribunal entered a trial. Angels are so wise, so strong, so full of grace. Christina was feeding off it, just like I hoped she would. Twelve lights of God, chasing away her darkness.

The back door of the court opened and Pahaliah entered. He stepped up to the bench and looked out over the court. He saw me and a subtle smile appeared on his lips. Pahaliah and I go way back. He presided at my trial. He leaned as much my way as he could without a mistrial being declared. I had to work harder to make my cases ironclad so the ruling would stick. But I could also get away with a lot more open baiting and frontal assaults on the Churches. It wasn't a fair trade, I actually had too much fun and came out way ahead on the deal. And I was going to take full advantage of it here.

Pahaliah sat down and banged the gavel. The Gallery and Tribunal sat. "Who is the Petitioner?"

Either Christina remembered she wasn't supposed to speak unless addressed, or she was too nervous to say anything. I declared, "The Petitioner is Christina Mermaid."

Pahaliah arched his eyebrows. "Her last name is what she is?"

"I'm not sure you should be asking that question of a woman named 'Singer.'"

"If your name was 'Advocate', you'd have a point," he smirked. Christina continued to feel stronger.

Pahaliah continued. "And who are her Advocates?"

"Joshua Hunter and Hannah Singer, acting as lead."

"And who Advoactes for the Church?"

"Mark Freedman, Giovanni Vasari, and Thomas Calvary, acting as lead," came the response from my left.

"Will the Petitioner please take the stand?"

Christina looked at me. She would be alone in the dock, without me to

123

hold on to if the Churches got bad. I squeezed her shoulder and smiled. She seemed to be drinking in my confidence. Then she walked out to the dock and climbed inside. She stood, looking at me, like a little girl watching her dad go away. I kept smiling. She closed her eyes, nodded, and I saw her straighten. She was going to be strong for me. Good.

The juniors sat down. "Advocate for the Petitioner goes first," Pahaliah said. "Singer? Your opening statements, please."

I had been thinking hard. The opening and closing remarks are the only time Advocates cannot be interrupted as they speak. That meant that, when Calvary made his statements, he could unleash everything on Christina and I couldn't do anything to stop him. This was really the only bump. If Christina could make it to the arguments, I could reduce the Churches to absurdity and nothing they said in their closing arguments would have any effect on her. But this? The Churches would get free shots at her. It was their best chance to make her will falter and they knew it. So I needed to make sure Christina could weather whatever was thrown at her. Two fronts to fight, Christina's sense of self and the Churches' zealotry. If I failed, a beautiful soul would vanish like ice in the summertime, three hundred years of effort, gone.

I knew what to do. I knew how to do it. I had to do it. I took a deep breath. I cleared my mind.

It's star time.

I started by turning dramatically to the left side of the court, where the Petitioner's exit would be in a regular Celestial trial. Instead, it was just a flat wall, showing the area outside the building. This side faced the Ancient Forest. The trees here had grown tall and proud, brought into existence at the same time as the Celestial Courts. "Look at those trees. Magnificent, aren't they? They're almost identical to such trees on Earth. One key difference, though: the trees here are constructs. The ones on Earth are alive. Well, sort of alive. They have no souls. When they die, they simply cease to be.

"When God created the Earth, he gave souls to humans. He gave them to all the different animals. Dogs, cats, even mice. They all have spirits. But he never gave souls to the trees. Not to the bushes. The grass. Plants don't have spirits. They don't have souls. Why is that? It can't be just because they are plants. God can do anything, there was nothing stopping him from giving them souls themselves. Why the omission?

"There is a simple but obvious difference. Plants don't really interact with the world. Beings with souls improve the world. Plants improve the world, but only by being used, not through any effort on their part. They are material. They are a resource. They have no will with which to volunteer, no imaginations with which to consider and make things better. Not even the ability to tell humans what their limitations are, so that they don't make bridge that can't support the horses. Others determine their use, from the birds nesting in their branches to the humans who use them to build homes or paint them as objects of art.

"Before God created the Earth, we were consciousness. Thought without form. We could vanish into nothing. In His wisdom, He made us more than just consciousness. We became souls, beings that could exist and operate on our own. We could exist outside His presence, going to Earth and being with others like us, helping to take a hunk of rock drifting through space and making it a home.

"Every being with a soul has an obligation to others. They are to provide something, anything within their capabilities, to make things better. Whether through protecting others or finding food or demystifying the world. Every being with a soul does this, living for others, not for themselves. And their reward is to become themselves, for their souls become truly whole. That is how entry to Heaven is granted, through selflessness.

"Christina is just like any of us here. She is just like any being on Earth, any animal. Like us, she started as a simple consciousness. But God simply granted us our souls. God would have granted a soul to Christina, but was not allowed an audience. She had to prove her sincerity. For three hundred years, she has done so. She has done nothing but help others, inspiring them, making their world better, over a period of several lifetimes.

"We were lucky. Our souls were simply granted to us. God gave them to us with nothing to justify His decision except faith. There wasn't even a world where we could prove He was right at the time. Christina has proven her worth. She has done so for three hundred years. The only difference is her timing was off. Had she existed back before the creation of the world, she would be granted a soul like the rest of us. Everything about her is identical to us, save for one tiny detail - she does not have a real soul. This trial is to correct this oversight. It's not that she has every right to a soul. It's not that she's earned a soul. She is a soul, made up of and doing everything that makes us souls. Her joy is real. Her sorrow is real. Her fear is real. To deny she is a soul is to deny everything that makes a soul what it is. She should not be denied just because she wasn't around when we were. We should make it official, make her complete. Her petition should be granted. Thank you."

I looked at Christina in the dock. She looked at me and I locked her with my gaze. I smiled slyly at her, trying to will as much strength as I could to her. She nodded, she got the message. Her lips vanished as she tightened her mouth and stood ready, like a house about to face a torrential storm. Would it hold up? Would it survive? It was just the two of us, putting our faith in each other. I put my hands behind my back and stood at attention. The way I held my hands made it easier to hide them in the sleeves of my robes. I didn't want anyone to see my fingers crossed.

Calvary focused his gaze on Christina. While she did look to the side, I didn't see her do more than that. She didn't gulp. She didn't start shaking. Hang in there, kiddo, you can do it.

"Her sorrow is real. Her fear is real." Calvary was sneering his words.

Pahaliah smashed the gavel, drawing Calvary's eyes to him like a magnet. "Are your comments for the Tribunal, or for Christina?"

I breathed an inward sigh of relief. Pahaliah was sharp as ever.

Michael would not have told him what I figured out about Calvary's strategy. It would have increased the risk of a mistrial. But Pahaliah pays close attention. If he didn't know exactly what Calvary was up to, he at least recognized he was trying to abuse Christina. Pahaliah doesn't put up with that stuff.

Calvary turned his gaze to the Tribunal, specifically the left side of the box. It put Christina in his peripheral vision. "She only thinks they are real. Same with everyone who thinks she deserves a soul.

"She is a formation. A simple accident. She should not exist. God did not create consciousness in the oceans, and even if he did, he would have given it form, not allowed it to choose a form. A half human, half fish creature? That is an abomination. All of God's creatures are complete. Here's one that wants to be human, but couldn't make themselves completely human. Why? What is the restriction that makes an ocean consciousness form a mermaid instead of a human?

"It's because they aren't human. They can never be human. Otherwise, they would do so.

"Had Christina reformed herself as a human, it would be different. But she couldn't, God did not allow that. So instead of just vanishing like she was supposed to, like all other mermaids, she clung stubbornly to a belief. But her belief is not truth. She is not human. She is not a soul. She is remarkably like one, but she is not.

"There is temptation to think of the three hundred years she spent helping others and feel sympathy for her. Three hundred years, wasted. But that is her fault. She has delayed her fate, she brings this sadness on herself and everyone else. No one wants to see her vanish. But that is the only option. She is asking for an exception to the rules, one that should not be granted, and trying to guilt trip everyone into going along with it.

"We are souls. We are created in God's image. She is not. She is a strange accident that is prolonging her own agony." Calvary turned his head to focus on Christina. She refused to look at him. "It is within her own power to end this emotional trial she is putting everybody through. She just has to do the right thing, and accept her fate as a mermaid. If Singer loses this trial, it will crush her. She might never recover."

I glared at Calvary. That was really low. He was trying to make Christina feel like an afterthought. The old "I'm so much trouble, I wish I'd never been born" bit. Bad enough he was dragging my emotions into it. I knew I could recover. Would Christina?

I looked at Christina. She was looking at me in outright desperation. I held my hand up like I had a quill in it and pretended I was writing something. Calvary was so focused on his prey, he didn't notice my actions. But he did notice Christina take a deep breath and look him in the eyes.

Calvary continued. "When she goes, she will simply cease to exist. But the guilt and depression and what if's will live on after her. What she is doing is cruel and unforgivable. She should not be rewarded for playing with everyone's emotions. She does not deserve a soul. She does not deserve to live.

Singer does not deserve what is being done to her. No one does. Christina deserves exactly what mermaids get in the end, exactly what she is trying to avoid. She deserves nothingness. Thank you."

I was still staring at Christina. The opening remarks concluded, she slowly looked at me. She gave me a sickly smile. The storm beat pretty hard and exposed some of the structure, but the foundation was holding together. I gave her a thumbs up, and felt her get a little stronger. I had to keep making her stronger. And the best way to do that was by making the Churches look foolish.

I looked at Calvary out of the corner of my eye. He looked at me out of the corner of his. I smiled. Christina didn't falter. She was still there. His best chance to get her, his free shot, the only time I was forbidden to run interference, was over. Anything he said now would have to survive a direct assault from me. He had gambled that dragging my emotions into it would be enough to push Christina over the edge. It didn't work.

I mentally rolled up my sleeves and spit on my hands. What should I do first, get Christina's spirits up a little higher, or make the Churches look like morons? Why, I could do both at once! I leaned over to Hunter and whispered, "Watch and learn."

Hunter watched me as I gave Pahaliah a sunbright smile. "Sir, Christina looks uncomfortable. Can she remove her robes so that she feels more at ease?"

Calvary looked like I just suggested another plague to finish off humanity. "She can't be naked!"

"Why not? What's wrong with nudity?"

"Man is not meant to be naked! Aaron and his sons were required to wear underwear in God's tent to keep their...stuff from showing!"

"That's was God's tent after the Exodus, there is no such restriction on the Celestial Courts. Besides, that's about proper decorum, not shame."

Michael started peeling off his bracers. "I need to feel free!"

Calvary stared in shock as Michael grabbed a handful of his lower robes and prepared to lift them. He screamed, "If God had meant for us to be naked, we'd have been born that way!"

It takes a lot to stop Michael when he's in the middle of messing with someone. That did it. Michael had stopped dead. His eyes, and the eyes of everyone else in the courtroom, including Christina's, were riveted to Calvary. Mouths were agape in sheer disbelief. From the Tribunal Box, I heard one of the angels say, "Oh, GOD, is he stupid!"

I checked the dock. Christina was looking like she was ready to burst out laughing. Calvary was fuming. I didn't want him to recover his wits. I looked at Hunter and said casually, "This case could be easier than I anticipated."

That was the wrong thing to say. Which meant it was the best thing to say. Calvary was so enraged he couldn't speak. Vasari decided to try a rescue. He got to his feet and said, "She should remain clothed to protect the angels."

Calvary spun around. "Shut up now!"

Pahaliah was holding the shaft of his gavel in his fingertips and moving them, making the head twirl back and forth. "Oh, no. Let him speak. I want to hear this."

Calvary stuck his finger in the leak. "No one else wants to hear him speak."

I raised my hand. "Move for a vote to be taken, supermajority or better to carry."

The lead Tribunal spoke. "Seconded."

Michael raised his hand. "Thirded."

Pahaliah looked lazily at Calvary. "So, you're telling us angels what we are thinking."

Calvary knew this was lost. He simply looked at Vasari and gestured out to the court, indicating he should speak. Vasari was oblivious to the trouble he was in. "It would be better not to tempt the angels and make them fall."

I winced. That was just insulting.

Pahaliah got a good grip on his gavel. "So, Calvary, aren't you going to beg me not to ban Vasari from advocating?"

Calvary looked at Vasari. He then looked at Pahaliah and simply said, "No."

"Barred from advocating, remove from courtroom 'til further notice." Pahaliah lifted the gavel up, holding the base by his fingertips. Gravity did the rest, dropping the head down. Vasari knew there was no point in fighting. He was already by the aisle when Michael sauntered up to him. Michael swept his hands in front of him in a "shoo" gesture as Vasari walked up the aisle and out the door. After a few moments, Michael came back in and resumed his place in front of the bench.

Christina waited a moment, then removed her robes. She seemed to relax a bit.

Calvary was looking at the door Vasari just left through. He turned to me, and his smile was pure ice. I immediately knew what he was up to. This was not over. I thought it would be downhill from here, but it was about to become a mountain climb. Christina survived his attack because of her faith in me and the inspiration I gave her. If he could tear me down in her eyes, she would be vulnerable, and her despair would do the rest. I had to tread carefully. Not only did I have to avoid a mistrial, but also doing anything that would get me kicked out of court. It was a tug of war with a knot of credibility, and whoever got it on their side would determine Christina's fate.

I started. "Should we just move to closing arguments?"

Calvary smirked. "Afraid of arguing against me?"

"Why would I be afraid of you?"

"Because you know you can't win."

"I'm doing pretty good so far."

"Not from where I sit."

I saw an opening and dashed for it, watching for traps along the way. "Your opening statements did not address a single point I raised, it sidestepped them. I'd say you're the one who's afraid."

"You aren't addressing any of my points, Singer."

"Fine. Pick one."

Calvary balked a little. His best hope was to keep the arguments general. Getting into specifics would give me a chance to argue and pull things my way. "That she deserves a soul."

Nice. He was still keeping things under a canopy of ambiguity. Time to get rid of it. I raised my banner and charged. "Has she killed anyone?"

"No." He actually lowered his head and shook it sadly.

"Ghengis Kahn did. Lots of people. And lots of other crimes. And he not only had a soul, he kept it. You're saying a world conqueror is more deserving of a soul than a peaceful mermaid?" I had another example, but I kept it in case Calvary went the direction I was expecting.

He did. "If Ghengis Kahn stood trial in this court, you would not resent him having a soul despite everything he did?"

"I didn't try to deny Tomas de Torquemada's soul, did I?"

That caught Calvary flatfooted. About a century earlier, I lead the opposition to Torquemada's petition and won.

Calvary paused for a beat. He gave me a disarming smile. "You really are good. Better than I thought."

I didn't let it stroke my ego, I was too busy taking advantage of it. I looked at Christina in the dock and said, "Told you you had nothing to worry about."

Calvary's smile got sly. "Getting desperate if you have to twist every little thing I say to your advantage?"

"If you want to sing a few more praises about me, be my guest."

I had completely forced him off topic. He had to get things back. "Do you agree that God made man in His own image?"

"Yes."

"So, we agree God gave His creations souls."

"Yes."

"So, we agree that, if God did not grant someone or something a soul, they are not supposed to have one."

"'We?' You got a frog in your pocket?"

"God gave us our souls. We didn't get them through a trial."

"The Courts didn't exist back then."

"So the Courts exist to violate God's plan?"

Only now did I relax. I had this in the bag. "If God doesn't want anyone He didn't create to have a soul, why did He create the shadow court?"

Calvary turned to stone in front of me. The only action was the widening of his eyes. My point could not be disregarded. He would have to argue God's will. He tried to salvage it. "The shadow court is not God's will, it operates independently of it."

"God created the Celestial Courts. He created the shadow courts. He could have simply not done so. God extends His love and mercy to anyone who wants it. He does not let details get in the way of that love and mercy. Not an

129

imperfect life. Not Atheism. And not someone that came to be on their own. He intends for individuals like Christina to have a soul." I looked at Christina in the dock. She was practically beaming. Christina could no longer be shaken. The Tribunal was already set to rule for Christina.

I smiled at Calvary. "It's over."

"Over my dead body!"

"You are aware you are, in fact, dead, right?"

He pointed at Christina and yelled at the top of his lungs, "SHE'S NOT HUMAN!"

"I will be," she said, confident and strong.

Calvary glared at Pahaliah. "She is not supposed to speak unless addressed."

Pahaliah looked at me. "Lady Singer, you are to speak for Christina at the moment. Calvary's last statement was, 'She's not human.'"

"She will be," I stated, simply and without fanfare.

Calvary shifted his eyes. He turned to look at Freedman. Freedman simply shrugged. Calvary faced Pahaliah and said, "The official position of the Churches is that Christina is not made in God's image and should cease to be."

Oh, no, you don't get off that easy. I was going to poison the wells and sow the earth with salt. I started my closing argument. "Calvary's case against Christina is a crime. Not in that he sought the destruction of a beautiful spirit, but in what motivated it. Calvary was inspired by arrogance. No one else can have a soul. No one can be more perfectly in God's image than humans.

"Calvary is like a man who posits that the sky may be blue, but it should be green. And anyone who does anything to keep it blue is violating the order God created. In actuality, it is a violation of Calvary's sensibilities. Those who trust in God and believe in Jesus are granted eternal life. It says nothing about that individual having to be a particular denomination, nothing about them being Christian, and NOTHING ABOUT THEM BEING HUMAN! Jesus sought to save anyone who wanted to be saved, he turned no one away. Not lepers, not the rich, no one. All they had to do was want to be better, and he would help them to be so.

"For someone to vanish into nothing is a horrible, horrible fate. Even God thinks so. While Celestial Advocates are free to come up with their own recommended fates, Eternal Nothingness is not an option. St. Michael will not only rewrite that portion, but he will kick you out of your position. God allows our spirits to live even after our bodies die, not to cease to exist. And this belief is reflected in the building and trial we are taking part in. Had God not wanted outsiders to have a chance with him, the shadow court would not exist, full stop.

"We know how this is supposed to go. We know what the outcome is supposed to be. Christina has suffered since her three hundred years of service ended, not knowing for sure if she had earned what she sought. End her suspense. Show her the kindness and love we are to extend to all who seek it. Grant her petition. Thank you."

I had barely finished when Pahaliah turned to the Tribunal. "You have heard the Advocates for Christina Mermaid state their recommended fates. You may now make your decision. You wish to confer?"

The lead Tribunal shot to his feet. "We are ready to rule."

"And what is your decision?"

"Petition is to be granted immediately."

Pahaliah didn't waste any time. He looked at Christina and smiled. "Get ready for this." He then declared, "So be it!" and slammed the gavel.

Suddenly, Christina's hair started billowing around like she was caught in the middle of a cyclone. She looked around in surprise, but not fear. As the cyclone got stronger, she started to rise up from the dock. Her eyes closed and her head fell back. From all around the court, golden specks of light streamed into Christina, going through her chest and into her heart. Soon, enough of the lights entered that the shape of her illuminated heart was visible. Then the light expanded out in a flash, temporarily bleaching out everyone and everything in the court to pure white. Eventually, regular vision returned. Christina was still floating above the dock, but her body looked like it was made of pure golden light. Her head tilted up and her eyes opened, the only part of her that seemed unchanged. She floated back down to the dock and landed on her feet. Her knees were wobbly, she had to grab onto the railing. The golden light didn't go away so much as absorb into her, leaving her standing with a look of pure rapture on her face.

Slowly, Christina's eyes raised to mine. Her voice was barely a whisper, but there was no mistaking what she said. "I'm human!"

"Congratulations, Christina," Pahaliah smiled. "Court is adjourned!" He slammed the gavel and he and the Tribunal filed out.

I quickly willed my wings away and rushed up to Christina in the dock. Michael came up as well. I looked at Michael. "She is okay, right?"

"She's better than okay," Michael smiled. "She's just...overwhelmed."

I thought about it. A trial with impossible odds, and the Petitioner pulled through. "Yeah, I know the feeling."

Michael came around to the dock entrance and helped Christina to her feet. She was still wobbly. Michael simply hefted her up and put her on his right shoulder. She squealed like a little girl, getting a ride on daddy's shoulder.

"You can't keep her up there," I told Michael. "You'll never get through the door."

"That's what you think, Hannah! Hold on Christina, here we go!" Michael tilted at an angle and started sliding across the floor towards the exit, Christina laughing the entire time. They were out the door and on their way.

I went into the dock and picked up Christina's robes so I could return them. When I turned around, Calvary was right in front of me, enraged. He still had his wings out, and had the whole "wrathful angel" vibe going. "How dare you."

"How dare I what?"

He was silent. When he finally spoke, his voice was a low rumble, like the warning growl of a tiger. "I'm sorry you won your trial. Bad enough doubters were getting into Heaven. But Atheists? And now a creature not of God's creation? Heaven was created as a reward for us. The faithful. You have no right to it. And you have no right giving it to others."

I leaned into his face. No way I was going to back down. "I don't give it to Petitioners. God gives it to Petitioners. I make sure you can't take it away from them."

"You've just made a powerful enemy," he said. There was no exaggeration, he stated it matter-of-factly. "You better bring your best the next time you go to court. Any case I'm not leading, I'll junior. You'll never win again, heretic. I might even get a retrial of your petition."

"Do your worst."

He stalked out of the court. Freedman had already gone. It was now just Hunter and I.

Hunter walked up. "I can't believe you aren't scared."

"Well, I am a little. Someone that mean? You bet they're going to try every one of those threats."

"You aren't as scared as I am for you."

I smiled at him. "Fear is powerful. But so is faith. And I'll put my faith in myself against Calvary's fear any day."

Hunter and I started walking out of court. We were in the hallway and about to pass through the door when Hunter stopped me. "Any chance I can junior for you some more? I think I can learn a lot more from you than I ever did from Lankshire."

"The way I do cases isn't anything you learn. You either have it or you don't."

His eyes drooped a little. "I understand."

"No, you don't," I told him. "Let's talk to Michael so we can find out if you do have it."

He smiled and I went outside with my soon-to-be new assistant.

Christina wasted no time in petitioning. She wanted to be born. The Churches tried to contest, but it was a waste of time. There was a fresh Celestial named David Acker who had only started out, he had juniored five trials and never lead. He lead for the Celestials (I juniored. It may have been in the bag, but no point in being careless). The trial itself was a joke. Because I was junior, I could watch the Tribunal. Angels are eternal beings. So when they're looking around and acting bored, you are definitely going on too long. Acker's opening argument was three sentences. The trial itself, he said nothing other than moving for closing arguments. His closing argument was four sentences. The Tribunal didn't even deliberate before approving Christina's petition.

Christina has been going around ever since. She loves life. While alive, she's unaware of her true nature. She's just a bright, sparkly, bubbly girl who makes everyone feel alive. She's still a muse, just living among the people she inspires.

Each time she died and returned, she remembered everything about herself, where she came from, and me in particular. Each time, she would ask me if I'd started writing anything yet. Every time she returned, from the late 17th century on. And she would keep urging me every time she saw me until she went back to Earth, my only respite from her enthusiasm. The Chinese water torture may be faster, but it's not as effective. That is the reason I'm finally writing these memoirs. She loves reading them when she comes back. Michael isn't as thrilled, though. He keeps looking at me and asking, "I'm not really that bad, am I?" Amazing. I'm finally getting back at my big brother.

Christina's case had wound up and she was on her way to be born for the first time. I finished up a couple of other cases and took some time to go to Earth. I went to the hills of Austria. I don't see a night sky very often. There was no one else around as I laid back on the grass and enjoyed the view.

I didn't hear Michael turn up, but I'm used to his sudden appearances, so I didn't even bat an eye when he asked, "Beautiful sight, isn't it?"

"Yeah," I said. "I used to love looking at it when I was alive."

"Good," Michael said, lowering himself next to me and laying down. "That's why God made it. A thing of beauty anyone can enjoy and no one can take away."

I let out a sigh. "One of the women in my village? She used to tell her son that the stars were angels. They were making sure things weren't completely dark while the sun was gone."

"Well, I think we know the truth, right, Hannah?"

"Yup. Balls of incandescent gas." We were silent for a moment before I spoke again. "So, which one am I?"

He swiveled his head to me. "Which one are you?"

I was still looking up. "Which one of those shining stars is me?"

Michael looked up and thought it over. He then pointed to the North Star. "There. That one is you. The star for anyone who is lost and trying to find their way."

I smiled. "Yup. Stars are definitely not angels."

"Nothing personal, Hannah, but as much as I hope you'll be an angel someday, I really hope that day doesn't come for a long long time."

I let out a snort. "Don't worry. They'd never allow it. I'll never be an angel."

"You said you'd never get into Heaven, either, and you have that waiting for you."

"That's Heaven, not being an agent of God. Big difference."

"If you say so."

And we watched until the sun came up.

There are two schools of thought when viewing humans. The first school of thought is that humanity is a marvelous creation, a constantly shifting and evolving testimonial to God and his genius.

Then, there's Hannah Singer point of view.

For the most part, I like people. I mean, as hard as I fight to keep them from being sent to Hell, I must like people, QED. But that is not a constant feeling. There are times that I wonder if that whole "free will" thing might not have been such a great idea.

I can usually tell when that mindset is going to set in. Usually, it's when I have a case where the Petitioner's actions really cause a headache. I shouldn't complain. I mean, I'm a grey. I'm supposed to handle these odd cases full of contradictions, a Gordian knot of personal ethics. But that doesn't mean I enjoy it.

I've been doing this for nearly seven hundred years. I don't venture among the living on Earth very often. So, the changes the world goes through can be dramatic. I tend to sort events into either "happenings" or "history". What does it take for something to no longer be a happening and become history? I start meeting a lot of Petitioners telling me about living through it. It's this collective that makes it what it is.

Discrimination exists everywhere. Anyone who says it is learned behavior is stupid. Mankind, by its very nature, is competitive. It's part of ambition and survival. When resources (land, love, opportunity) are harder to come by, not everybody can get a slice of the pie. No one spreads it around because not much can be done with a meager portion, it has to be bigger. It starts with making sure they get their own slice, and quickly evolves into getting other's, either to make sure they never get it or because they figure it would be a waste for others to have it. After all, what are they going to do with it? So much more can be done by someone who already has momentum.

As a result, discrimination occurs. People find any reason they can to validate their behavior. Whatever makes people different is extrapolated into proof that they are not the same as them and should not be treated as such. Some will do it based psychological factors, such as economics. Class warfare is a VERY old problem, the rich thinking the poor deserve their fate and poor thinking the rich are stuck up. Others do it based on physique, such as gender. Saying women are weak or men are pig headed and it's genetics or hormones or whatever. Some will base discrimination on sociology, such as gatherings, be they social or even how they worship. People that want to discriminate will simply find any convenient reason, it doesn't matter how illogical or preposterous it is. And the easiest way is by appearance. What "race" you are.

One of the most tumultuous periods of history was America's civil rights movement that started in the mid-1950's. Everybody up here knew it was coming. America has always been racially different than the rest of the world. My native England has some absurd leaps of logic for who qualifies as "white". With everything so firmly entrenched, progress is very very slow. America, however, got culture shock from the influx of immigrants looking to make a better life. Ethnic neighborhoods sprang up to insulate themselves from others who didn't understand them. This lead to the creation of economic bases and political bases. People were able to move away from being considered second class citizens. Everyone wanted that opportunity, to be regarded as what they felt they should instead of what others said they should. Black people started demanding decent treatment.

And all Hell broke loose.

The conflict took many forms. There were lynchings, murders, putting people in jail on trumped up charges, riots...but the worst was the death of trust. So many friendships, so many bonds, so many families. They never happened and would never happen. Everyone became defensive. I remember Clarence Jones. He was the first black Celestial. No discrimination, everyone else wanted to claim their Heavenly reward, and I don't blame them. He was the first to actually volunteer to put his on hold to join our side. The first time he juniored for me, he actually said during a review, "Bet you're surprised to see a black man doing this."

"No more than you are to see a woman doing this," I shrugged.

He had noticed that very few women had ever become Celestials in the history of the courts. In fact, I was one of only three active females at the time. "Oh. So you don't have a problem?"

He got his first glimpse of the infamous Hannah Singer temper. "Do you want me to regard you as a black man, or as a Celestial Advocate?"

He blinked. "Celestial."

I shoved a handful of scrolls at his chest. "Then start asking questions that will help save this guy's soul."

It did break the ice. We became good friends after that.

It was the cusp of the New Millennium, the name people on Earth had for the dawn of the 21st Century. I'm aware of the changes on Earth because of the advocacies I do. Talking with Petitioners, I get personal accounts of how the world changes. Many don't even realize the significance of the events they are living through. It's only when you know the scope that the impact hits you. Of particular interest to me was the Civil Rights movement. Life is a struggle to extend liberty and rights to everybody, and I'm frankly surprised America didn't collapse. Trials here that hinged on discrimination quieted down towards the end of the century, with only the occasional blip to deal with. Those few cases were usually handled by others. Ethics and morals among the living were becoming murkier every day, and St. Michael wanted my efforts focused on the harder cases.

So, when Michael came up to me with a million candlepower smile and a scroll, I wasn't expecting what I got. I skimmed it quickly, then looked at

Michael. "You like this guy, don't you?"

"Yeah. Which is why I'm giving you this one. It's going to be a minefield. I mean, I love what the guy did. But I also see how there's going to be a LOT of problems."

I thought about my case load. I was almost clear, five more hearings total. "Can you stall this a little longer? I'll be able to really focus soon."

"I could probably stall this until the Trump Of Doom," Michael said. "Any ideas?"

I looked back at the scroll. "Some ideas, but nothing firm. Winning this one will take a position that the Churches can't undermine at trial. I'll not only have to sell the Tribunal on the recommended fate, but keep from doing anything the Churches can feed off of."

"Let me know when you get something."

I gave Michael a salute with the scroll and walked away.

I finished my cases and went back to my quarters. I put on very large pot of jasmine tea. I knew I was going to be drinking a lot of it as I read about Jayden Elijah Brady and how he used the Civil Rights movement to scam an entire section of Alabama for over thirty years.

Jayden Elijah Brady was pretty unremarkable for most of his life. Growing up in the South, he did what he was supposed to. He was a dedicated son, he did his service, he took over the family business. "Jeb", as everyone called him, was a good, solid citizen, just moving through life.

The problem was, no one likes just moving through life. They want to get ahead, to do something more than just go day to day. Jeb was sort of hemmed in. The social circles he moved in were all about connections, knowing somebody who knew somebody. Business and government contracts, the kind that could help him move forward, were sewn up and no one was letting them go.

It was when he was in his thirties that the Civil Rights movement exploded. Jeb was pretty apathetic. He didn't really have an opinion. He didn't care to. He knew some black people. They seemed okay to him. He knew white people. They seemed okay. That is, when they weren't giving him the "Aw, too bad" about not getting any business.

And then, one day, Jeb decided to run for Governor. He was sold on the idea of an ordinary man representing the people. However, he didn't have enough money. The other candidate for the nomination had money rolling in from his business and church connections. And while trying to campaign, listening to the crowd of white voters complain about the encroaching Civil Rights movement and how it would be the end of the American Way, inspiration struck. He started campaigning as an opponent of the Civil Rights movement. Integration? Bad. Voting rights? Bad. He didn't care, politicians broke promises all the time anyway. But people felt that he represented their interests and pledged to help him fight the scourge. They gave him money. Gobs and gobs of money.

Jeb lost. The businesses didn't want to lose their fixer, and made sure Jeb couldn't mount a credible threat. Jeb started to worry. He spent a lot of money just trying to start his campaign. If only he'd gotten all that money at the beginning, he wouldn't be looking at losing his house, his business, his life.

Another small time politician suggested Jeb pay off his debts with his campaign funds.

"But that's campaign money," Jeb said.

"Doesn't have to be," his friend explained. "As long as you pay taxes on it, it's your money to do what you want with."

And that was the light bulb moment.

Jeb became a professional candidate. Never won once. But he got plenty of money. And he would dutifully render unto Caesar what was Caesar's before living off of it. He was subtle about what he did as far as expanding his businesses or getting better amenities. He wasn't stupid. He knew full well people would realize he was duping them. Any office that was available and people were looking for a champion, he stepped up.

By now, his rhetoric was noticed by other leading lights in Alabama. He was accepted as one of the boys, getting to go to fancy functions and so on. The entire time, he wondered what would happen if the truth ever got out.

As far as the black families Jeb knew, they knew him well enough that they figured all along it was a put-on. At first, they disapproved, regarding Jeb as a political opportunist. Then they saw money that would be going to buying things to keep away from black families or efforts to chase them out being focused elsewhere, enabling them some breathing room. Jeb became a beacon for the whites and an inside joke for the blacks.

Jeb eventually was introduced to the daughter of an old Southern family. She was his age, never married, and she was smitten with the idea of this man with so much social standing possibly being interested in her. Because she saw more of the private man, she soon figured out Jeb's game. She kept her mouth shut, however. As his girlfriend (and eventual wife), she had social standing that evaded her because of her relative age. As long as she was a social focal point, she didn't care.

They soon had two kids. Jeb made sure the kids had a nice college fund and the chance to go where they wanted. Kids are sharper than adults give them credit for, and noticed Jeb's secret. To them, racism was a weakness to take advantage of. They didn't want to be taken advantage of, so they played along when convenient and took off for less oppressive vistas when they got the chance.

When a new group of politicians came of age, Jeb was kind of put aside for this group with more fire. He did, however, have more than enough and his businesses still survived, so he was comfortable. And his wife continued to work the crowd. Each of them got what they wanted.

Jeb died recently. His wife was a great cook, and he packed on pounds. Clogged arteries, his heart just about popped like a zit. Nice funeral, with people condemning him as part of the "old South" and how everyone had moved forward. Completely misrepresented his character, but let's face it, that was his fault. Now, he was in the Valley Of Death, and everyone was wondering what would happen.

I just sat there, staring at the scroll without reading it. By now, my tea had gone cold. In fact, a quarter of it had evaporated. I needed a change of scenery. I took the scroll and headed for the Blooming Meadow.

I found a nice place beside a duck pond, leaning back against a rock. I put my feet in the water and dove into the scroll again. My attention had refocused. So much so, I didn't realize I had company.

"Is this a table for one?"

My head snapped around and I saw Clarence. He had a worried look on his face. He was stuck with a bad case. I gestured next to me, and he sat crosslegged.

"Whatcha got, Clarence?"

"Guy who ran a dog fight ring," he answered in disgust. "Both sides contesting. How about you?"

I passed Jeb's scroll to him. "Con artist."

Clarence started reading it. I knew when he got to the good part, because he burst out laughing. He was laughing so hard, he fell over on his side. He lost his grip on the scroll, which promptly curled up and started rolling towards the water. I had to pounce to grab it.

In between guffaws, Clarence choked out, "White people are sooooo stupid!"

I looked at him and held out a handful of my blonde hair. "Excuse me?"

He immediately straightened up. "Present company excepted!"

I just smirked at him, then gave him the scroll to finish reading. He still had to stop and let his laughing jags subside every once in a while.

When he finally passed the scroll back, he was still laughing. "Why don't I get cases like this?"

"You're not a grey," I told him. "It takes rare skill."

"If they were all like that, I'd make sure I had it."

"Just because some cases are fun doesn't mean they all are."

He rolled his eyes. "Okay, all right, fine." He then leaned over and whispered, "Any chance I can junior this one?"

I just looked at him. "No. You can watch from the Gallery like all the other Advocates."

"I can be a help to the case. I already know who's going to lead."

"Yeah. Jeff Fairchild." Fairchild was the most senior Church and my counterpart for the opposition. Whenever one of us turned up in court, the other wasn't far behind.

"You are wrong, Jasmine Breath."

"Oh, really? Tell me something I don't know."

"James Callahan will lead."

Clarence and Callahan mixed as well as gunpowder and an open flame. Callahan was a white Southerner who died during the Civil War or War Between The States or whatever they called it. He was very adept at using Scripture as a shield. Lesser arguments bounced right off him. His nickname among the Churches was "Ol' Ironsides." We Celestials had another nickname for him. "Ol' Ironfist may junior, but he'll never lead. Fairchild will never throw anyone else against me."

"You're dealing with a Southerner who took advantage of the old boy network," Clarence said. "Callahan will want a piece of him."

"Fairchild won't allow it. It'd be a snap for me to shape Callahan's arguments as a personal vendetta with nothing to do with the case at hand. I'd have the case in the bag as soon as opening arguments finished. No, he'll junior."

Clarence looked to the side, nodding his head. "You sure I can't participate in this somehow?"

I gave Clarence a good look. "Hmmmmm. Maybe you can."

"How so?"

"You'd make a great distraction for Ol' Ironfist."

Clarence just smiled at me.

I stood up. "All right. I'll select you as a junior. But remember your duties. You are to keep Callahan busy and distracted. Whatever Fairchild uses for his arguments, he'll leave the Southern culture thing to Callahan. The main points are for me."

Clarence shot to his feet. He stood ramrod straight and slapped the edge of his right hand to his forehead. I held my right finger and thumb in the shape of an L and slapped it to my forehead. We spun around and marched our separate ways for now.

The build-up to trial was uneventful. Meeting with Jeb was pretty casual. He was a good guy, although he was nervous. After all, he technically lived his life by taking advantage of others. Whether or not they volunteered for it.

"That's the part that concerns me," I told Michael in his chambers.

I was seated in front of Michael's desk, eyes closed. It wasn't that I was that focused on the case. Michael was behind me, standing at a foosball table that hadn't been there last time I visited. He was using his will to control players on both sides. I carefully said he was playing against himself because I almost used another preposition that could have been taken a way I did not intend.

"How does it concern you?" he asked, splitting his attention between three things.

"The most obvious angle Fairchild is going to shoot for is personal responsibility. That people should not victimize others, no matter how reprehensible they are."

"Objectivism is a tough sell with angels."

"It'd still sink this case. The old, 'Just because you can, doesn't mean you should.'"

"You could always go for a lesser fate. Something easier to defend."

"No. The Churches are bringing out too much firepower. Fairchild will use any fate other than approving petition as proof that we know Jeb erred. Callahan will use his rage to overpower my reasoning. Sure loser. They wouldn't get Casting Down, but they'd still get something that puts Jeb through the wringer."

"Options?"

"Not clear yet. I still have plenty of time to request trial. I'm trying to consider everything."

"You can't take too long once petition has been filed."

"I know. I just need a golden thread, something that I can run through all my arguments. If I just argue without staying some sort of course, Fairchild will know I'm grasping at straws."

"He can use your own arguments as proof that you have no arguments."

"Yeah. He's too sharp for that. I need something really slick that he'll never get a grip on."

Suddenly, a horn blared that made me jump from the chair. I looked behind me. One of the sides in the game scored a goal. Michael had his arms raised, pumping his fists in victory and mimicking the sound of a crowd cheering. I had just opened my mouth to yell something when Michael pointed at me and said with a smile, "Language, Hannah."

I could only fume at my big brother.

Jeb's scroll indicated he was pretty sociable. But he was quiet during our consultations. I recognized the guilty look. The first thing he said to me was, "I shouldn't be going to Heaven."

"That's for the Tribunal to decide," I told him.

He was silent for a beat. "You don't really believe I deserve Heaven, do you?"

I had been reviewing another scroll looking for angles to help him. I put it down. "Let me explain something to you," I said as gently as I could. "The way the courts work is that the Churches are supposed to get what they ask for. In this case, Casting Down. You think you deserve to be Cast for what you did?"

"Well...maybe...."

"No, you don't. Okay, you didn't live a perfect life. But you didn't live in a way that deserves Hell. My job isn't to get you into Heaven, it's to keep you out of Hell."

"You're saying I might not get what I want, but I should get what I deserve?"

"You got it. The angels are wiser than us. If they feel you deserve Heaven, they'll give it to you. And you shouldn't argue with them anyway," I smiled.

He nodded. He smiled, although the guilt seemed to increase a little bit.

I worked on Jeb's defense every spare moment I had, even while waiting for other trials to start. I was leading the opposition of a lawyer who specialized in nuisance lawsuits. Usually, I look at the Tribunal of angels at trials and feel nothing but envy. Now, I just felt depressed. Angels have great senses of humor. I had no doubt they would think what Jeb did was a hoot. But that was immaterial. It wasn't that they wouldn't approve petition, they couldn't. In order for them to rule the way I wanted, I had to give them a good reason to. I had to show Jeb to them in a way that could make them....

My eyes popped. A smile appeared on my face. I slammed my fist on the tabletop and yelled, "Yes!"

I then remembered I was in the middle of a trial. Every eye was looking at me, wondering what my problem was. Camael, the presiding angel, glared at me and readied his gavel. "Care to clarify your statement, Singer?"

I made myself look contrite. I didn't want Camael to bar me from advocating right now. "I apologize for the outburst, sir."

"What was that about?"

I thought quickly. "You will see as my defense unfolds, sir."

That seemed to buy me time. I did my usual work and potted the guy, reincarnation, hard labor, he'd have to work for the rest of his life, no lawsuits. Camael didn't adjourn once the verdict was reached. He just looked at me. "That defense was what you were so excited about?"

As long as court was in session, he could bar me if I stepped out of line. He was clearly looking for one last shot. I bowed. "My apologies. I thought it was really clever."

"Don't let it happen again. Court is adjourned." He slammed the gavel and stomped out.

I raced out of the courtroom as soon as I could do so and made a beeline for Michael's chambers. We talked for a couple of minutes about my defense. When we were done, Michael put in the request for trial and I was on my way to round up one more junior.

I strode to the courtroom with a smirk on my face. I didn't want it there. There was a very real possibility that my idea wouldn't work. I was going to have to hit the Tribunal with it and redress every point Fairchild and his flunkies made within its context to make it work. At this point, the only question was who would be the presiding angel. That was the only unknown in the equation. Well, that and how it would end.

I got inside and saw the Gallery was a little busier than usual. Usual number of Advocates and stragglers watching, but a distinctly higher number of angels. Once again, they have great senses of humor. Word got around about what Jeb had done, and they not only wanted to see what would happen, but how I would make it happen.

I looked to the Celestial table. My two juniors were already there. Clarence was in the second seat from the aisle. He was my goto guy to keep Callahan in line. The other was Galileo Galilei. Galileo had a long history of sparring with the church on philosophical grounds, fighting by hook or by crook.

He was my emergency fallback, to supply me with another angle in case I really got stuck.

I got to the lead Advocate seat and smiled at them. "Got your crash helmets ready?"

Galileo smiled. "According to the Churches, I have a very thick skull, so I'm not sure I need one."

Clarence also smiled. "We're on your side. I don't think we're the ones who need the helmets."

I looked to the Church table. Fairchild and his team were already there, talking feverishly amongst themselves. I saw Callahan right away, the permanent scowl on his face a little darker than I remembered. He was really mad. Also there was David Tucker, another generic Church that Fairchild frequently drafted to junior. I smirked. Everybody at the Celestial table had approved petitions, and no one at the Church table did. I made a mental note in case I could use it later.

Eventually, my ears picked up three sets of footsteps, two heavy ones walking in perfect sync and a softer set. The Guardians were bringing the Petitioner in. I looked at my juniors and flicked my hand at them, shooing them down. By the time Jeb got to us, the Petitioner's seat was open. I gestured to it and he sat.

Jeb sat with his shoulders hunched and head down low, like he was trying not to be noticed. I took a quick look at the Church table. Ol' Ironfist looked me in the eye and gave his left palm a quick punch. The noise caught Fairchild's attention. He looked to see Callahan separate his hands and go back to the scrolls in front of him. Fairchild looked at me, and his expression said it all – can't get good help these days.

We all continued to go over our scrolls and strategies until the chimes sounded. Everyone stood and we deployed our ceremonial wings. Although our wings aren't real, they behave like they are. They aren't attached, so we can't control them or move them. But they still move with us and we can still feel some basic touch with them. I felt my right wing shift a little bit. I stole a quick look at Jeb. He was actually hiding behind my right wing, like a kid hiding behind his mom when meeting someone new.

"Down in front," I told him. He sheepishly crept out from behind it.

The door by the Tribunal box opened and the twelve angels entered. I just stood for a moment and enjoyed the view. I momentarily forgot my problems as I reveled in the integrity, strength, and grace of the Heavenly beings.

The back door opened, and the presiding angel entered. Aw, frick! It was Jegudiel! Jegudiel is the angel who guides people in positions of authority and responsibility, from kings to generals to police. Looking close, you could see where he kept the whip at his side under his robes. Jegudiel was big on people who worked hard and earned their keep. In other words, sense of humor or no, he was not going to be thrilled with Jeb. Proof came when he got up to the bench, looked at us, and his expression turned to one of distaste when his gaze drifted over the Petitioner.

Jegudiel cracked the gavel once and dropped onto his seat. It was still controlled, he was stone still as soon as he hit, no bounce. The Gallery and Tribunal sat as well. Jegudiel called out, "Who is the Petitioner?"

"The Petitioner is Jayden Elijah Brady," I called back.

"And who are his Advocates?"

"Galileo Galilei, Clarence Jones, and Hannah Singer, acting as lead."

"And who advocates for the Church?"

"David Tucker, James Callahan, and Jeff Fairchild, acting as lead," came the call from my left.

"Will the Petitioner please take the stand?"

Jeb carefully walked out, tripping on his feet under the harsh gaze of Jegudiel. He knew full well that this was going to be rough. He looked at me hopefully over his shoulder. I just nodded to him. My brain was already charting the course I needed to take.

Once Jeb was in the dock, I asked Jegudiel, "May I have a moment to consult with my juniors, please?"

He nodded. "You may."

Clarence and Galileo moved over one chair each so they were next to me. We put our heads together. I unfurled a scroll and held it in front of us so no one could see what we were saying. I got right to the point. "I'm going to need you two to really step up on this."

"Instructions?" Galileo asked.

"I need to focus on Jegudiel and nullify him. He'll lead questioning towards hammering Jeb. Fairchild is the lesser problem right now. You're going to have to take the subtler points and his juniors."

"Should I try to snipe Callahan?" Clarence asked. That meant tricking an Advocate into getting themselves thrown out of court.

"No. Fairchild doesn't like Callahan. We can use him as a disruption. Bait him, but keep him in the hunt."

They both nodded and sat at their new seats. I faced the bench.

Jegudiel said, "Your opening statements, please, Miss Singer."

I steeled myself. I took a deep breath.

It's star time.

I swept my arms out like a showman. "Welcome to the revolution! An entire group of people, relegated to secondary citizen status, began to organize and unite and stand up for liberty! No more separation! No more preferential treatment! Equality for all!

"Now, in order for there to be a revolution, there has to be a power structure to oppose. One that denies what is demanded. Not what is asked. Asking isn't a revolution, it's a movement. 'Could you please treat us equally?' Revolution happens when people are tired of asking and being told, 'No, because we say so.' Things are kept as they are for no reason, acceptable or otherwise. Opposition to the power structure takes a variety of forms. There is social pressure, through boycotts and sit-ins. There is philosophical pressure, trying to educate people and change their minds. There is political pressure, preventing people from thinking they are exempt from the law. And there is economic pressure, costing those doing wrong the only thing they value as much as power and control – money.

"Jayden Elijah Brady, or 'Jeb', as he was known, was a part of this revolution. He penalized people for their intolerance. They gave him money. Lots of it. Money that could have gone to any number of positive things, like schools or art or science. Instead, it was offered as a tool of oppression. Jeb took it and used it for a variety of things, none of which had anything to do with its intended purpose. It's no different than government fines, where people and businesses give up money that is then used for things beneficial and wasteful, all at the discretion of the collecting body.

"It was a tax on stupidity, and Jeb was the collector.

"Jeb was unfairly shut out by the system. So he exploited it. Should he have resisted? After all, people are not supposed to take advantage of each other, they are supposed to be principled. However, that is with other decent people. People that should not be taken advantage of, that you should feel guilty for exploiting. The poor. The sick. The disenfranchised. Jeb's targets were none of those things. They had everything and sought to hold on to it. The sin of greed was theirs, not Jeb's. Jeb's sin was a reaction. It was justice. His petition should be approved. Thank you."

I looked at Fairchild so I could listen to his opening statements. I had clearly gone in a direction he wasn't expecting. He was just staring at me, mouth partly agape and an unfurled scroll in his hands that he seemed to have forgotten about. After blinking his eyes a couple of times, he closed his mouth and rolled up the scroll. He held it out and dropped it to the side on the table. He pinched the bridge of his nose for a moment as he started speaking.

"This is a joke. It has to be a joke. Brady wasn't a revolutionary. He was an opportunist. That's all. Any other suggestion is laughable.

"He wasn't a revolutionary. He never sought to create change, he upheld the current system because he benefited from it financially. He wasn't a rogue like Robin Hood. Robin Hood gave his stolen goods to those who needed it. He also actively fought to end the reign of a corrupt ruler. Brady kept the money for himself and only appeared to challenge corrupt rulers. He wasn't even a prankster. What he did was funny, but ultimately mattered to no one but himself.

"He was a con artist. No more, no less. He acquired things under false pretenses, from money to his wife. Lying is a sin. Living a lie is a crime. He exploited, he deceived, he stole. None of what he received would have been given to him had his true intentions been known. He's a thief, plain and simple, one who does not accept responsibility for the situation of his own creation. He has violated every rule of God, especially helping his fellow man instead of hurting them. He should be Cast Down. Thank you."

Oh, great. Fairchild was cheating. Opening arguments are the only time you are not allowed to interrupt the speaker. He had thrown out several arguments that I would potentially make and shot them down, giving me no chance to refute him at that moment. If I didn't readdress each point during regular arguments, he could use it as proof that I didn't have an explanation or excuse for Jeb's behavior. And with no explanation or excuse, the Tribunal would never rule against the Churches.

My best option was to make Fairchild bring the fight to me. I'd never counter all his interpretations without the Tribunal's eyes glazing over. If I could really sell Jeb as a revolutionary, Fairchild would have to address my points instead of me addressing his. It would give me the momentum in the trial.

But first, I had to get past Jegudiel. Fairchild knew it, too. When he finished his statements, he just kept facing the bench instead of turning to argue with me. Jegudiel would be asking questions and doing the heavy lifting for him.

Jegudiel dove right in. "A revolutionary, Singer?"

"Yes, sir," I said with a slight bow.

"He couldn't have worked and made a living like other people do?"

"He was too busy being a revolutionary. He couldn't serve two masters."

Jegudiel actually started rubbing his temples. Congratulations, Hannah, that's a first for you. He sounded pained when he spoke. "You don't think you are misrepresenting Brady at all?"

"How else can he be represented?"

Jegudiel got quiet. Angels are allowed to ask questions and can guide things certain ways, but they cannot overtly inject their ideas into the proceedings. The baton was passed back to Fairchild. "How about lazy?"

I turned to face him. "Revolutionaries aren't lazy. It's a long, hard mission they've chosen."

"How convenient his revolution enabled him to not have to work."

"On the contrary, he worked quite hard finding people to give him money."

"Okay, he wasn't lazy. He was a very industrious thief."

The weapons Fairchild and I were using were semantics. I had to keep describing Jeb as receiving things given to him. Fairchild had to keep describing him as taking things from others. If either of us could get the other to say otherwise, even on accident, it would give us a clear advantage in the trial. "He didn't take anything that wasn't being offered."

"He took it under false pretenses. It was given to him for one reason and he used it for something completely different."

"So, you're saying he should have been discriminatory and oppressive?" Nine ball, corner pocket.

"He did tell them he would represent their wishes."

"'I'm not usually a terrible person and under other circumstances, we could probably be friends. But this is business, they sign the checks.' Oh, yeah, that's MUCH better."

Now, Fairchild started rubbing his temples. I wasn't really proving my case, but I was still preventing him from making his. Gaining momentum in this trial was becoming more and more important by the moment.

Suddenly, Fairchild straightened. Inspiration struck. "He wasn't a revolutionary. He was just underpaid."

Uh-oh. Fairchild found a weak point in the armor. He was going to attack Jeb's motives. And Jeb's life made it very easy. I started running through options in my mind, hoping to derail this train.

Galileo shot to his feet. "All revolutionaries are underpaid. If they were happy with their lots in life, they wouldn't be revolting."

I kept quiet. Galileo was a revolutionary himself, so he knew the mentality and could argue it better than me. It would also buy time to get my thoughts in order for when things shifted back to me.

Fairchild wasn't about to give up. "So revolution has nothing to do with doing the right thing, but to be bought off."

"Buying off? Or getting what they think is fair? Revolutionaries stop their campaigns once they get what they sought."

Fairchild glared at him. "Or once they are forced into submission."

Galileo gave him a mouth-full-of-teeth smile. "It still turns."

"They sure don't make revolutionaries like they used to," Fairchild responded. "Instead of sticking to their principles, they agree to a false life. One they know is wrong."

A philosophical argument. Break's over, back on the clock. I said, "Living a false life wasn't either of their choices. It was forced on both of them. They had to live false lives." Galileo sat back down.

"He could have lived a perfectly acceptable life if he had put some effort into it. He didn't have to con those people."

"He tried. He fought the system for over thirty years and he still couldn't get ahead. He wasn't entitled. He was worn out. How can you fault someone for being tired of failing?"

Fairchild was silent. In that moment, his position as a Church had fallen away. I saw the emotions in his eyes. Human concern. Compassion. Understanding. Duty or no, he didn't want to do this.

Callahan sensed the impact my point had. He shot up from his seat. "He defied God's will! God's will was for him to suffer!"

I wasn't about to let that point stand. "God doesn't want any of his children to suffer."

"Suffering is the way to Heaven! It teaches humility!"

I answered quickly. I wasn't going to give Fairchild a chance to silence Ol' Ironfist until I got a piece of him first. "Suffering teaches resentment!"

"Serving others is our first duty! Being a servant is a noble endeavor!"

I coated my words with sarcasm. "Which is why so many volunteer to do it!"

"If being a servant or slave is so horrible, why does the Bible encourage slaves to be happy and tell masters how to handle them?!?"

I immediately looked at Jegudiel. "Move to strike servant, slave, and master arguments from consideration!"

"On what grounds?!?" said Ol' Ironfist.

"The precedent has been established that slavery has no place in the modern world!" I jabbed my finger at my chest for emphasis. "I established that precedent! They have been rejected for almost a century and a half and should not be introduced now!"

"Hannah Singer should be removed from this case!" he returned.

"On what grounds?!?" I shot back.

"She is trying to enforce her values on an established culture and social order with no consideration of history and situation! She has no right to tell others how to live!"

"I get kicked, you get kicked, too! Your whole argument is telling Jeb how he should have lived!"

"I'm telling him how he should have lived within the existing order, I'm not rewriting that order!"

Clarence shot up. "Even if the order is heartless and wrong?!?"

The Guardians reached for their swords. Fairchild and I looked worriedly at each other. We were standing on deck with two loose cannons rolling around. Even at our most confrontational, our goal was trying to do what was right, not get into an ego-driven hissing match. We both turned to our juniors and barked, "Shut up now!"

Ol' Ironfist looked at Clarence and said two words, "Uppity" and a derogatory noun.

Clarence said two words, a four letter verb and the pronoun, "You."

Jegudiel slammed the gavel so hard, I was surprised the walls were still standing. "Both of you are barred from advocating until further notice! Guardians, get them out of my courtroom!"

Suddenly, I had an idea. I looked at Jegudiel and said, "Move for mercy, sir."

Jegudiel glared at me. "You disagree that your junior was out of line?"

"Not for Clarence, sir." I jerked my thumb at Callahan. "Him. Please allow him to stay."

Everyone was shocked. Except Fairchild. He knew a set-up when he heard one. "Mercy should be denied!"

I just smiled innocently at Jegudiel.

Jegudiel eyed me carefully, then declared, "Mercy granted, Callahan may stay." He hit the gavel, and the Guardians came to escort Clarence out. Clarence looked at me as he left, guilt evident in his eyes. I would deal with him later. Right now, I had a trial to win.

I decided to take advantage of everyone's uncertainty after the eruption. "Move for closing arguments," I said.

Fairchild simply nodded. "I concur." He thought for a few moments, then started. "Brady is guilty. We all know it. He lived a false life. He took what didn't belong to him. He lied. He swindled. He has done nothing to warrant a Heavenly reward. Does it matter what else might have been done with the money? With the effort? He didn't teach what people did was wrong. He didn't even try to set things right. He just did his thing, and that was it.

"It is hard for a rich man to enter the kingdom of Heaven. It is even harder for a rich man who never earned what he received. He wanted money. He got money. He wanted prestige. He got prestige. He did nothing to prove he deserved these things. He lied by omission. He has proven his view of humanity is poor. Otherwise, he wouldn't have done the things he did. Man is to be guided and educated, not exploited. He should be Cast Down. Thank you."

I launched into my arguments as soon as he was done. "The question we have to answer is, how could Jeb have done this? What can possibly justify what he did? How can we possibly understand the path he chose?"

I pointed to Callahan. "THAT is the reason why Jeb did what he did. Callahan is from Jeb's area. Even if we just restrict ourselves to this trial, we see the mentality of the time and place. People get what they deserve. Notice how its always those who get the benefits who says everything is deserved, it's never those who lose it to them. We have seen the contempt he feels for people with nothing making them different other than the amount of melanin in their skin. We are in the Afterlife, in the Celestial Courts, and he STILL lets his racism occur. He can't even keep it quiet in the presence of Heavenly hosts."

The Tribunal examined Callahan like he was a bug under a microscope, a pest that caused a horrible infestation. I continued, "These are the people Jeb exploited. These were not people who didn't understand. They saw no reason to understand. They saw no reason to change their views. The first step of any war effort is to dehumanize the enemy. Racism is the easiest tool to achieve this end. Jeb's behavior didn't dehumanize anyone. They had already done that to themselves. In order for there to be a crime against humanity, there has to be humanity. There was none. He does not deserve to burn because other people hated. His petition should be granted. Thank you."

Jegudiel looked to the Tribunal. "You have heard the Advocates for Jayden Elijah Brady state their recommended fates. You may now make your decision. You wish to confer?"

The angels in the Tribunal whispered amongst themselves for a few moments. Then the lead Tribunal stood. "Yes."

Jegudiel looked out at us. "Court is in recess." He banged the gavel, and everyone stood as the angels walked out.

Once the doors closed, I sat in my seat and sagged. I hated this feeling. I knew it. Knew as sure as I knew the sun would rise. Jeb would never get into Heaven. The question was, what would he be doing instead?

Jeb came out of the dock and tried engaging me in conversation. Galileo did most of the talking. He knew how these things affected me. I could take judgments, but when there was a delay like this, it just got to me. Admittedly, I knew the case was almost guaranteed to fail. I mean, Jeb was a con artist. But that didn't make it any better. And I honestly thought I could have pulled it off.

Fairchild was waiting patiently. The only thing I could hope for was that I somehow kept Jeb out of Hell. Anything else, he'd get another shot at Heaven later on. I just focused within my mind and hoped.

Times like that, the only sound that will penetrate my consciousness is the chimes that reconvene court. I heard them and stood with everyone. Jeb went back to the dock. The doors opened and the angels came in. Jegudiel sat at the bench and tapped the gavel. He looked to the Tribunal. "Have you reached a judgment you are all in agreement on?"

The lead Tribunal stood. "We have."

"And what is your judgment?"

I took a deep breath.

"Petition for entry into Heaven is suspended."

My eyes flew open, and my breath came out as a sigh of relief. There were three ways to approve petition. Simply granting it sent the soul to Heaven. Pending meant the soul had to do something like repent or some other straightforward act. Suspended meant the soul would be assigned some task and would be admitted to Heaven whenever they completed it.

"What are the terms of the suspension?" Jegudiel asked.

"Petitioner is to be sent to Earth as an agent," the lead Tribunal said. Jeb would be given a physical form so he could interact with the living instead of being reborn. "He is to work for an anti-discrimination group. His task is to raise funds for them. When he has acquired twice as much for them as he did for himself when he was alive, the suspension will be lifted."

Jegudiel looked a little relieved. He said, "So be it. Court is adjourned." He tapped the gavel, and everyone stood as the angels filed out.

We willed our wings away and I watched the Guardians walk over to the dock to escort Jeb to the Petitioner's exit. As the Guardians stood, he started talking to them and pointed to me. He had something to say to me.

The Guardians brought him up to me. He was smiling. A genuine smile. I felt terrible. I mean, his suspension was a breeze. He'd be on his way to Heaven before he knew it. But I'm not supposed to give the trials my best. I'm supposed to win. "I'm sorry," I told him.

"Don't be," he said, sounding a lot happier than I'd heard him since he got to the Afterlife. "To tell you the truth, I don't think I deserve Heaven just yet. I mean, I was a con artist. Here's my chance to earn my place."

It took the sting off. We shook hands and he walked to the Petitioner's exit.

Jeb didn't take long to satisfy the conditions of his suspension. The terms of his suspension were vague, so he could have easily picked some big name group in a major city and been done in about a week. Instead, he chose an obscure rights group and threw himself into his work. In fact, he raised twice the amount of money he was supposed to. He finally decided he'd done enough and forgave himself, and he was on his way. A man of rare integrity. He definitely deserved Heaven.

Clarence, on the other hand, was avoiding me for a while because of the scene in the courtroom. I intercepted him coming out of Jegudiel's court one day. He had apologized and was given a penance to perform. He'd be able to advocate again once he finished it. Clarence had just opened the doors when he saw me and stopped dead.

"Come on, Clarence," I told him. "You know you don't have to be afraid of me."

He just looked at me.

"Okay, be afraid of me right now. Consider it part of your penance."

He walked with me and we hashed things out a little bit. We were good after that.

I then walked back to Michael's chambers. I knocked lightly on the door and he told me to come in. I entered and saw Michael was alone, going over petitions. I closed the door and leaned against it.

Michael smiled at me. He stood up and went to the two high back chairs in front of his desk. As he retrieved the whoopee cushions from them, he asked me, "What bringest thine furrowed brow to mine office?"

Thanks, big brother. I went over to one of the chairs. "Is there any hope?"

"What do you mean by that?" he asked, sitting at the same time I did in the other high back chair.

"You know, I've seen so many souls over the centuries, and it seems like Earth is getting better. People are caring and loving and becoming more aware. And then you run into things that remind you they haven't come so far after all."

"The flaws of humanity disappoint you," Michael said.

"Yes."

"It's the whole reason for life, Hannah. To get those impulses and behaviors under control and eliminated so they can get into Heaven. Heaven's more important than Earth. You spend a lifetime on Earth. You spend eternity in Heaven."

"It's just…some people aren't ready even after that lifetime. They don't really progress, do they?"

"Everybody's ready when they are ready," Michael told me. "Everybody gets there in their own time. Some like you get an early jump. And for the rest? Well, that's what we're here for."

I just leaned back, and the two of us became lost in our own thoughts for a while.

CUNNING STUNTS

You will be forgiven if you skip this particular reminiscence.

Let me explain something about death. A lot of people are afraid to make jokes about death. Or to look at the lighter side of it. And there's a reason for that. Death is big. Scary. Merciless. It strikes without warning. All your hopes, all your goals, all your dreams, everything you've done in life? Over.

It is the transition that makes death so scary. But once you're on the other side of it, it's not so bad. You can always tell the rookies up here because they still hype when you make light of death. St. Michael and I were making jokes one day in the presence of a newly-minted Celestial Advocate name Clark Horvis who hadn't been dead for very long.

"What case do you have, Hannah?" Michael asked me.

"The late Neil Campbell."

"'Late?' Oh, good. His family gets their next Neil Campbell free. How did he die?"

"Boating accident. Fell overboard."

"Drowned, huh?"

"I'm filing it under 'drank himself to death.'"

Clark gasped at that point. Michael and I just looked at each other and said in unison, "Tenderfoot." We then went back to our banter.

We're not morbid up here.

Really.

Swear to God.

It's just that, after a while, death loses its intimidation. It's something that simply happened to you. After about a century, it becomes just another piece of data about your life. And when you've been dead for almost seven hundred years like I have, it can become a source of real fun.

Clark was still getting the hang of things up here. The proximity of his life was still close. So Michael took me aside and told me to take him down to Earth for some shore leave.

"Why me?" I asked.

"Your case load is lightening up, Hannah. Besides, you have the best chance of enjoying whatever he wants to do."

He had a point. There were a lot of things that weren't my cup of tea. For example, country music or American football. But when you're there, you can't help it. You start feeding off the crowd. Everybody is having a great time, and you start having a great time. What the event is doesn't give it value, the people do. I mean, I still have a ten-gallon hat and a football helmet I'm not entirely sure what to do with. This isn't to say I always enjoy the crowd having a good time. Michael, for some unknown reason, enjoys roller derby. I couldn't wait for that one to be over with.

So I went to talk with Clark. A little time back on Earth got his interest right away. When people make their first return to Earth, the places they pick fall into one of two categories. Some will pick someplace they never could have visited in their lives, like cities in other countries. Others will pick someplace that they would have gone to, reliving old times, if you will. I'm pretty good at guessing who will pick what. I figured Clark would fall into the latter group.

"What day is it on Earth?" he asked.

"Thursday. I think. Maybe," I told him.

"No, I mean the date."

I thought for a second. The Afterlife has no real concept of time, so I honestly didn't know the answer. I knew it was around mid-July, but I couldn't be any more precise than that. I held up my hand, one finger extended. A putto, Mary, flew up. "Yes, Miss Singer. How may I assist you?"

"What is the date on Earth right now?"

She told me. Clark's eyes shot open. "We can still see it!"

"Thank you, Mary," I said, sending the childlike angel speeding away. "We can still see what?"

"The Mid-Iowa Stunt Spectacular!" Clark's shoulders were actually bouncing a little bit, like a kid talking about an upcoming Christmas. "I went to it every year when I was alive! It's this weekend!"

And so, a short time later, Clark and I materialized outside a stadium. I declared, "Well, here we are in Iowa, a celebration of corn and internal combustion."

Clark was blinking his eyes repeatedly. He hadn't become completely physical, so he was seeing the world with a mixture of his regular Earthly senses and his spiritual ones. I gave him a quick crash course, and we both became physical. We had already acquired tickets and some cash. He bolted for the entrance as I walked behind him.

The stunt spectacular wasn't exactly a stunt show. It was vehicular mayhem. Michael would have loved it. The first event was a demolition derby. I quickly shifted to my spiritual senses and saw how reinforced the vehicles were. The drivers were in no danger, other than getting shaken up like a can of house paint. It was actually pretty fun to watch, although, if anyone actually won anything, I couldn't tell.

There were then some other stunts, little ones at the edges. The middle of the field was being prepared for what Clark had come to see -- Thomas "The Hawk" Fawkes, a daredevil in the Evel Knievel mode. They were setting up ramps and pyrotechnics and school buses and all kinds of things, like an obstacle course you went over instead of through. I did a quick spiritual view. It was definitely doable, but it would be tricky. I took a quick look at Fawkes, standing in a black T-shirt and jeans and checking over the set-up. He was scared. That was normal. But he was also focused and steady. He knew exactly what to do and how to do it. He could very well pull it off.

Finally, the big moment arrived. Fawkes had changed into his stunt costume, white with a stars and stripes cape that hung just above his belt. Good.

154

Less likely to catch on something. The crowd went wild, anxious to see this motocross race with steel and flame. Fawkes took a couple of laps around, carrying an American flag and whipping the crowd up even more. I'm not the kind to cheer and do other crowd things, and even I was on my feet, getting into it.

Fawkes finally went to the elevator that would lift him to the start of the run as the announcer described what was going to happen. The start was on a raised platform. Halfway down was a loop. Fawkes was going to shoot through the loop, the momentum carrying him through and boosting his speed to the jump ramp over a string of school buses. He'd land on the far ramp and hit another ramp, angled to shoot him almost straight up vertically. Gravity would cancel his momentum, and he would land perfectly on the platform. Each part he went through would be accompanied by an explosion of fireworks.

The run was mathematically precise. There was no room for error. I took another look at Fawkes. He was keeping it together, steady as a rock. The guy had guts. I couldn't help but admire him.

The signal was given. Everything was set, all that was needed was for Fawkes to go. Fawkes revved the engine a few times, then kicked it into gear. He sped down the ramp like a bat out of Hell (no, I'm not be hyperbolic). He flew through the loop, fireworks and explosions around him. He didn't falter. I could sense a sort of tunnel vision on his part, where all he could see was the line he had to ride to make it through. Another explosion of color and sparks erupted when he hit the jump ramp. He arced through the air over the buses. It was just amazing to watch. He landed on the far ramp, another burst of pyrotechnics greeting him. He rode fiercely through it, hitting the last ramp. It worked exactly as it was supposed to, slowing him down while moving him forward just enough to jump onto the platform. He went off the lip, landing expertly on his back tire, braked, and killed the engine. As his fists shot into the air in victory, the biggest pyrotechnic display went off.

And that was when I gasped.

While everyone was paying attention to other things, additional fireworks had been added for a big finish. The heat and shock was too great. Part of the platform bent. Fawkes spilled off his bike, grabbing onto the railing for dear life. The bike slid off the side instead of down the ramp, hitting another bank of pyrotechnics. The gas tank blew. All the other fireworks were out of control, blowing up and imploding the platform. It dropped, taking Fawkes with it.

The crowd had stopped cheering. They knew this wasn't part of the show. A riot of red, orange, and yellow rose up as the collapsing platform hit the ground. I knew Clark had switched to his spiritual senses because he gasped when he saw what I did. No one else in the stadium noticed the faint wisp of blue that rose out of the flames, like a ribbon of silk drifting up instead of falling down.

A departing soul.

Fawkes' departing soul.

I shifted to my spiritual voice, something that living beings would not be able to hear, but Clark would hear just fine. "Doesn't he leave anything for the second show?"

Clark just looked at me, too stunned to say anything.

I ignored his reaction. "Time to go. Now."

He didn't move.

I rolled my eyes. "What are you waiting for?!? The encore?!? Let's go!"

Clark snapped out of it. Everyone was so focused, clinging to the unrealistic hope that Fawkes somehow survived, they didn't notice the man and woman in the audience that simply disappeared without a trace.

We made it back to the Afterlife. I knew it would still take time for Fawkes to drift up into the Valley Of Death. I held up my hands above my head, only the index finger on each extended. I then crossed them in an "X" above my head. Immediately, a group of Guardians appeared. I instructed them to locate Fawkes. Michael came up. He heard the hubbub and knew what was happening. He stood politely aside, smiling, as I dispatched the patrol. With them on their way, it was now Michael, Clark, and me.

Michael was silent for a beat, then asked, "So how was the show?"

I gave him a thumbs up. "It was killer."

"Really? I thought he died on stage."

"Nah. He really brought the house down. Or a significant portion of it, anyway."

"WHAT IS WRONG WITH YOU?!?" Clark screamed at us, catching us both by surprise. "A man has died!"

Michael slapped his hands to his cheeks. "My God! That's never happened before!"

"Shouldn't we be a little more reverential?"

"Why?"

"His life is over!"

"Everyone's life ends," Michael said. "There are far more tragic deaths, deaths with far more impact on the world, and his death is literally one in a million. He lived a good life, he's on his way to Heaven, his family is working through their grief, and frankly, that's all I'm really concerned about."

"It's just...it's just...."

Clark sulked off. Michael and I just looked at each other. We knew what he meant. Life is precious. It's the whole point. People sometimes wonder what the point of life is, given all the hate and anger and stupidity and suffering and other bad traits of humanity. It's to actually live. To experience things you can't as a spirit. Otherwise, there'd be no point, spirits would simply be created directly in Heaven instead of being born on Earth. It's also why there is so much focus on the Afterlife instead of life -- life is temporary, fate is eternal.

A Guardian zipped up to Michael and me. "We found him. We let him know what's happening, he's getting an escort to the clerks' office. He'll be petitioning soon."

A sudden thought hit me. "No! Don't let him petition!"

The Guardian looked at me in shock. Michael was staring straight at me, like he was trying to see the thoughts inside my head. "If he doesn't petition, he can't stay at the Interim," the Guardian said. The Interim was where Petitioners stayed while waiting to hear what would happen.

I looked at Michael. "Can he stay at the Archives?"

Michael nodded. "I'll make the arrangements." He looked at the Guardian. "Please bring Fawkes to my chambers and wait for me there."

The Guardian bowed and took off. Michael looked back at me. "What are you going to need for this little scheme of yours?"

"Fawkes' scroll. The Churches don't even know to look for it yet."

With the speed of angels, Michael vanished, then returned with the scroll. He held it out to me triumphantly. "Got ya covered."

"Thanks. I'll talk to you in a bit, I just want to clarify my thoughts." Michael nodded as we went our separate ways. I had to do a lot of planning, and I needed all the time I could get.

One of the ways people cope with the hard times, bad luck, or when life is more sorrow than happiness, is to think that God has a plan. It provides comfort, because no matter how bad things get, they figure it's supposed to happen. Some react by figuring they did something to deserve what is happening to them, other react by figuring whatever is happening is only temporary and will soon be gone so the plan can get back on track. The first philosophy offends me because it says God likes to hurt people. I know Him. He doesn't like seeing His children suffer, and He certainly doesn't like being the one to make them suffer.

So this idea developed that people suffer because they deserve it. And because some souls do get born into roles that they either are assigned to or volunteer for, there's a corollary philosophy, that those that are suffering asked for it. These philosophies are not necessarily mutually inclusive, like a homeless person who is supposedly there to remind others that they should be considerate of their fellow man. This paints an ugly picture of God, and a worse one of the viewer. The idea that everything exists in the world in relation to them is an ego trip. No one goes to Earth for a lifetime of pain, frustration, and suffering. That's not even handed down as a fate at trial. It's not like people want to not succeed. That's not noble suffering, that's psychosis.

The whole idea of predestination and being born to suffer has always been around, especially during the Old Testament days, but it took on a new life about the time of the Protestant Reformation. The Catholic Church, the largest Christian body of the time, was being seen as too casual and lenient. So you had people dragging things back to the hard lines of the Old Testament days and the Pharisees that Jesus fought, when strict adherence instead of mercy and understanding were the orders of the day. It's bad enough to think you're holier than thou, but it's worse when you try to actually quantify and prove it.

The Catholics, seeing their followers leaving, started adapting its stances to be equally stringent (I had never seen St. Thomas Aquinas genuinely angry before). You were to work hard for the glory of God, you weren't supposed to live for yourself at all. This continues to the current day with certain professions. Church officials will view certain occupations as more leisure than actual work. Things like designing toys. Or acting in movies. Or being a daredevil stuntman.

I have to deal with these cases frequently, so I know them inside and out. All you have to do is establish that leisure is not a sin, and that's actually pretty easy to do. But there's a wrinkle to consider. Jeff Fairchild, the lead Church, had a special argument cooked up for times like these. It combined too much leisure, not producing anything worthwhile, with Wanton Disregard, intentionally putting yourself in harm's way. Wanton Disregard doesn't get used often. For example, anyone who tried to argue it for soldiers or police officers or firemen would get laughed out of court. Selfless sacrifice, it's a key component of Noble Death. Except in rare cases, Noble Death means automatic entry into Heaven. But when the person isn't doing it for that reason, like, say, a frat boy belly flopping into a kiddie pool from the roof of the frat house and something goes wrong, Wanton Disregard comes into play. It's a nice way of saying, "This person was stupid and got what they deserved."

Fairchild liked to trot it out. He was successful with it for a while. Then he tried it against me in a case I was leading. It was the first time I'd heard it, and I promptly demolished it. Any time it looked like he was going to use it, I was made defender. I had been trying for decades to establish a precedent that would prevent Fairchild's one-two punch from being a valid stance, but I had never gotten any closer. Until now. Fawkes' death could be the opportunity I was looking for.

Michael and I marched to his chambers. Clark sort of fell in with us. Along the way, we picked up Harold "Smack" Kowalski. Smack had been a sportswriter on Earth for fifty years when he died. Astute, insightful, and funny, the things that made him so popular in the newspapers served him well as a Celestial. And his fedora made him look quite dapper. I had never really heard Smack crack any jokes about death, so I had no way of knowing how he would react. I had my suspicious, but I didn't actually know.

Turns out I was right. We entered Michael's chambers, where Fawkes was sitting and a Guardian was standing by. Former chain smoker Smack stuck his pen in the corner of his mouth, lifted his hat from his head in salute, and said, "Congratulations on finally quitting smoking."

Fawkes smiled. "Yeah. It feels like a weight has been lifted from my shoulders. And my chest. And my arms. And my...."

Clark gasped.

Fawkes looked at Clark innocently. "What? I'm not supposed to make those kinds of jokes?"

Smack dropped his hat back on his head. "Too hip for the room. Save

158

them for the roast."

I spoke up. "Try singing torch songs instead."

Clark looked at Michael. "I don't suppose you have anything to add."

"They haven't tagged me yet," Michael shrugged.

Clark closed his eyes and muttered, "If you can't beat 'em, join 'em." He opened them and said, "Well, you gotta kill yourself to make it in show biz, so you're halfway there."

Fawkes jumped out of the chair and strode up to Clark, slapping him on the back when he got close enough. "That's more like it!"

The Guardian was dismissed to give us a little more room. Michael took his seat behind the desk, I stood next to it on his right. Fawkes went back to his original chair, Clark took the other, and Smack stood in between them.

"So, mind if I ask what the delay is?" Fawkes asked. "I mean, I lived a good life. I didn't rip anybody off, I went to church, I made people happy...."

"Well, except for your last performance," Smack opined. He puffed on his pen like George Burns puffed on his cigar.

I laid out the plan and what I was up to. I wanted it in chambers because Michael would be integral to the plan, too. Michael thought it was a great idea. Fawkes was excited. Smack couldn't wait, and Clark simply rolled his eyes, but he was still smiling. "You sure this will work, Hannah?" he asked.

"We do this right, you bet. Michael? You have any place Fawkes can stay yet?"

Michael looked at me innocently. "You don't think he should stay in here?"

Smack's jaw dropped and the pen fell out of his mouth.

Fawkes looked insulted. "I'm not going to do anything to an angel's stuff!"

"It's not you we don't trust, it's Michael," I explained.

"Why wouldn't I be able to trust an angel?" Fawkes asked.

I arched my eyebrows. "Fawkes? Please stand up and check out your back."

Fawkes stood up. He craned his neck, and thought he saw something. He reached behind him and pulled off a piece of paper that had been hung off his back with tape. The paper had two words -- "bed wetter."

Fawkes smirked at Michael. "Very funny."

Michael smiled back. "No, that's just amusing. THIS is funny." And Michael stood, his hands stretching out a pair of men's briefs.

Fawkes' eyes flew open and his hands immediately covered his crotch. He finally said, "You are GOOD!"

Michael aimed the briefs and released the one end, sending them flying across the room.

Fawkes sat back down. "Well, when I'm away from home, I AM used to having my own trailer."

"Riders?" Michael asked.

"Minifridge, for starters."

"Done, and done. What do you stock it with?"

"Regular iced tea in a whiskey bottle."

Clark looked at him. "That isn't whiskey I watched you drink?"

Fawkes looked at him. "Alcohol before a stunt show? That's a good way to get yourself killed."

Clark started laughing. Fawkes started laughing, choking out, "I didn't mean it like that!"

Smack started laughing.

Michael and I started laughing.

And it was a while before we finally stopped.

Everything was set up as well as could be. Now, I just needed Fairchild to jump in. I gathered a bunch of scrolls for review and headed for the Water Gardens. I didn't pick my usual spot. It's secluded. I went to a higher traffic area and sat on the ground, leaning against a stone bench. I wanted plenty of others to be able to overhear my discussion with Fairchild. It would help keep Collusion charges at bay.

Collusion is the greatest crime that can be committed in the Celestial Courts. Cutting a deal with anyone for any reason at any time is unforgivable and gets you automatically Cast Down. We don't even want to be accused of it. Advocates who are rather adversarial go out of their way to make sure they are in the clear. And given that I was basically trying to manipulate Fairchild, I wanted to be very careful.

I had been there for a while when I heard Fairchild's footsteps approach. I rolled the scroll up and had it retied when he spotted me. He looked annoyed. Good start.

Fairchild spoke with his usual imperiousness. "Let me guess, you aren't going to contest Fawkes' petition?"

"We aren't planning on it, no," I smiled.

"You've been lucky so far, Singer. But I can make Wanton Disregard stick this time."

"You're sure of that, are you?"

"Yes. He should have known how dangerous what he was doing was."

"He did. He wore a helmet, didn't he?"

Fairchild drooped his head and pinched the bridge of his nose. I pulled out another scroll and unrolled it. As I read, I said, "There you go, taking death seriously again."

Fairchild sounded pained. "You should take death seriously."

"And where in my job description does it say that?"

"Fawkes' family is taking it seriously. They're trying to find a place to spread his ashes. They had him cremated."

"Well, Fawkes did give them a head start on that."

"Will you knock it off?!? Jokes like that are in poor taste! It's bad enough Fawkes did those stupid stunts and acted like a...like a...." His voice trailed off.

"Flaming idiot?" I offered.

"Burn!" Fairchild screamed at me.

"Didn't you just say jokes like that were in bad taste?"

Fairchild was silent for a beat. He then screamed unintelligibly at me and stormed away.

It was all going according to my master plan.

Ah, the corrupting influence of leisure. Even Churches that believe in the "all work and no play" philosophy have downtime. Eternity does get dull after a while.

There are a variety of things for those who work the Celestial Courts to enjoy when they finally get some breathing room. Given the sheer number of angels, there are choirs all over. Guardians practice their combat skills. Some people play music or put on plays. And, of course, there's my favorite place, the library. There are plenty of other things, and they all have one thing in common – they are dignified ways to kill time.

So, when Fawkes decided to cut loose, the Churches weren't really expecting what they got.

In the Afterlife, you are pretty much impervious to damage. The laws of physics and limitations on what the body can do are also different. For someone like Fawkes, who pushed his body to its limits every day, this was a whole new world to explore. And he couldn't wait to get started.

Fairchild was walking through the Campus, the area where the Churches resided, when he heard a commotion. It came from the border between the Campus and the Archives. He stalked over, trying to figure out what was going on.

When he arrived, he saw several Advocates from both sides standing next to a Celestial Residence. It's a large building, eight stories tall with a decorative band where the sixth floor is (no one wants to stay there). Everyone was chanting, "Jump! Jump! Jump!"

Suddenly, Fawkes sailed over the edge at the top of the building, bungee cords around his ankles and trailing behind him. He fell gracefully through the air as the cords started to tense. However, he misjudged the length. Sploot! His head went straight into the flower bed dirt like a lawn dart, burying him up to his shoulders right next to where I was leaning against the wall and watching. It was enough to support his weight. His arms and legs went a little limp, like he wasn't entirely sure what to do at this point.

I started buffing my nails on my robe. "And the British judge gives him a three. Didn't stick the landing right."

All the other Advocates were hooting and laughing at this. Fairchild realized that his Churches, who he worked hard to shepherd and mould, were getting some very questionable ideas. He looked at me, and saw me grabbing one of Fawkes' legs. "Uh, Fairchild? Little help?"

Fairchild stomped up and stood across from me, grabbing the other leg. Then he froze. His hands flew off the leg like it was covered with thorns. He

161

screamed, "WHAT AM I DOING?!?"

"I hope you didn't think you were going to make a wish," I told him.

"Whose bright idea was this?!?"

Fairchild was focused on me. He didn't realize Michael was bungee jumping at that moment. He drifted right behind Fairchild, licked his own index fingers, then jammed them in Fairchild's ear holes. Fairchild let out a very unmanly shriek and reacted like he had a live octopus in his underwear. By then, Michael was on his way back up.

By now, Fawkes had pulled himself out of the dirt. He was sitting on the ground, smiling like a Buddha. Fairchild glared at the crowd. "Back to your quarters!" he bellowed.

The Churches slinked off, casting occasional glances at the building as they went. Fairchild's expression said it all – they were thinking of trying to bungee jump off the building, too.

Fairchild looked up the side of the building. Michael was simply hanging there, back to the wall, upside down, and about halfway up. Fairchild snarled, "You aren't acting like an angel."

Michael willed his wings to appear. He wrapped them around himself like a bat and started saying, "Blah blah blah."

Fairchild stalked off, clearly trying to figure out how to put the toothpaste back in the tube where his Churches were concerned. Once he was gone, I looked to Fawkes and Michael. "Okay. Time for Phase Two. Fawkes? Let's file your petition and get you repented."

Michael extended his wings and started flying, apparently forgetting he still had the bungee cords attached to his ankles. Due to his strength, he got pretty far when the cords snapped back, hauling Michael with them. He smashed face first against the side of the building. He just hung there, shaking his head and laughing at his situation.

Suddenly, from out of nowhere, Metatron appeared. Metatron is almost Michael's equal in every way except sense of humor – Michael is a clown, Metatron is dead serious. Metatron was standing a distance away with one arched eyebrow, looking at Michael. He vanished, then reappeared holding an easel, a canvas, and a brush. He quickly set up the easel and the canvas. Staring at Michael, he focused and touched the brush to the canvas. A vibrant image of Michael hanging from the cords as Fawkes looked on in confusion and I fought to keep from laughing appeared. Metatron held the canvas so Fawkes and I could see it, and intoned, "A thing of beauty and a joy forever." Then he vanished, taking his art supplies with him.

Michael twisted around and yelled, "Likeness rights! I get a cut of the sales!"

Everything had to move quickly at this point. Fawkes filed his petition and went to repent. Michael entered "no contest" as soon as it came to him. However, he didn't ask for a trial. Just as I instructed him.

I was marching along past one of the gardens. I knew right where

Fairchild was, I had asked a putto to locate him. As I walked by, whistling a happy tune, Fairchild looked up from his Bible and saw me. I waved cheerily to him. He closed his book a little too harshly, but didn't seem to notice or care.

He stalked up to me. "So, where's your buddy?"

"Fawkes or Michael?"

"Yes."

"They're over on the pitch, blowing off some steam."

"Why would they need to blow off steam?"

"Fawkes petitioned. I'm his defender. I'm trying to come up with a winning defense. Fawkes is a bit jumpy, so Michael had a suggestion for some fun."

Fairchild's eyes flew open. The sentence, "Michael had a suggestion for some fun," doesn't usually bode well.

Fairchild ran faster than I'd ever known him to. I was actually having trouble keeping up with him. He made it to the pitch and just froze.

The pitch had originally been set up for a bocce tournament. However, everything was moved aside. Michael and Fawkes were on opposite sides of the field. Each sat on a dirt bike. One hand revved the engine, the other hand held a lance with a boxing glove on the far end. Michael was dressed like Fawkes in jeans and a T-shirt, presumably to keep his robes from getting caught in the dirt bike's machinery. Fawkes had a baseball catcher's mask as a face guard, Michael was wearing an upside down fishbowl. For one brief moment, I wondered if Michael had finally gone over the edge.

Smack walked calmly out between the two jousters, pen in his mouth. He stood between them and took the pen out of his mouth, dropping it on the ground and grinding it with his foot. He lifted his fedora off his head. He held it out by the top, ready to drop it, when his head quirked to the side. He looked at the two mighty warriors, and changed his grip on the fedora so he was holding it by the brim. He tossed it up in the air and ran away from Ground Zero as fast as his seventy-five year old legs would carry him.

The fedora hit the ground, and the engines roared to life. The two bold and stupid men hurtled towards each other, but somehow, things were happening in slow motion. I knew what would happen, but I couldn't stop watching. Fawkes' lance hit the solid mountain of man that is Michael and splintered into pieces. Meanwhile, Michael's caught Fawkes square in his rib cage and angled up. The bike went one way, Fawkes went the other, up and back. Michael hoisted his lance, and soon he had Fawkes balanced perfectly on top. Michael started riding around, holding his lance like a banner. This went on for a few moments, then Michael gunned the engine. He raced off the pitch, dust trailing in his wake.

I watched as Smack walked out to recover his precious hat. As he dusted it off, Fairchild intruded on my thoughts. "Where is Michael going?"

"I don't know," I thought absently. "I mean, that's the path you take if you want to go to...."

Fairchild and I looked at each other and said in unison, "The Water

Gardens!"

We streaked to the Water Gardens, eventually hearing and following the sound of Michael's idling engine. Michael had done a physics experiment, using the momentum of the bike to launch Fawkes into the air. Fawkes traveled and landed dead center in one of the water pools, fish and ducks scattering. When we arrived, Fawkes was clambering out of the water and stalking up to Michael, a look of sheer disbelief in his eyes. He got up to Michael, looked him in the eyes, and said, "You really think I can do that to you?"

"Aw, come on! At least, give it a try!"

I just blinked. After all, I did ask for this.

Fairchild's outrage had been replaced with a stunned expression. "How exactly did you get internal combustion vehicles up here?"

Michael smiled. "Angelic privilege," he said. "I brought quite a few bikes up, if you want to try it."

Fairchild's mouth moved, but I could barely hear his voice say, "Quite a few?"

Fairchild ran off, heading back to the pitch. I gave chase. As we got closer, we heard several dirt bike engines going. Sure enough, several were holding jousting tournaments. Including several Churches. Thankfully, they were off duty. Physically attacking an on-duty officer of the court is grounds to automatically Cast Down.

Fairchild went to the middle of the pitch, waving like a madman to get everyone's attention. It was only after everyone had jousted and knocked off another rider, ending the match, that everyone looked. I guess they found jousting each other more interesting than Fairchild. I can certainly understand that.

"Get off those bikes now! What is wrong with you?!?"

I stepped up. "Yeah! You're creating a disturbance! If you're bored, you can bungee jump with the others!"

Fairchild looked at me like I had just announced the Apocalypse will begin in five minutes, good seats still available. He ran for the Celestial Residencies. He was greeted by the sight of several Advocates, Churches and Celestials, leaping off the tops of the buildings, including a couple who didn't bother with the bungee cords.

I caught up with Fairchild just in time for us to see Michael and Fawkes come around the corner of the building, heading for the Blooming Meadow. Both of them had giant red skyrockets strapped to their backs. Michael was talking excitedly. "That was a cartoon. They were trying to be funny, not accurate."

Fawkes looked equally excited. "Good. 'Cause I've always wanted to try this."

Fairchild looked at me. He was despairing right now. "He's filed his petition?"

"Yes...."

"And you didn't contest it?"

164

"That's right...."

Fairchild bolted for the Campus. I took off after Michael and Fawkes.

The daredevil duo was standing on a bluff, aiming themselves to fly up and over the Blooming Meadow and come down God only knows where. I stood back, helpless, as they did their pre-launch inspection. What they were actually inspecting, I have no idea, but they were checking things over for something.

Suddenly, a Guardian appeared in front of me, holding a document. I recognized what it was. It was the Churches' decision on what to do with a petition. I saw the three things I was hoping for – Fawkes' name, "no contest," and Fairchild's signature.

Michael and Fawkes noticed the Guardian and went to check out the document. While this was going on, Fairchild came up. "There! No contest! Nothing preventing you from going into Heaven! Now get out of here!"

Michael and Fawkes looked at each other in disappointment. Then, they grinned evilly at each other. Michael snapped his fingers and the fuses on the rockets lit. They aimed themselves away from us. Fairchild, the Guardian, and I all took a few steps back.

The rockets ignited. Michael's rocket took him a short distance into the air, then crashed him into the ground, using the archangel to plow a short, shallow trench before finally burning out. Fawkes, meanwhile, had made it into the air when the rocket exploded. He plummeted to the ground, landing with a thud and leaving a small impact crater. He and Michael were laughing like loons as they extracted themselves. As they stood together, Fawkes looked up at the fireworks display and said, "That brings back some memories!"

Fawkes then smiled at my little group. "Okay. I'm ready to go now."

The Guardian went up to him, touched Fawkes on the shoulder, and they vanished.

Fairchild shot his hand up, holding out three fingers. Three putti appeared. Before they could even ask how they could assist him, Fairchild barked to them, "I want a bunch of Guardians to put a stop to everything and have my Churches return to the Campus immediately!" The childlike angels flew off and Fairchild stormed away.

I went over to Michael, who was smiling at me. "Any chance we can do this again?" he asked.

"Not bloody likely!" I said, trying to be stern but smiling back.

"You sure you don't want to try it? It's really fun."

I reached up, grabbed Michael's ear, and pulled him after me towards the pitch.

Order was finally restored. All the dirt bikes, save for the one Michael was now sitting on, had gone away. The Celestials were disappointed the fun was over and went back to the bocce tournament. The Guardians broke up the bungee jumping. Michael gave the order that it wasn't allowed now, and everyone had no choice but to go along with it. It was only Celestials around right now. Every Church had been recalled to the Campus, presumably so Fairchild could scream at them for acting like idiots and to never do it again.

Fairchild eventually came by. Michael was still revving the dirt bike engine like a little kid, so I left him to his toy. I walked up to Fairchild, fighting to keep my smile down.

"Well, Singer, that should do it," he said with finality. "Everyone is back under control as they should be. I hope you're ready for some payback."

"Payback? What did I do?"

"You think I don't know this was some plan on your part? Create such a disruption, I'll approve petition, and Fawkes gets into Heaven without standing trial. I may have figured it out too late, but I did figure it out. I'm too smart for you. And the next time you get a stuntman, I'll make sure he stands trial."

"You can't do that anymore."

Fairchild looked at me in shock. He knows better than to think I'm bluffing. All he knew was that he'd missed something.

I let my smile burst onto my face. "By not contesting his petition, you've created a precedent. Any other stunt people that come in that weren't as insane as Fawkes? They're as good as in now. After all, you didn't contest Fawkes, why are you contesting them?"

Fairchild's mouth dropped open so wide, I could actually count his teeth. I held up my forearm, looking at an imaginary watch. "Whoa, is that the time? Must dash." I stuck out my thumb like I was hitch-hiking. Michael pulled up on the dirt bike. I jumped on the back of the bike, sidesaddle like a proper lady, and wrapped my arms around Michael's waist as he popped a wheelie and took off.

Couldn't tell you what happened immediately afterwards. Michael and I went joyriding for a while.

All humans, regardless of race, gender, or even religion, have certain things in common. Certain reactions. Certain values. Certain questions. And among those questions, the most frequently asked one is, if God is all loving, why does he allow so much suffering in the world?

There are two answers to this question. The first answer is that it is the first step to undoing reality. God created the world so we could live in it, and also Heaven, a place with no suffering, no harm, no fear, so we can be rewarded with it. If He does the living for us, preventing all the bad things that go with life, there's no point to living at all. This is why Divine Intervention, where God directly intervenes in events on Earth, happens so rarely. It changes too much, making the world an extension of God instead of us, especially when His actions violate the very laws of physics and such that govern the realm. He doesn't like it, but He has to remain hands off. If He doesn't, everything from the Earth to Heaven itself will fall apart.

That's the complex answer, the philosophical one, the one that provides a peek into the mysteries of life and why things are the way they are. The second answer is far simpler -- no good deed goes unpunished. For every act of Divine Intervention that occurs, there is a person that, if they can find some way to take advantage of it, they will.

I was in my quarters, getting ready for another batch of trials. Three defending, one opposition. I had been reviewing the life scrolls of the Petitioners, coming up with great cases, and getting ready to argue. I enjoyed a nice cup of jasmine tea, letting the flavor and aroma calm my mind. I grabbed the life scrolls and case history scrolls off the top of my modest bookcase. I smiled. "Look out, Churches! Hannah Singer's on the move again!"

As I walked to the Courts, I continued to turn things over in my mind. Only two cases where I was facing Jeff Fairchild, the senior Church Advocate and the closest thing to an archenemy I had. He was leading the case I was opposing. The last two cases had different Churches. One was the typical kind, fire and brimstone and moralistic outrage. The other was rather laid back. Open and shut, the Petitioner as good as in, the Church was just putting up a token case. I usually gauged how I did in those cases by how many sentences I said total before the Tribunal granted petition. My average is seventeen.

I had just gotten onto the steps leading up to the main court building when I saw them. St. Michael was coming out of the entrance, three Celestial Advocates behind him. I was off to the side, so it was obvious they were coming towards me. I kept climbing, adjusting my path so I could meet them halfway. I figured something was up. Michael usually dresses casually and fun. He was wearing his regular robes and his face didn't have his usual humor to it.

When we met, I asked, "Looking for me?"

"Yes. Your cases are being reassigned."

I immediately handed over scrolls to whichever Celestial Michael indicated. Once things were divvied up and the Celestials on their way, I looked at my boss. "I'm guessing I need some prep time?"

"Yes," Michael said. "You're leading a trial by God."

I straightened up a little more. Even among those worthy to stand in the presence of God, not many could argue cases in front of Him. I was one of the chosen few. It's always an honor and an incredible experience to stand before Him. Unfortunately, being assigned a trial by God means you are about to get a really sticky case. "Particulars?"

Michael reached in his robe and produced four life scrolls, none with ties. Whoever they belonged to, they were still alive. "Start with these."

I examined each scroll in turn. All kids, related through their mother, only the two oldest shared the same father. Ages ranged from thirteen to five. Started out lower class, mother worked her way up into a respectable life, providing the kids with school and other important elements of life.

I looked at Michael, rolling up the last scroll. "So what's the problem?"

Michael took back the four scrolls and handed me another. This one had a tie. "The problem is in here."

I took the scroll, untied it and started reading. The mother's name was Marianne Hutchins. White, lower class, divorced, barely passed high school. Worked what they called the "pink collar ghetto" -- mostly beauty salon stuff with low pay, few benefits, high risk of unemployment, and no hope of getting ahead. Not the most conscientious parent. Tried using the kids as leverage for spousal and child support. Casual drug user. Heavy drinker...

My eyes popped. I looked at Michael over the top of the scroll. "Died about five years ago?"

"The spirit currently in her body is an angel, trying to provide for those kids so they have a chance at a better life. He's actually turned things around for them. Hutchins never petitioned. She's requested a trial by God because she wants her life back."

"Her life as it is now?" It was a rhetorical question. No way she'd go back to how things were before.

"Got it in one," Michael said, annoyance detectable in his voice.

I gave my big brother a salute with Hutchins' scroll. "You can count on me."

He placed the kids' life scrolls in my arms and saluted back. We then went our separate ways as I considered the strange case of Marianne Hutchins.

In life, there are no guarantees, only opportunities. Making progress in the world depends on recognizing them and taking advantage of them. Well, sort of. Just as there are opportunities to make yourself into something good, there are opportunities to make yourself into something bad, and frequently, the same opportunity can go either way. It really depends on your self-image and what you want it to be.

Marianne Hutchins grew up in a small town. Not a lot of chances to advance in the world there. She noticed from an early age that people wanted to make excuses for her and fix things for her. That became her primary approach. She did everything with an eye towards being seen as sympathetic. Cheating on a test? Well, she's an average student, she's just under pressure. Treating other kids poorly? Well, she's insecure, it's just her coping mechanism. Getting caught driving drunk while still underage and in a dry county? Well, she's led a sheltered life, she's just acting out.

Hutchins was a natural charmer and had no trouble keeping people around her. She juggled a few boyfriends at once. They went along with it because she was giving them sex. That taught her the powerful sway sex held over boys. She pursued one of the boys who had managed to get a scholarship to an Ivy League school. She figured that she just had to wait patiently, he would graduate, they'd be married, and she'd be set for life.

Unfortunately, life didn't work out that way. Hutchins' boyfriend changed during his freshman year. On the one hand, he wanted a girlfriend more appropriate to his new station in life, someone he could impress his buddies with. On the other hand, he was no longer as dazzled by Hutchins' limited offerings. He dropped her like a hot rock. Devastated that her meal ticket was gone, Hutchins was having a crying fit when she was spotted by a college football player. He misinterpreted her grief as a broken heart instead of lost life goals. She played it up, keeping him around her while she checked him out.

The new guy was a jock, but he was also a gentleman. That didn't mean anything to her, all she could see was a football player at a big college. He got plenty of perks, resulting in a comfortable lifestyle. He was also being scouted by professional sports teams. They became an item. Learning her lesson from her last boyfriend, they eloped over spring break. She was thrilled and just waited for the gravy train to pull into the station.

As time went on, Hutchins became pregnant. The husband had no problems with the idea of Hutchins being a mother. Michael? To say he had misgivings about how she'd handle motherhood is an understatement. He assigned a guardian angel, Onmyhml, to the baby. Meanwhile, a war between sports teams had broken out, each wanting to pick the husband in the draft and offering all kinds of bonuses. Then, disaster. Her husband got hit hard during a game, completely snapping his leg at the knee. Surgery couldn't give him his old knee back, and his football career was over. So was his life – he was mostly taking blow-off courses for easy A's to keep on the team.

Hutchins decided to jump. She lent her "support", and got pregnant a second time. Onmyhml's workload doubled. Hutchins then served the divorce papers. With one kid and another on the way, Hutchins got a sizable portion of her husband's pay, however meager it was. He wound up working two jobs just to keep his head above water.

Hutchins continued to scout for new men. She parlayed some of the leftover cash and perks from those halcyon days and got some touch-up work done to her face. She headed for the business districts, where her good looks and charm got a good amount of attention. Her kids? Her family babysat, problem solved. She knew exactly who would be receptive and who to target. She'd never compete with the women that could throw themselves at the top execs, but there were plenty in the middle she could go after. One started getting stingy, so she got pregnant again. He settled with her to make her go away. She then did it again with another guy who was already married. She had him over the barrel and got hush money from him every month.

Hutchins enjoyed alcohol and drugs. Reasoning that all she had to do was stick with what she could handle, she miscalculated one day. The pills and the booze hit her body hard, and she started slipping away. Onmyhml wasn't sure what to do to help his four charges. Divine Intervention to keep Hutchins from dying was out, so Onmyhml prayed to God for the next best thing. God granted it. It had to happen fast.

Hutchins died. It was only for a split second, but it was enough to sever the link between her body and her spirit. Onmyhml entered her body and linked with it before it started breaking down. The body suffered no ill effects and revived. It was a good thing it happened in the middle of the night. Onmyhml, suddenly deprived of his usual spiritual senses, was a bit disoriented and needed some time to get used to being alive. He pulled it together enough, though. The kids noticed something odd. Mommy simply said she wasn't feeling well. The kids hugged her. Onmyhml started crying. It wasn't an act, he loved those kids.

Onmyhml was now in a position to really help those kids, and he did. He worked hard, planned shrewdly, and "Hutchins" started climbing out of the pit of her life. The kids were responding to the change. They discovered self-respect, and starting turning themselves around, too. "Hutchins" got a job in a fast food place. The intelligence, planning, and responsibility impressed the right people. "Hutchins" got promoted to assistant manager. She never made manager, she made regional. In less than two years, she had a position that may not have shook the world, but it provided well and made her respectable. She even dropped the payments made by the kids' dads. She didn't need them anymore, and the men were free.

"Hutchins" was also getting attention from men, including her exes who used to hate her but noticed she wasn't the woman she used to be. Onmyhml wasn't sure how to handle it. Some of them could make great fathers for the kids, but since they wouldn't be with a real woman, would that even be right? God reassured him that, as long as the love was genuine and not just to add a missing element, it was okay. Besides, human love isn't the same as divine love. With God's blessing, "Hutchins" started dating. A wonderful man found her, and things started getting serious.

Meanwhile, in the Afterlife, the real Marianne Hutchins was cooling her heels. She didn't bother to petition, figuring she was as good as nailed (not quite, but a Heavenly reward was definitely not going to happen). Somehow or another, she learned about the switch that occurred. At first, she didn't even care. All she knew was she was dead and stuck. But as Onmyhml started making gains, Hutchins got jealous. Now, "Hutchins" was about to get married

170

to a great guy with a supporting income, she had a great job with respect and good pay, and the kids absolutely adored her.

Hutchins started demanding to be sent back into her body. Her kids needed their mother, not the impostor currently there. The Churches were getting sick of listening to her. The Celestials were getting sick of listening to her. Michael consulted with God, and God told him what to do. Hutchins was to be told to ask for a trial by God.

And I was to be told to lead the opposition.

Trials by God can literally occur at any time. You never know when they'll happen. He doesn't start things until everyone is ready. But that's the part that gives you anxiety. He knows when you're ready, but you may not have a clue.

I carefully considered my trial strategy. Hutchins had no knowledge of the Bible. I mean, zilch. I could probably quote from the Book Of Armaments and she wouldn't have a clue. All she knew came from watching movies like "The Ten Commandments". Don't get me wrong, great film, but took a lot of liberties with Biblical and historical fact. Who exactly was the Pharaoh, Moses being loud, Ramses casting Moses out of Egypt in the wrong direction...it was the funniest movie Michael and I had seen until "Caddyshack" came along. The sad part is, it put Hutchins' Biblical knowledge on par with most Christians on Earth.

This trial would not be won or lost on Biblical accords or precedents or anything official. I had to not only beat Hutchins, I had to convince her she'd been beaten. I knew her type. They would do anything, say anything, grasp at anything, to create even a shred of doubt that they could capitalize on. I had to completely shut her down.

Michael noticed me being a little nervous around him. My big brother knows me too well. "What do you want to ask me, Hannah?"

We were sitting in his office, him in his chair, me in one of the visitor chairs. I took a deep breath, and promptly chickened out. "It's nothing."

Michael leaned forward, folding his arms on his desktop and resting his chin on his bracers. "Come on, you know you can ask me anything."

"...I don't want to insult you."

"Thinking I would never forgive or understand if you make a mistake is a bigger insult."

He had me there. I took another deep breath and asked, "Would you junior for me at Hutchins' trial?"

I thought he might be at least a little annoyed. He's an archangel, and he's being asked to junior by a lowly human. But nothing of the sort. He smiled warmly and said, "No problem, Hannah. Although I'm curious what you need me for."

"Unless I miss my guess, she's going to drag angels into this. For the more egregious errors, I'd like to see her face down the real thing."

Michael nodded. "You can count on me."

I worked at getting into Hutchins' head, figuring out how she thought

171

and why she thought it. I wasn't about to lose this case. Four innocent lives were at stake here, as well as the love of a good man. I refused to let selfish arrogance destroy this family.

I was sitting in my quarters, trying to relax. I had just gone over the life scrolls again and jotted some notes. I'd brushed up on my Bible just in case there was anything there I could use. I took another long drink from my tea cup. I closed my eyes, trying to think if there was anything I'd overlooked. I then padded over to my bookcase and looked for something to read. Hmm...Sir Arthur Conan Doyle. Can't go wrong with Sir Arthur Conan Doyle....

Suddenly, I felt it. A pulling sensation, right around my heart and reaching out, growing in strength as it went. The time of trial was upon me. I was nervous and excited. Standing in the presence of God is something you never get used to. But I had to force that from my mind. I had a trial to argue.

As the feeling grew, I felt it changing my very being. I was dissolving, every piece of me turning into an element of light. My vision changed as my eyes themselves began turning. Eventually, everything went back as it was before. The only difference was my location. It was a beautiful crystal courtroom, shaped like a semi-circle. The Advocate tables curved along with the back of the room, facing the flat side. In the middle of the flat side was a simple, open space. That was where God would appear once He was done. God was taking everyone in the Valley Of Death out of time. Every word, every nuance, every action, everything the Advocates did would be known to everyone in the Afterlife.

I looked around. I was the first one here. After a few moments, Michael turned up next to me. He was wearing proper robes. He would never attend a trial by God in anything less. He gave me a smart salute and said, "Greetings, boss!"

I smiled back before looking to the curved table to my left. "Just be ready for me to pass off to you at any time. You see an opening, you go for it."

"I won't step on anything, will I?"

"You know how I argue, I'm sure you'll be fine."

Shortly after I finished speaking, Hutchins appeared. I hadn't moved, and she was turned just right. Her very first view of the crystal court was my gaze drilling through her.

"So, you're trying to stop me, huh?" Actually, she had a lot more curse words in there, but I'm not allowed to repeat them.

I felt Michael's breath on my ear as he leaned in and said, "Fight the urge to punch her."

I smirked. "No problem. Blocking her will feel better and will last longer."

Hutchins gave me a couple more curse words and turned to face the opening, giving her hair a casual flip with her hand as she did so. The temptation to treat her like a child was strong. But I've argued against her type before. Their thought process is so desperate for anything self-affirming, they will come up with amazing leaps of logic. Ideas that seem random to normal people make perfect sense to them. I had to run faster than her at all times so that I wouldn't be left behind when she inevitably reversed direction.

That was pretty much the best strategy to use. I basically divided the trial into two parts. The first part, I went defensive, letting the other side make arguments and me nullifying them. Then, when they started running out of steam, I started throwing out my arguments. By then, they'd usually fed me enough that I could contradict them or just tie them up in knots. I had to overwhelm her so that, when the end came, she would simply surrender. Otherwise, she wouldn't accept anything else other than victory. It was going to take a while, but I was up to it.

After a few moments, all was apparently ready. We felt the presence of God. Michael and I faced forward and deployed our wings. A form of pure light appeared in the center of the far wall. I allowed myself a few good feelings. Being in the presence of God is too wonderful to deny that.

"You have requested this trial because you feel you should be returned to life," God said.

I briefly wondered what Hutchins would hear. How you hear God's voice depends on how you relate to Him. To me, He's gentle and soft spoken. To the Churches, He's booming and authoritative. I figured, given how distant Hutchins was to Him, His voice would be faint and small. I snuck a quick look at her out of the corner of my eye. I think I guessed right. She was actually leaning forward a little with her head slightly turned, trying to gather extra sound into her ear. People could have such amazing relationships with God if they would just treat Him differently.

"Yes," Hutchins said. "My death was an accident. It shouldn't have happened. I should be returned to life to live with my kids. I miss them so."

I came out swinging. "Which is why it took you five years to request a hearing on it."

Hutchins told me to shut up and described me as a female dog.

I gave her a second helping. "You can't even show respect in the presence of God, and you expect Him to return you to life? Are you doing anything besides wasting our time?"

Hutchins looked from me to God and back. She turned and bowed in an exaggerated fashion to God, ignoring me completely. Her words were full of sugar as she said, "I'm sorry, I didn't mean to swear in front of you, God. Please forgive me."

"I forgive you, but Hannah has a valid point," God said. "It is important for parents to teach their children about respect. For their parents, for themselves, for other people, and for whichever god they choose. Do you really think you can teach them this?"

She actually said, "I can teach them better than the angel currently in my body."

My jaw dropped. My eyes went wide. This is a very sore spot for me. Was she actually suggesting she was better than an angel?!?

God said, "Uh...Michael? Would you please?"

Michael reached over, put his index finger under my chin, and gently lifted my jaw closed. I didn't realize what had happened until Michael returned to his position.

God asked, "You find her statement difficult to believe, Hannah?"

That snapped me out of it. I turned to Hutchins, full of rage. "Oh, you bet I find it difficult! What makes you think you can teach your kids better than an angel?!?"

"I was with them all their lives. I know them better."

"Onmyhml has been with them all their lives, too."

"Who's Onmyhml?"

I forced my temper down. I couldn't let her get to me. "The guardian angel assigned from the day your oldest was conceived."

"That's an angel, not a living being. Angels don't understand life."

That was actually a good point. Better shoot it down in flames. "For someone who doesn't understand life, he's doing pretty well. The kids have become B average students, they're healthy, a man who is husband material and will make a great father...."

She pounced. "That's why! The angel is male!"

Michael looked amused. "Angels are asexual."

"There are boy angels and girl angels," she responded. She pointed to me in an accusatory fashion. "She even called him a 'he.'"

Michael didn't even blink. "Whether we are masculine or feminine is based on our personalities, not our sexualities."

"It's still enough to make that angel a 'he.' That means he's getting into a gay relationship, and being gay is a sin!"

I argue these kinds of points against the more fundamentalist Churches all the time. I looked at Michael and smiled. "Mind if I take this one?"

He nodded politely. "Oh, by all means."

I looked at Hutchins like she was the slowest kid in class. "Homosexuality isn't a sin."

"Yeah, it is! It says so in the Bible!"

"What does it say in the Bible?"

"That gay men should be put to death!"

"You're misquoting. You want to look it up?"

Hutchins looked lost. She said, "Sure." A Bible appeared on the table in front of her, and she began skimming through it as fast as possible.

While she was distracted, Michael tapped me on my shoulder. When I looked at him, he was just staring at me. He quietly asked, "'Misquoting?'"

I was equally quiet. "Technically, that's true. I never said she was misinterpreting, just misquoting."

Michael rolled his eyes. "Oy gevalt...."

"Questioning your lead. Some junior you are."

"Burn," he sniffed.

"Ah, ha!" Hutchins declared triumphantly. "Leviticus 20, verse 13! 'If a man lies with a man as one lies with a woman, both of them have done what is

detestable. They must be put to death; their blood will be on their own heads!'"
She stuck her tongue out at me.

You have to do better than that, Hutchins. "Uh-huh. And what about lesbians?"

Hutchins quirked her head to the side. "Same thing."

"Chapter and verse, please."

The only place in the Bible where lesbianism appears is in Romans 1, verse 27. I was musing that it was going to take her a while to get there when I smelled something. I looked down at the table in front of me. God had created a nice cup of jasmine tea for me. I bowed humbly and picked it up, taking a sip and enjoying its effect on my senses. That was when I had proof God gave me the tea. No matter how much I drank, the level of the tea in the cup never got any lower. Michael's good, but he's not that good.

Eventually, Hutchins found it. She read aloud, "'Even their women exchanged natural relations for unnatural ones.'"

I carefully set the tea cup down. It vanished as soon as my fingers left it. "God doesn't have a problem with homosexuality, the writer of Leviticus does. Homosexuality is a sin in the eyes of man, not God."

"Romans said 'natural relations for unnatural ones.' Homosexuality is unnatural."

Nice try. "That doesn't mean it's wrong or a sin, it's just not how sexuality usually goes."

"'Unnatural' sounds wrong to me."

I held up a fistful of my hair. "Most of the people where I came from had brown hair instead of blonde. Technically, I'm unnatural. Does that make me a sinner?"

"Hair has different natural colors."

"And human sexuality has different natural aspects. People engage in all kinds of sex acts that many may find strange or repulsive but the participants are just fine with." I gave her a glare of pure ice. "Two guys at once, props, things like that."

I heard Hutchins gulp audibly.

"That was a warning shot," I told her. "I've read your life scroll. You sure you want to cast the first stone?" Come on, be smart, don't do it....

"There was nothing unnatural about what I did."

Why do they always have to do it the hard way? "Just because there were opposite genders involved?"

"Yes. It was natural. It was normal."

"If it was natural, why did you have to be coerced into it?"

"I wasn't coerced."

"You had sex with several guys because they had given you expensive gifts or money. You had sex with several guys and convinced them to give you expensive gifts or money. You even forced some guys to keep giving you money for giving them sex. You traded sex for goods, services, and money. There was no love or fun, it was commerce." I put the cherry on top. "You were a prostitute."

Suddenly, Hutchins was frozen in place, a faint golden light around her. God had frozen her. She was clearly ready to attack me. I could have taken her. Her scroll mentioned a glass jaw that stopped her from being a school bully. But making chin music is not exactly a nice thing to do in the presence of God.

God's voice drifted over us. "If you want to try to convince me to grant your request, you must conduct yourself properly."

I guess Hutchins communicated to God that she would be nice. The glow vanished and she could move again.

She looked at me, pure fury in her eyes. "It's my life. It's my body."

"You died. Your life is over. It's not your body anymore."

"It was an accident!"

"People die in accidents all the time, and they don't get their lives back. They have bigger families than you did. They don't get their lives back. They accomplish more with their lives than you did. They don't get their lives back. Why should you be the exception?"

"They need me! They love me!"

"No, they didn't, and you know it. They were just props to you, you were a resource for them. There was no love."

"That's only because of how life was!" She was getting desperate. "Now that things are better, I can be the good mother they need!"

"So, you weren't a bad mother, you just wanted someone else to do the hard work."

She was starting to plead. "They need me back."

My face steeled. "Do not make me do this."

"Do what?"

"Prove you wrong."

"Scared you can't?"

"It will scar you, mentally, emotionally, and spiritually. Stop now. Don't take this any further. Show some restraint for once."

I realized too late that I'd made a harsh mistake. She was reading my hesitation as a bluff. The truth about Onmyhml could destroy the family. I looked to God, sending a silent prayer. "Please. Make her stop. She doesn't realize what she's about to do. As bad as she is, I don't want to do this to her."

The voice of God echoed in my thoughts. "I cannot. It is her decision, they are her consequences."

Hutchins sneered the words I dreaded. "Prove it."

I closed my eyes and took a deep breath. I opened them, and asked God, "Please bring Onmyhml, the children, and the fiancée."

In a flash, they were all taken out of time. The four kids appeared first, then the fiancée, standing in the open space in the middle of the courtroom, facing away from God. They looked around in confusion. When they returned to Earth, they wouldn't really remember anything more than impressions, there's no frame of reference for the living mind to recall the Afterlife. They would also all be able to speak clearly here, especially the youngest, since they weren't restricted by earthly bodies and limited vocabularies. They all seemed good. I started hoping that, when the big reveal hit, they wouldn't freak out about who had been the woman in their lives.

They got their bearings and saw Hutchins. Everyone looked confused. The fiancée spoke first. "Marianne?"

"Yes," she smiled. Full teeth, beaming attitude, the whole show. "I'm coming back to you."

The oldest kid asked, "What do you mean, coming back to us?"

"That's not your real mother on Earth. I'm your real mother."

A long, long beat. Finally, the fiancée asked, "Then who is that on Earth?"

Against the back wall, right in front of their field of view and between Hutchins and I, Onmyhml appeared. He looked scared. How would they react to the truth?

The youngest practically burst with joy. "I knew it! Mommy's an angel!" He dashed from the group and wrapped himself around Onmyhml's leg. Onmyhml stroked the kid's head, looking at the rest of the family, fear thick enough to feel.

The other kids looked in confusion. "He was right."

"What do you mean, 'he was right?'" the fiancée asked. He wasn't angry, just unclear.

The oldest spoke. "Every once in a while, he says mom is an angel. Just like the ones in the churches."

"Babies still have their spiritual senses," Onmyhml said quietly. "Eventually, their regular senses take over. I was hoping he'd forget."

They all looked at each other. Everyone was trying to figure out what to do. Finally, Hutchins broke the ice. "Now, wouldn't you rather have your real mommy back, not some guy?"

The youngest freaked out. He moved so Onmyhml was now between him and Hutchins. A purely defensive position. "No. He's my mommy. Not you."

I looked at the rest of the group. They all looked a bit shocked and surprised. But I saw something else.

Acceptance.

Despite how strange the situation was, they wanted it more than the normal situation.

Hutchins' face fell. She was being rejected.

"I'm your mother," she told the kids. "How can you prefer this...thing," she said, gesturing angrily to Onmyhml, "over me?"

The fiancée looked shocked. "You're calling an angel a thing?!?"

"You're sleeping with a guy!" she retorted.

He thought for a second, then said calmly, "An angel that loves and wants to be with me, or you? I'll take the angel."

"He's a guy!"

"On Earth, he's the woman I love."

177

Suddenly, the golden glow returned. Hutchins had gone over the edge.

I looked at them. When I spoke, their heads jerked to me, like they finally noticed I was there. "You sure you're fine with this? You won't know the truth up here," I said, pointing to my temple. "But you'll know the truth in here." And I pointed to my heart.

They all looked at each other. Onmyhml was standing straight and proud, eyes closed, like he was facing a firing squad. "It isn't my life. It is yours. Whatever choice you make will be the right one."

The youngest wrapped himself tighter around Onmyhml. The other kids came up and started hugging him. The oldest said, "And Billy was bragging his dad works for a Fortune 500 company. We've got an angel!"

The fiancée came up. With trembling fingers, he reached out for Onmyhml's face.

"What are you doing?" Onmyhml asked.

With nervousness clear in his voice, the fiancée said, "I'm going to kiss you."

Onmyhml was confused. "But you're not gay."

"I know, but I want to prove to you that I'm fine with this."

The fiancée and Onmyhml sort of kissed. As soon as their lips met, the fiancée started weirding out. His shoulders hunched a little and he looked like he'd been sucking on a lemon.

Michael and I both laughed. They all looked at us. The fiancée said defensively, "Look, I don't have anything against gay people...."

"We know, we know," Michael interrupted. "It's just not how you're wired up. How about we put you back in your familiar situation?"

Everyone was still holding on to Onmyhml. They weren't letting him go, figuratively or literally. "I think we'd all like that," Onmyhml said.

A flash of light, and they were gone. The golden glow around Hutchins vanished, too. Her only movements were for her expression to fall and her shoulders to sag. She couldn't deny it. They didn't want her.

The voice of God drifted out to us. "Returning to life would only benefit your sense of luxury. Onmyhml wants to do right by them, you want what you feel entitled to. The request is denied."

Prisms of light radiated out from God. My vision got brighter until everything was bleached out, even my hands in front of my face. When the light faded, I was back in my quarters, sitting at my table, my Sherlock Holmes collection open in front of me, and a fresh cup of jasmine tea next to it.

Hutchins took the rejection pretty hard. She eventually petitioned. She didn't put up much fight. Both sides opposed, she got reincarnation to try and get it right this time.

Life on Earth for Hutchins' family was a little odd for a bit. They didn't know exactly why everything seemed different now, but it did. Only Onmyhml remembered what happened. But things eventually settled back down. All except the youngest. He was more insistent than ever that mommy was an angel.

Onmyhml could only roll his eyes and say, "Kids."

It took me a little while to shake off the trial. I hated proving how much Hutchins' own kids didn't want her. But it had to be done.

"For the good of her family?" Michael asked me.

"Sort of," I responded. "She wasn't really evil. She was just...self-absorbed."

"That can be just as bad as evil at times, Hannah."

"You know," I told him, "there are times when my arguments aren't just arguments. They are me actually passing judgment. I have determined which people are deserving and which aren't. Am I supposed to actually enjoy that?"

"In which case, why did Hutchins' trial make you feel so bad?" Michael finished.

"Right. Or, is it wrong for me to pass judgment, and I'm just as self-absorbed at my other trials? I mean, God says we aren't supposed to be judgmental, right?"

Michael smiled at me. "In general, people aren't supposed to be judgmental. The fact is, there are times when you have to be judgmental. When not only is it okay, it is expected of you."

"When you have someone to take care of?" I smiled back.

"That's one time," Michael nodded. "Don't forget your job, Hannah. You are taking care of souls who want to get into Heaven, of a court system that protects them...you have to be judgmental. You are one of the ones God wants to be and trusts to be judgmental."

"But what if I go to far?"

"If you do, you'll reel it in. That's the difference between you and people like Hutchins. Your judgment isn't the important thing, doing right is. Judgmental is one thing. Obsessed is another."

All I could do was nod my head.

ABOUT THE AUTHOR...

Peter G is a card-carrying Renaissance man. When he's not working his office job, he is either making his own computer games or creating stories. A comic book fan since the black and white boom, Peter G's first officially published credit came in the Morbid Myths 2007 Halloween Special. Since then, his comic output has included dark superheroes (The Supremacy), an online comic strip about the office environment (Stress Puppy), an existential fantasy series (Head Above Water), and his first all-ages comic about a little girl who becomes friends with a mermaid (Sound Waves). He also writes reviews and articles for Video Game Trader magazine. He lives in Illinois where he spends most of his time complaining about politics and watching movies.